PRAISE FOR
—— BROTHERS BOUND ——

"*Brothers Bound* is a poignant, deeply moving account that stirs a mixture of sorrow for Buck's losses and awe at his resilience and capacity to impart profound life lessons derived from his harrowing experiences. The story presents an emotionally rich and transformative journey of a Vietnam vet who grapples with the psychological and physical scars of war. This story not only sheds light on the often-overlooked aspects of military operations but also delves deep into the human element, exploring themes of duty, brotherhood, and the indelible mark of war on the human soul. Through the physical imagery of scars and the psychological depths of memory rooms and emotional breakdowns, the story touches on themes of survival, the enduring human spirit, and the redemptive power of love and hope. *Brothers Bound* is a must-read for anyone who would understand the emotional trauma of war and resilience of love."

—**Charles Templeton**, author of *Boot: A Sorta Novel of Vietnam*

"Bruce Berger's novel places two American soldiers inside small cages in a brutal Vietnamese prisoner of war camp and seems to throw away all hope of rescue or escape. But that's not how the story ends, it's only the beginning. These two men will stretch the bonds of brotherhood and share a combined spiritual strength that will not allow either to give up as long as they still have life inside them. Bruce Berger has given us, in this work of human survival, a truly unforgettable love story."

—**Bill McCloud**, author of *What Should We Tell our Children About Vietnam?* and *The Smell of the Light: Vietnam, 1968–1969*

"Brothers Bound is a short, terse, and remarkably rich, precise story of human survival. The irony of going from the Casualty Branch to Graves Registration, (both jobs few readers can imagine or have even given any thought to) is an astounding focus in itself, but then for it to morph into an epic fourteen-month prisoner of war struggle is a superb exercise in the finest imagining of what human survival can reduce to. The critic James Wood once wrote that his grandmother, nearing her death, fell into a condition of 'bewildered silence.' Closing the final pages of *Brothers Bound* leaves this reader in a similar condition. It's a remarkable piece of work."

—**Joseph Heywood**, author and Air Force navigator in the Vietnam theater

"Every so often a narrative arrives that allows us to understand—in the most vivid, visceral way—how war is experienced on frozen battlefields, coral islands, or in this case, a POW camp and a desperate escape through the steaming jungles of Vietnam. Bruce Berger delivers a triumph of storytelling about war, the bonds between soldiers, and the human spirit, with a brilliant twist in the conclusion."

—**Mark Harris**, former VP of Comms, IBM

"I thought I knew a lot about the Vietnam War, but Bruce Berger's writing brings into sharp focus the horrific world of captivity, the brotherly love of two men for one another, and their indomitable will to survive."

—**Don Tyler**, author of *Tough Guy and Other Poems*

"This is a rich book of inspiration, courage, survival, and brotherhood. As a proud Vietnam veteran of the 101st Airborne Division from the year 1970, I find this to be a must read for *all*."

—**Jim Thompson**, veteran

"Bruce Berger tells an essential part of the Vietnam story—the business of death as American forces worked to send soldiers' remains home and notify their families. Berger's brilliant descriptions force the reader to experience every feeling, sight, sound, and smell his heroes encountered when trapped in a brutal POW camp. Just as his character, Hues, was 'everyman,' Berger infuses his characters with the DNA of a multitude of soldiers in Vietnam, generating compassion and empathy for our soldiers in a winless war."

—**J. Suzanne Horsley**, PhD, professor, author, and widow of a veteran

"Bruce Berger gives readers a vivid idea of the costs of war as he develops the bond between Buck and Hues. *Brothers Bound* is worth the read for the POW story of war. But Berger's writing offers readers a much larger experience. He is using the fifty-plus years since Vietnam to help unpack lessons of war. This is not a book just for Vietnam vets; it is wisdom that can help most of us as we negotiate the jungles of today. And I believe many readers will feel those lessons in the poetry of the psalms attributed to Hues. This is a book that can move you."

—**Richard Puffer**, US Marine infantry platoon commander in Vietnam 1969–70

"Bruce Berger turns the clock back more than fifty years and reminds us of the horrors and sacrifices endured by our Vietnam vets. The redeeming outcome of this tragic conflict is the binding brotherhood of Hues and Buck—two guys who meet in a bar minutes before their tour of service begin. What follows is an intense friendship and the two become each other's family, brothers that put their lives on the line for each other . . . and more. They are indeed Brothers Bound. Sometimes heart wrenching, sometimes joyful. Always difficult to put down."

—**Sue Neumann**, retired corporate communications leader

"Bruce Berger's storytelling of Buck and Hues's bond amid the brutalities of war is profoundly moving, showcasing the indomitable resilience of the human spirit. Their unbreakable brotherhood, forged in the crucible of adversity and forged through daring escapes, serves as a testament to the transformative power of friendship in the face of overwhelming challenges. This book is an absolute must-read for anyone seeking inspiration and a reminder of the profound strength found in unwavering dedication, especially during life's most trying moments."

—**Eyun-Jung Ki**, PhD, professor, author, and past president of the Korean American Communication Association

BROTHERS BOUND

Brothers Bound

by Bruce K. Berger

© Copyright 2024 Bruce K. Berger

ISBN 979-8-88824-340-4

All rights reserved. No part of this publication may be reproduced, stored in a retrieval system, or transmitted in any form or by any means—electronic, mechanical, photocopy, recording, or any other—except for brief quotations in printed reviews, without the prior written permission of the author.

This is a work of fiction. All the characters in this book are fictitious, and any resemblance to actual persons, living or dead, is purely coincidental. The names, incidents, dialogue, and opinions expressed are products of the author's imagination and are not to be construed as real.

Published by

3705 Shore Drive
Virginia Beach, VA 23455
800-435-4811
www.koehlerbooks.com

BRUCE K. BERGER

BROTHERS BOUND

VIRGINIA BEACH
CAPE CHARLES

Dedicated to all brothers and sisters who serve or have served in the US military and placed their lives on the line for our nation and each other. A special salute is given to those who were prisoners of war and suffered severely yet survived courageously in a deeper, darker layer of hell in life on earth.

AUTHOR'S NOTE

This book is semiautobiographical fiction. I was not a prisoner of war (POW) in Vietnam, but I served there in 1970 with the Casualty Branch of the 101st Airborne Division at Phu Bai. I was the next-of-kin editor who wrote hundreds of sympathy letters to grieving families back home about the death of their soldier. Sometimes I joined a Graves Registration team to gather fallen soldiers and help them begin their final journeys home.

I experienced little combat in the field, but I was immersed daily in the words, images, weight, and limitless reach of its aftermath—the injured and dead. I also was deeply moved by the power of good memories, the incredible depth of brotherhood love, and the presence of human spirits. In many conversations with soldiers in Vietnam, and more after the war, they said good memories helped them survive—took the edge off their pain and fear, gave them hope.

Brotherhood among soldiers is neither new nor surprising. Soldiers are trained and organized in squads, platoons, companies, and other "family" units. They depend on each other for physical and mental support, protection, medical help, and so much more. Soldiers may argue, disagree, curse, and sometimes even fight. But when the shit hits the fan, they've got each other's back. They'd give their life in an instant for a fellow soldier, and they don't leave brothers or sisters behind.

And then there's the power of spirits. Have you ever felt the spirit of another? Maybe someone alive but not with you in person? Or someone who died but still lives in your mind and heart? Or the spirit of a higher power? Some soldiers spoke of their brothers' spirits that lived on after their death. Others said the spirit of Christ, or the light of the Lord was with them every step. Several said the spirit of a family member or close friend was with them every day. As one seriously injured soldier told me, "Mom is with me; I feel her hugs. Her spirit is always with me, though she died three years ago."

Think of the pilgrimage of Buck and Hues, the two central characters, as a symbolic journey we all undertake in life—when we live with pain, fear, grief, uncertainty, depression, constant anger, or believe the end is near. We may reach the end of our journey abruptly.

Or, like Buck and Hues, we may hang on during those difficult journeys and discover the hope and power of memories. The rich embrace of another's light and spirit. The incredible love and strength of a brother or sister who is there for you. Ready to carry you every step of the way.

The names of all characters in this book are fictitious.

PART ONE

— **14 MONTHS IN THE CAGE** —

CHAPTER 1

—— **THE BROTHERS** ——

Hues and I met after a nasty fight in a bar. We were both drafted into the Army on the same day, December 3, 1968—our shared Christmas present, we later commiserated—and completed basic training in different units at Ft. Knox, Kentucky. But we didn't formally meet until the night before we shipped out to advanced training at Ft. Polk, Louisiana. We were on twenty-four-hour passes at the time.

That night, at a run-down bar on the edge of Armory, a small town ten miles from the Army base, I saw Hues get drawn into a fight. He was one of only three Black people I saw in the place. The bar was packed with country music lovers dressed in cowboy hats, vests, and neckerchiefs. Thin wood planks covered the walls and ceiling, creating a rustic look and feel. Small chandeliers hung from the ceiling, and dozens of deer antlers and horseshoes decorated the walls above the booths and tables. The dance floor was painted black and layered with sawdust.

Shuffling boots on the floor, clinking glasses, and loud laughter and singing voices blended into a noisy bin of life. A giant Victrola jukebox flashing red, blue, and yellow dominated the room, sitting atop a low platform at one end of the floor. It sat blaring out music from the 1960s—"Stand by Your Man," "Okie from Muskogee," "Tiger by the Tail," and Roger Miller's "Chug-a-lug" when the fight broke out.

Hues had just stepped away from the crowded bar with a mug of beer in his hand, not twenty feet from where I stood drinking. He stumbled when he turned, nearly fell, and splashed most of his beer on a heavyset man who sported patched work jeans, a sweat-soaked green T-shirt, and a black hat that read in big white letters, *White Chicks Only!*

"Man, I'm sorry," Hues yelled above the noise, trying to apologize. "Wanted to drink that beer, not spill it on you. Sorry 'bout that. I'll buy you another beer. Make up for it."

The big man sneered and threw his beer in Hues's face. "Drink this," he yelled. He then punched Hues hard on the cheekbone, knocking him to the floor. "Get the hell out of here, asshole," he bellowed. He loomed over Hues while his three buddies circled them and waved other customers back from the men.

Hues pushed himself up, shaking his head. "Man, the Lord works in mysterious ways, don't he?" Hues asked loudly. "Here we are meeting like this. Two strangers: one Black, one White. Same place but two totally different worlds." He smiled, shook his head slowly from side to side, then pointed at the man's hat: "May I ask, did you learn to read in the local KKK school? Or are you really just a big dumb fat ass?"

Lightning quick, Hues kicked the big man in the balls, who screamed and bent over. Hues then kicked him hard in the head. The man dropped heavily to the floor. The fight was then on between Hues and the big man's equally large friends. Hues held his own up to a point, but he was backed against the bar with little room to maneuver. The three men kept crowding, hitting, and kicking him, closing in for a nasty takedown.

I imagined the Black man was probably an Army man, given his clothing and shaved head. And a Black man fighting a White man in a room full of White folks—the odds were pretty damn long. I admired his courage and cool. *What the hell*, I thought, *we might end up together in Vietnam. Who knows?*

I stepped up near the fight and grabbed one of the attackers. The man's arm in my grasp, I spun him around and twisted it sharply, flipping him into the air. He crashed to the floor, and I lined up a kick straight to his ribs.

"Enough!" I bellowed above the music. "Leave my Army brother alone!"

One of the other men cursed loudly and swung at me. I ducked under his swing, spun again, rolled down on the floor, snapped my leg back, and kicked the man's knee from the side. He collapsed in pain on the floor. Then I spun again. Jumped up. Twisted in a blur and smashed my right elbow into the third man's nose, breaking it and effectively ending the fight.

I slowly circled the floor, eyeing all others with what I hoped was a tough, fearless smile because I sure as hell wasn't fearless in my mind. I was praying no one would step up to fight because the odds would then be long for both of us. Fortunately, no one moved. No one said anything. Only the loud music spoke in the room—Johnny Cash was singing about a ring of fire.

I touched the soldier's arm and smiled. "Let's find a quieter place for a drink," I said. I put my right arm loosely around his shoulder and walked him outdoors into the cooler night.

"Man, I owe you," he said. "Thank you. How'd you know I was an Army brother?"

"No big mystery," I said. "We both got shaved heads, right? And wearing black Army dress shoes and an Army belt? In a bar? Near an Army base? Simple deduction, right?"

He smiled, "Right!" He held out his hand. "I'm Jameis Jones, but call me JJ—or better, Hues. That's H-u-e-s. My family blood is black, brown, white, and yellow. I'm every color, every hue. I'm everyman. Know what I mean?"

"Sure, Hues," I said and smiled. "Sounds good to me. I always wanted to meet *every man*. I'm Brian Charles Kinder. Most call me 'Buck,' an abbreviation for my full name. You can too, if you want. You headed to Ft. Polk tomorrow too?"

"Yeah, Buck," he said. "Ft. Polk for a couple months, then probably the big bird flies us to Nam, right?" We smiled at each other and firmly shook hands.

That was the beginning of our friendship, which grew stronger every day after we were assigned to the same training unit and barracks at Ft Polk. We also flew together in the big plane that transported us and several hundred other soldiers to Vietnam in late May 1969.

As we grew to know each other, we learned we were different young men who'd grown up in strikingly different circumstances. Yet, we felt a strong bond with each other. We felt like old friends. Family members. Brothers.

I knew others with similar experiences. You know, you meet someone for the first time, begin talking, and suddenly feel like old friends who've known each other for years? There's a sense of physical familiarity and a kind of shared mental wavelength. It's like you just picked up from wherever you left off in your last conversation some hours, days, months, or years ago, even though you've never met before.

We also learned we shared some things in common. Like intelligence. Growing up in Michigan. Loving loud music and moving poetry. And feeling strongly about religion, though on different sides. I was a religious cynic who'd lost my faith at age fourteen when my married preacher, a man I greatly admired, ran off with another man's young wife. Left his four little kids and lovely wife behind. Hues, on the other hand, became a true believer at about the same age when his father was shot to death before his eyes. From that point on, he devoted himself to becoming what he called "a full-time street preacher" in Detroit. That sounded weird as hell at first, but Hues seemed totally sincere.

Overall, we sensed something in each other that linked us. Hues eventually summed it up this way: "I don't really understand it, Buck, but it's like you somehow complete me, you know? When you're around me, I just feel bigger, better. I feel a little more peace with things. You on the same page?"

I nodded. "Yeah, Hues. Like we've been brothers forever, though we just met. And I'm glad. I'm glad we got each other's back. We really gonna need each other in Nam, man."

"Sure as hell," Hues said. "Got your back, brother."

"And I got yours."
We dapped fists.

HUES

He was twenty years old and a junior college student with an unusual ambition: he wanted to become a minister, specifically a street minister who interacted daily with homeless street people. That ambition grew out of a challenging life growing up on the tough streets of River Rouge, Michigan, on the southwestern edge of Detroit. River Rouge was a small city jungle of concrete and brick buildings, boarded-up homes, and blackened streetlights. It was home to a blend of angry, uneasy, and frightened people, many Black—both criminals and victims—walking the streets. According to Hues, the most common possessions of Black folks living in that racially charged city in the late 1960s were stunted dreams and hopes. "If stars in the heaven are hopes, their nights are pretty damn dark," he said.

At an early age Hues developed an unerring sense of danger on the streets because he saw so many bad actors and crimes, he told me. He once saved an old lady from having her purse stolen by two teenagers. He noticed them observing her closely and nodding at each other as she hobbled and wobbled her way toward them with a cane from across the street.

He instinctively knew they were going to grab her purse and run. She probably had little or nothing in her purse, but Hues decided to help. It was the right thing to do—an issue he wrestled with daily. He ran past the two teenagers watching her, politely took her by the elbow, turned her around, then helped her back across the street, telling her softly that the two men were intending to rob her.

Hues was a thin man, a little over six feet tall, with smooth brown skin and friendly brown eyes filled with big light. He also possessed a big voice and an even bigger smile that often seemed fixed on his face, even in grim times. "Call me JJ or better, Hues," he said to everyone he met, just like he'd told me outside the bar in Kentucky. "That's h-u-e-s.

Like my momma said, I'm Hues because I'm all colors. Grandmama was White and Asian, Grandpappy Black. Mama Hispanic and Black, and Daddy White, Black, and Yellow. All hues of color, that's me. I'm everyman, so I prefer Hues, but call me JJ if you want. Just no disrespect, hear?"

He loved music, poetry, and the church, though it wasn't always that way. At age ten his mother and younger sister, whom he deeply loved, died when they were struck by a speeding car in a police chase. His mother died quickly, but his sister lingered on for eight days, aging Hues much too fast as he sat beside her in the hospital around the clock. At age fourteen he killed a man in self-defense just after the man fatally shot his father in the chest in a robbery attempt in an alley in downtown Detroit. Hues had sprung at the man, twisting and wrestling the gun from his hand before shooting him twice in the chest.

Witnesses had testified the shooting was self-defense. He did no jail time but spent several months in a juvey home to get his act together, he told me. Then he moved into a Baptist minister's home in River Rouge with his wife and two grown children. They all embraced him. It was a turning point in his life, he said. They helped him focus on life and a purpose.

He first told me this story at Ft. Polk, then referred to it often in other stories.

"Reverend Brown, now he got a passionate voice. He been to hell and back several times in his own life," Hues said. "The two years he did in prison got him focused. Life's really about choices we make, that simple, he told me. And three really big choices stare you in the face in Detroit: One, be a criminal or a mean, angry man livin' on the street, probably die young. Two, give up on yourself and blame the world for every damn thing; drown in alcohol or drugs and self-pity. Three, embrace the spirit of the Lord and the love of his son, Jesus, and make good differences in the lives of others."

He continued. "'Life ain't just about you, Hues, don't believe it,' he told me. 'No matter what you see on TV or people claim, true life means something bigger than just your little damn self, you hear? It's about making the lives of others better. You get it? So, forget what you lost in life, Hues. And Lord, I know it's already been a lot, son, a helluva lot. But forget what you lost. Focus on what you still got and can give. Best gifts we can give? Hope and love. Costs you nothing but grows your heart and soul. Okay? I won't talk about it again. Just think about your choices. Then make some damn good ones.'"

Hues had indeed given it a lot of thought, he told me. He went back to school and helped the minister at his church when not in school: everything from washing windows and mopping floors to tending the small playground behind the church. The loss of his mother and sister, the brutal shooting of his father, and the words and deeds of Reverend Brown helped focus his life.

He learned how to honestly talk to himself, and to stop losing and complaining. "So many homeless, hungry, and hopeless people living on those mean streets," he said. "I saw them every day—faces angry, sad, broken. People crying and fighting on the streets. So, I decided to become a street preacher. I wanted to carry my music, words, and smiles to them, you get it?"

For a few minutes each day, he could brighten the lives of others . . . and brighten his day too. He'd found the spirit and light he sought when cheerfully psalming as he walked the streets of the city, which became his church. And his thinking was reinforced often by the Reverend.

"If you don't believe in and follow the light, what the hell is there, people?" Reverend Brown argued in every Sunday worship service, according to Hues. "That takes a lot more courage and strength than blaming, cursing, harming, lying, cheating, and stealing from others! Believe in yourself and grow your damn spirit! What the hell's so difficult about that?"

Hues wrote and memorized more than thirty of what he called his "MoCity Street Psalms," short poems drawn from the biblical Psalms and set to a rhythm he'd learned on the streets. He possessed an uncanny ability to adapt his psalms to the current moment without losing his hypnotic rhythm. He could confront a situation and rap or sing a psalm—what he called psalming—and change the words to better reflect and illuminate the moment they were in. And he psalmed in a deep, compelling voice that touched others. It haunted me when I first heard it one morning in infantry training. Then I grew to love it and look forward to it.

So, he often walked the streets of River Rouge, or downtown Detroit, or occasionally Belanger Park, where elderly folks gathered on benches to watch their past lives flow past in the river's steady current. He greeted all and shared the psalms and his personal light. Younger people especially ignored him or told him to get the hell out of the way. A few thought he was crazy, a druggie looking for a handout or a fix. They told him he should get his ass into a real church if he was truly a goddamn preacher.

Older people and others like me found Hues to be an intelligent and talented musical man who embraced everyone, no matter their age, gender, or color. He simply wanted to make people feel better, even if just for a moment each day with his psalming and big, sunshine-bright smile. Okay, maybe he was a bit crazy, but he was a good crazy—or maybe crazy good.

Older people especially liked Hues because he was so alive with music and hope. They looked forward to seeing him in the streets. He told me several regular street walkers and bench sitters carried coffee in their thermos to share with him while he sang and cracked his silly, lousy jokes—which somehow rendered them even funnier, as I discovered.

Hues graduated from high school and earned a small scholarship to Henry Ford Community College in Dearborn. He studied woodworking, poetry, and the Bible. He met a young Mexican lady, Juanita. They grew close and imagined a future together. He really loved her, he told me. But then she and her family moved back to Mexico when their grandparents died. They inherited a sprawling cattle ranch. Juanita and Hues continued to correspond until she informed him she was pregnant. With another man's child.

Hues was an intelligent, well-spoken, very articulate man. But sometimes, as he later told me, he'd draw upon what he called his "ghetto grammar" to make a point depending on the audience, setting, and his mood or frame of mind. "I want to connect with people, communicate," he said. "Language on the street, that's real too. Got to speak and understand it. And sometimes those words, they're like music, no? You shorten your words or drop some verbs to make a point and make it sound like music at the same time. For example, 'Fo sho she one done it BIG time, yo?' Now, tell me that ain't musical poetry, Buck."

Hues also earned certificates in first aid and CPR, skills he believed might be useful to his street parishioners. His first-aid teacher was a young South Korean lady, Sena Park. She was completing her RN program and hoped to work in a maternity clinic. They met early one morning for coffee before class began and enjoyed laughing and talking. A week later they met for dinner in the Seoul Garden, a Korean restaurant in Dearborn. They enjoyed a wonderful evening of exotic food and rich laughter.

Two weekends later she walked with him on a street-preaching Sunday afternoon. She marveled at what he did and how happy the people seemed to be when he was with them joking, talking, and psalming. At the end of the day, she placed her small hands softly on his cheeks, then gave him a long hug. "You are special man, Hues," she whispered.

Then he'd been drafted. They still exchanged letters every few weeks. They'd planned to reunite on his break between infantry training and leaving for Vietnam. But her grandmother died in South Korea. She and her family returned there for the funeral. He didn't see Sena again before he headed to Vietnam. They'd only spent time together for a couple months, but Hues told me Sena was likely the woman he'd marry. She had a huge heart, which he said he saw every day in his mind.

"Big as a planet, man. I want that heart in my life forever," he said. I believed him.

BUCK

As I told Hues that first night we met, I was nicknamed "Buck" at an early age. At the time we met, I was twenty-two years old and a graduate of Western Michigan University. I was drafted in late 1968, just four months into a new teaching job at a small high school in central Michigan. I was a little over six feet tall, with strong arms and fast reflexes. I was a football player and wrestler at my small high school in Michigan. I grew up in a family of five, including an older sister and younger brother, in the village of Farewell, one of many small farming communities in southern Michigan.

My first job was at age five. I picked and gathered strawberries and other fruits and vegetables at a neighbor's small farm for several hours each morning. I can still recall the old neighbor man, Mr. Rudy, smoking a cigar and sipping homemade red wine each morning as he reluctantly gave me my standard quarter for a morning's work. Over time I became a hard and disciplined worker, much like my father. I was also a friendly and reasonably intelligent guy. And religious for a while.

The small community where I grew up included a handful of churches spread across the six blocks that constituted the downtown area. The town included the high school and elementary school buildings, several historical and imposing brick homes, a county courthouse encircled by giant maple trees that dominated the village center, dozens of small houses, two trailer parks, and fewer than one thousand inhabitants. The town was surrounded by fields of wheat, corn, soybeans, oats, and rye. Stands of majestic oaks and red maples towered like sentinels above the yards and fields. Along with squares of planted pine trees, they shaded the back roads and small rivers I loved to wade and fish in for bluegills, sunfish, bass, and catfish.

I started fishing regularly with my father at age three, he told me later. Even at that age I sensed something special about fishing and nature. I remember at age five when I went fishing one Saturday morning with my father. When he turned over our boat on the riverbank he discovered a small, coiled massasauga rattlesnake waiting for us. My father calmly picked up an oar and smashed the snake's skull. "Just a lesson to remember," he said to me. "Don't ever forget about danger. Especially when you don't expect it."

My ancestry was largely European. My father, German and Scandinavian, taught me the value of work and discipline—and a total focus on the task at hand, no matter how difficult. As a teenager, I worked several summers with him in his plumbing and electrical work in homes. My mother was mostly English and Irish, and she inspired my love of literature and music. When my sister, brother, and I were young children, Mom read us poems at bedtime—everything from Yeats to Whitman to Shakespeare—not the standard Dick, Jane, and Spot stuff. I didn't really understand poetry when I was a youngster, but I loved the musicality of the words, their rhythms, and sounds. She also hummed hymns constantly, "Amazing Grace" being at the top of her list.

I was closest to my mother, who I learned later in life was badly crippled, suffering, and near death from severe polio when she brought me into the world. She reminded me often how lucky we were to be alive and to cherish the life we were given. "You only get one life, so live it every minute," she often told me.

Given my mother's strong influence, I was active in church and Sunday school. I sang in the choir. At age fourteen I was elected the student representative on the church's administrative board. Several months into that experience, my minister, a man I admired greatly, had an affair with a young married woman, just twenty-two. When discovered, they simply ran off and disappeared.

My belief shattered. I couldn't equate the preacher and his robust proclamations of the words of the Lord with the man who ran away from the church and his own beautiful family. How many ministers and preachers were like mine, who said one thing and lived another? How many so-called religious men were just con men in robes, their praying words lost in their lying, cheating, denying, scandalizing? I believed in a higher power, but the Lord? I bottled up my religious belief. Capped it with cynicism and anger. Stashed it away on a dark shelf in a dim corner of my mind. I wouldn't reopen the bottle until my time in Vietnam with Hues.

I loved the outdoors and spent increased time in nature in my high school years—hunting, fishing, camping, learning about wildlife and tracking, and testing out survival techniques. I possessed an eerie sense of direction, wherever I was. I learned to read the sun, moon, and stars as easily as most read road maps and street signs. I camped and fished often for trout in cold rivers and streams in central and northern Michigan when I was a college student. I often felt closer to nature than I did to people. If I had a church then, it was nature.

Okay, I occasionally smoked a joint or two, loved beer at an early age, and was a big rock and roll fan who could listen to loud radio music endlessly. I dated several young women, one of whom I grew close to. Jeanie possessed long blond curls, a mischievous smile, and a lush body. My private nickname for her was "Curvy," which I shared with no one, not even Hues. She insisted on calling me by my given name, Brian, rather than Buck.

Our first real kiss, on our second date, was filled with so much passion that we believed in the moment that the other was special—we wanted and needed each other. We became lovers who frequently spent weekends planning and dreaming about a life together.

In the spring of 1968, I earned my BA in Education and began teaching that fall at a small high school in central Michigan. I was drafted into the Army at the end of the year. Hues and I flew to Vietnam in late May 1969.

CHAPTER 2

—— PHU BAI ——

We felt close to death shortly after we landed in Vietnam, but not in the way we had imagined. Given our infantry training at Ft. Polk, we'd anticipated being assigned to combat infantry units somewhere in the country. We hoped for the same unit. But it didn't play out that way. I was assigned to the Casualty Branch of the 101st Airborne Division, which managed communications with families back home regarding the thousands of soldiers in the 101st who were killed or injured in the long war.

Hues was assigned to the Graves Registration unit of the 101st. Their primary task was to gather American soldiers who died and take their bodies from the battlefields to Phu Bai. After identification, the soldiers were transported to one of two US military mortuaries in the country, where their bodies were prepared and then shipped home. Both the Casualty Branch and Graves Registration were located at Phu Bai, home of the 101st Airborne Division Admin Center.

Phu Bai, roughly translated as "valley of graves," was several miles southeast of Camp Eagle, where the 101st Airborne was headquartered in I Corps, the northernmost region of South Vietnam. The base supported major operations and Fire Support Bases (FSBs) in the Ashau Valley, the stronghold of the North Vietnamese Army (NVA), along with some Viet Cong (VC) soldiers. It was the setting for many tough battles with both enemies. The countryside was hilly and densely jungled—ripe for booby traps, tunnels, ambushes, and assaults on remote firebases. It was also home to deadly predators and withering diseases.

The Phu Bai camp was surrounded by many guard stations and bunkers along its big, multiple-mile perimeter. The camp included the 85th Evacuation Hospital and the Graves Registration Center, a fighter-jet capable runway, multiple helicopter landing pads, numerous sand-bagged living hooches for several thousand soldiers, latrines, mess halls, transient barracks, two small clubs for officers and enlisted men, dozens of dirt roads, and a complex of administrative offices.

The complex included dozens of cubicles for the Casualty Branch, Payroll, Personnel Records, Legal, Transportation, Military Police, Processing Centers for incoming and outgoing soldiers, and so forth. Many offices were located in a corrugated sheet metal building about thirty feet high in the center and stretching nearly three hundred feet long.

I reported to the Casualty Branch the afternoon I arrived at Phu Bai. I was directed to Sergeant Moretti's office in the Administration Center.

"PFC Brian Kinder reporting for duty, Sergeant Moretti," I said.

The sergeant, a short man in his forties with graying hair and piercing brown eyes, looked me up and down and nodded. "Welcome to the Casualty Branch, Private Kinder. I read your records recently. How'd you end up here?" he grinned.

"Well, that's my question too, Sergeant. I was sure I'd be assigned to an infantry outfit, given my training," I said.

"Maybe the college degree," he said. "Many in the branch have a degree or some university education, which is important because your job involves a lot of writing. And typing. Along with some patrolling and guard duty. And maybe a little shooting and some mortars and rockets once in a while. But probably a lot more writing than shooting." He grinned again.

I nodded. "Okay. What kind of writing?"

"Sympathy letters."

"Sympathy letters," I repeated.

"You're the new next-of-kin editor, Kinder. You write letters to families whose son, brother, father, husband, or other kin died here in Nam. You done a lot of writing?" he asked.

"Lots of writing, yes. But no experience with . . . sympathy letters."

"Don't worry. You'll have more help than you want. And you'll learn fast, right?"

"Fast, yes," I said.

"Good," he said as he stood. "Let's go meet Captain Randall, our fearless leader," he grinned. "And be on your best behavior," he winked. "Just a tip, PFC."

When we entered Captain Randall's office at the back of the Casualty Branch room, he held up his hand for us to wait. He appeared to be writing a note. We waited for several minutes.

"Come in," he finally said.

Sergeant Moretti saluted him. "Sir, I want to introduce you to our newest member of the Casualty Branch team, PFC Brian Kinder."

I followed the sergeant's lead, and his tip, and saluted the captain. "PFC Kinder reporting for duty, sir."

Captain Randall slowly looked me up and down. "At ease, Private." He waved the sergeant out of the office. "I want you to understand the important role the Casualty Branch plays in the war," he said. "We don't get involved much in combat here on the base unless we get hit. And sometimes we do. But what we do get involved with every day are injuries and deaths suffered by soldiers in our division. We deal with the aftermath of combat for soldiers in the 101st. who die in combat or accidents or are seriously injured. We're the key link between them and their families back home."

"Yes, sir," I said.

"Your specific role: write the letters to families to inform them their soldier died in combat or some other manner, maybe an accident or a suicide. We had one just last week—a kid who wouldn't go up a hill anymore. Blew his brains out. Think about that, Private. You write the official military letter of death. It has to be perfect. No spelling errors, no wrong names. Not too much and not too little detail. Just enough. And then you go big on praise for his service, his courage and honor. Not too much but enough. Do you understand me, Private?"

"Yes, sir. I understand."

"Well, I'll make sure you understand because I sign off on all your letters before they're sent off. When you think your letter is done, you bring it to me. Clear?"

"Yes, sir."

"And if you've screwed up the letter in any way, I'll let you know. Loud and clear. So, I hope you're a damn good writer."

"I am, sir."

"I hope you weren't a history major, or worse, some damn drama major in college."

"No, sir. English major. Lots of writing and editing experience. Just not with letters about dead soldiers."

The captain rose from his chair, came around his desk, and moved close until his face was no more than six inches from my own. His deep brown eyes were lit with disdain, while his thin lips framed a perfect sneer. I'd seen a few of those in the Army already.

"Just remember, Private, I'll be watching you. I'll be looking over your shoulder. At all times. I've got a minor in English, which is probably worth a lot more than your major from one of those weak directional schools. What was it? Western or Eastern Michigan?" he sneered.

"My writing skills are excellent, sir."

"We'll find out, Kinder. Just don't mess with me. Now go meet your team and get to work. You're dismissed." He walked back to his desk, sat down, and picked up the phone.

I gave the captain a slow salute, turned, and left his office.

Sergeant Moretti met me outside the office door and walked out with me. When we were clear of the office, he whispered, "You managed that well. He's the only real prick on our team." He laughed and led me off to meet the others.

Eight men worked in the Casualty Branch, most of whom were college graduates or college students who'd been drafted. Carl was a farm boy with a degree in biology from the University of Iowa and a new wife working in the fields of his father's farm. "Tiny" Jenson was a small man with big glasses and a bigger degree from MIT. Harry Weaver, who loved a joint or two each day, grew up in the "best fishing country in the world" near Eugene, Oregon. Monty Clarkson, the ever-nervous "married man" from Galveston, Texas, was drafted two months after his wedding. His wife announced she was pregnant two days before he flew to Vietnam.

Pierre Barrilleaux, a hulking blond with a broad smile and deep voice, possessed an accent so Cajunized he was virtually impossible to understand, even when he spoke slowly, which he seldom did. But if you asked him to repeat what he'd said, he'd just smile at you like you were a moron and flash you the middle finger. Virgil Rossi from Brooklyn, a tough kid on the streets, earned his marketing degree in night classes at CUNY. Norman Williams, a Black man from Chicago, was drafted after his junior year at Loyola University. He told everyone he was triple majoring in guitar, women, and marijuana. Wink, wink.

My new buddies in the Casualty Branch told me Sergeant Moretti had more than twenty years of service. They said he was a tough but good man with a laugh he was unable to stop once he got started. So, they all worked hard to make him laugh at least once an hour.

On the other hand, they all rolled their eyes when they talked about the captain. Tiny described him as "a preening non-smiler with an empire-state-building-sized ego that toppled on at least one of us daily." Several months earlier, Tiny had set up a betting pool early each morning to determine which soldier the captain would shit on first that day. The winnings were split between the predictor and the dumped-on-soldier.

The walls of the Casualty Branch office were marked by a montage of unusual, eye-catching images in addition to the standard calendars and family pictures. One large map depicted several dozen firebases in the Ashau Valley, the locations of the 101st Division units, and soldier populations at each firebase.

Another large chart provided a sobering scorecard of the number of American soldiers in the 101st who'd been killed in action (KIA), wounded in action (WIA), missing in action (MIA), non-battle deaths (NBDs), and so forth.

A smaller scorecard listed DEROS rankings (date of estimated return from overseas) of men in the Casualty Branch. Pierre was the short-timer with only thirty-four days left in Vietnam. He happily informed me I was now at the bottom of the list—nearly one year to go.

"Probably won't make it," Pierre said. He winked and gave me the middle finger.

Most striking of all was a roughly six-foot-by-six-foot square, crude but colorful painting depicting a mountaintop covered with snow that was lit by a pink full moon in a dark blue night sky filled with hundreds of jagged silver stars. Stark. Vivid. Haunting.

Harry told me he painted it one weekend when he pulled a forty-eight-hour weekend shift as penalty for smoking a joint in the office.

"It's my gift," he said. "My gift to all our living and dying brothers in the jungle heat in this country, man. It's an icy cold mountain top under a pink neon moonlight that leads up to heaven, and it cools you the hell off on the ride there. It's the high road to heaven, man, if you get my meaning."

"Ask him how many joints it took," Tiny said.

"Five," Harry said. "Or maybe more than five. I wasn't really counting, you know? All I do know—it was sure as hell a huge high for me!"

"Where in the world did you get paint for it?" I asked.

"There's an old, old one-legged Vietnamese man who lives in the space beneath the little barbershop," Harry said. "If you got cash, he can get about anything you need or want. Except an early flight home."

"And the captain approved it?" I asked.

Tiny giggled. "It was done before he got here," he said. "For whatever reason, Sgt. Moretti loved it. He told the captain 'hands off' because higher-ups on the base approved it."

My primary task was to receive the killed-in-action (KIA) reports via phone, gather relevant personnel information and records, and then write personalized sympathy letters to their families back home. Tiny led me through the process the next morning when our phone rang about 0730. He picked up the phone, which was in the middle of a big desk: I sat on one side, and Tiny on the other. An old Remington typewriter sat in front of each of us. As Tiny picked up the phone he whispered to me: "Listen closely and make some notes. Write exactly what I say." Then he began the conversation.

"Casualty Branch, 101st Airborne Division Airmobile. Specialist Jenson speaking. May I help you, sir?" He listened for a moment then repeated what the other party was saying. "Okay, you're reporting from the bush not far from Firebase Henderson. You have two Ethers and three Friars to report." Granny wrote it down and whispered to me, "Ethers are killed in action; Friers are wounded in action."

"Got it," Tiny said on the phone. "Please name and spell the Ethers . . . okay . . . William H. Bentley, B-e-n-t-l-e-y, a private. Correct? Okay. And the second Ether is . . . Richard M. Washington. That's W-a-s-h-i-n-g-t-o-n, a corporal. Correct?

"Okay, and the Friars are . . . Thomas Murray, M-u-r-r-a-y, a sergeant E-5, correct? And then Miguel Santiago, S-a-n-t-i-a-g-o, a private. And the third Frier is Gerald, with a G, Arnold, A-r-n-o-l-d, a corporal, right? And the estimated times of death and injuries? Okay, between 0600 and 0700. Got it. Anything else? Okay, take care."

Tiny hung up the phone and looked at me. "That's your first report," he said. "It's a perfect day when we have no casualty calls."

"How often does that happen?" I asked.

"Not often enough. Maybe three, four times in the eight months I've been here. Okay, read the report back to me."

I did so, then asked, "Ethers are killed in action, and Friars are wounded in action?"

He nodded. "You're wondering why the code names?"

"Yes."

"We do it because others like the enemy might listen in on our calls. Doesn't happen often, but it can. So, we use those codes and others for missing in action (MIA), non-battle injuries (NBI), non-battle deaths (NBD), etc. We don't want the enemy to nail down our locations or anything else."

"Okay, I get it."

"Now, the next step is to get personnel files on the five men," he said. "We'll do that at the records office at the other end of the building."

We rose and Tiny led the way to the records office, where we waited a bit to obtain the five files. Once we had them, we double-checked the names and ranks again before we returned to the Casualty Branch. Tiny then opened a file drawer containing labeled cover sheets for the files. He taped ETHER cover sheets on files for Bentley and Washington and FRIAR cover sheets on those for Murray, Santiago, and Arnold. He handed the two ETHER files to me and kept the three FRIAR files.

"I work on the Friars; you work on the Ethers. I'm sure you were told you're the next-of-kin editor," Tiny said.

I nodded.

"We do them a bit differently, but no need to discuss it right now. I'll get you some copies of recent next-of-kin letters and show you where they are. First thing, take a long look at each file. Double-check everything. Again. Then review the previous letters. They'll help guide your first drafts. And here's my personal summary of do's and don'ts for the letters," he said as he handed me a thin file. "They can help guide you too. I'll review your drafts before they go to his highness." He grinned. "Any questions, Brian?"

I grinned back. "Not yet. Thanks for your help, Tiny. Oh, and you can call me 'Buck,' if you want to. Most of my buddies do."

"Buck. I like it." He nodded and we went to work.

Tiny's summary directions were simple and clear: write brief, clean letters. Provide a few details about where (generally), when, and (very,

very rarely) how the soldier died. Laud the soldier for his service to the nation. And especially, ensure the letter sounds sincere and is mistake free. If you make a typing error, you can't erase it. You start over. Letters must be error and erasure free.

I understood. This was the official Army letter to the family confirming the death of their loved one, so it had to be done right and promptly. Later in the day, I learned that sometimes when fighting was intense and casualties in the field mounted, I or others from the Casualty Branch team would join the Graves Registration (GR) team to gather bodies of soldiers killed in the field.

That's where Hues was assigned: the GR team at Phu Bai. He briefed me on his role and team when we met up after our first two weeks at the camp. We were housed in sandbagged hooches about a mile apart on the big base, but we stayed in touch via phone and tried to meet once a week at one of the chow halls in the camp. Sometimes we'd meet for drinks at a small Air Force bar, which was open to all military members. We always talked about our shared memories and discussed the oppressive weather, the letters I wrote, and the bodies he evacuated.

As Hues described it, he was one of seven men in their team, most of whom were graduates of the Army's medical specialist training program. They were led by Captain Fowler, a quiet man of strong convictions, and Sergeant Williams, a longtime soldier who'd "seen too much to resign and die," he told others convincingly. They were a diverse group in every respect, but they were all touched and sobered by their work, which was vital, nightmarish, and spirit-numbing. It was so likely to produce posttraumatic stress disorder for years that the unit was the only one in the Army where soldiers could step away to another military occupational specialty (MOS) if they wished, Hues told me.

At least that was the rumor. One of many rumors in the Army. Just like elsewhere.

Their tasks included gathering dead American soldiers at fire bases or other battlegrounds during or postcombat (and sometimes seriously injured soldiers too), wrapping the bodies gently into zippered black body bags, carrying them carefully but quickly onto the helicopter (a big target for the enemy), then transporting them to the GR Center at Phu Bai. From there helicopters or other aircraft would take them to two large American mortuaries in Vietnam—one in nearby Danang and the other in the south near Saigon at Tan Son Nhut.

Medical specialists at the mortuaries confirmed identity through dog tags, wallets, fingerprints, medical records, or written confirmations from fellow soldiers. Once done, the next-of-kin were notified of their soldier's death. Personal effects were also inventoried—watches, photos, rings, letters, and other items—then shipped to the Quartermaster Department in the US, where they were cleaned and sent on to next of kin. The bodies were cleaned and embalmed. Fully prepped, the soldiers began their long journeys home to grieving families.

"Our goals never change," Hues told me. "We recover bodies as quickly as we can. We positively ID them. We prepare and ship them home as soon as possible. And we do everything, *everything* with respect. We treat them like they are our *real* brothers. Period. So damn simple, Buck. And so damn sad and difficult."

I nodded. "We meet the same dead soldiers but in separate ways. You do it with your hands and heart, me with my words and images. Apart from being a combat soldier or pilot in the field, Hues, you got the toughest job. You're living every day with the dead in your arms."

"Maybe. But those dead brothers, they *live* in both our heads," he said. "Forever."

The days were long at Phu Bai, though we felt blessed every morning we weren't soldiers out fighting in the jungle. They were up for death every minute of every day. They were our real heroes in the war. We prayed for them.

Our twelve-hour days were sometimes followed by twelve hours of night guard duty on the big perimeter of the base. Occasional rocket or mortar attacks happened, which killed several soldiers. But the enemy launched no massive attacks on the big base while we were there.

I spent long days with KIA reports that summer, as there was a great deal of fighting in the northern area. I felt compelled to learn as much as I could about each dead soldier before writing his letter. I first read every word in his personnel file. His height and weight. The color of his hair and eyes. I'd stare at his picture, a formal Army portrait often taken during basic training, heads and faces clean-shaven.

Every face was different, yet too many were much the same: too young to die too young for the grave. Barely a young man, really just an older boy, now no more. Dead. Soon flown home to trigger forever grief in his family. His bones were likely planted in a cemetery in his hometown. Watered with tears and showers of memories. He'd gotten in the way of a bullet, a grenade, a mortar, a booby trap. Or he'd died an accidental death. Or was the victim of a rare suicide or homicide. Didn't matter. In the end he was dead. His grave became part of their lives.

I checked his hometown address, phone number, mother and father, or perhaps his wife—their next of kin. Sometimes it was someone else, a son or a daughter, a brother or sister. So many people would be devastated, left empty for the eternity of their lives. Their young man had died thousands of miles away in the jungle in a country they knew only through loud TV news reports or local protest marches.

Their young man utterly wasted.

The reach of death, limitless.

I wrote each letter carefully. Briefly described when the young man died, possibly a general "where" he died, or a general "what time" he died, and, sometimes how he passed, especially if he died trying to save the life of a brother.

I tried to incorporate something specific in each letter to make it less impersonal. Pay honor with some words. After all, he was a brother, though known only in death. Finish the letter and proofread it closely. Had to be perfect.

I then gave the letter to the captain, who'd read it closely and often attack or nitpick a word or phrase I'd used. As an English major in college, I demonstrated to the ever-sneering captain I well understood writing, word choice, and grammar. Better than he did. I was always respectful but rarely buckled under the captain's withering, glaring challenge. What was the captain going to do, send me to Vietnam?

The letter was then forwarded for signature to the soldier's relevant field officer, who signed it and sent it home. I placed a copy of the final letter in the KIA folder, which thickened daily. My last step was to stand and give a long, slow, solemn salute to every new KIA letter before I placed it in the folder. It was my simple way of saying, "Thank you, brother, for giving your life to the service of our nation. Bless you and your family."

I couldn't imagine my mother receiving and reading my KIA letter.

Hues's days with Graves Registration were filled with moving and evacuating dead soldiers rather than writing moving words about them. I spent one day working with GR about a month into my tour. I experienced in one day what Hues experienced virtually every day.

When the call for help came in, usually from a firebase in the midst of, or following an enemy attack, or an ambush or firefight in the field, Hues and sometimes another soldier accompanied a crew of typically four men—a couple pilots, a crew chief who kept the helicopter in top condition, and a medic or medical specialist from GR. The specialist led the identification work with the deceased soldiers and assisted Hues in loading bodies into the helicopter. Hues's primary tasks were to enclose bodies in the black zipped bags (if available) then carry and place them carefully in the chopper. A trained infantry soldier, Hues was arms and legs in the GR unit because there was a growing shortage of trained medics.

The crew flew to the battle location in a "Huey," formally the Bell UH-1 helicopter that was part of the 326th Medical Battalion. These air ambulances provided basic medical care capabilities for injured soldiers—IV fluids, oxygen, bandages, and tourniquets—as well as transportation for deceased soldiers.

The recovery and evacuation work was dangerous, difficult, and depressing. Hues was no stranger to death—his sister, mother, and father having all died before he was fifteen. But each body he gazed upon, then carefully lifted, bagged, and carried onto and later off the chopper, was a real person. A life suddenly ended. Alive only for grieving now. But alive forever in the memories of family and friends and his own mind, which he often visited.

He described some bodies as blasted, utterly wasted—just pieces of arms and legs to clutch and gently place in the bag. Other bodies were barely marked, showing a single hole or cut. All now quiet in death, eyes closed or open and waiting to be shut. Locked forever in the growing Vietnam memory room in his mind.

When the chopper lifted off a firebase to return to GR, Hues told me, "I give a slow salute to each body—man—and silently thank the soldier for his service, for giving his life for the rest of us. Then I pray to the Lord to embrace him in his eternal light."

In late August 1969, nearly three months into our year in Vietnam, I called Hues and invited him to meet me that night at the little Air Force bar. I wanted to surprise him with some incredibly special news I'd received just the day before. We both liked that bar because a beer cost just a nickel, and it was air-conditioned. Cold beer and cold air—pretty much at the top of every soldier's wish list in Vietnam, apart from *not* being there.

We met around 2000 hours, and shared a brief hug. After we received our beers, I raised mine in a toast.

"Hues, I got three toasts tonight. And I wanted you with me since you're involved. Or I *hope* you'll be involved."

"Sounds good, Buck. Toast away," he said, raising his beer. "Definitely up for some good news, any kind today."

"First, here's a toast to my future wife, Jeanie, who I proposed to in a long letter I wrote just last night and sent out this morning. I'm sure her answer will be *yes*," I said, winking at Hues. "To Jeanie!"

"Hear, hear, Buck," Hues said smiling and tapping our beer cans. "Congrats! But maybe we wait a little bit to share a toast? Like . . . until she actually *says* yes?" He laughed and took a long drink.

I ignored his question but laughed too. "Second, here's a toast to my first baby—boy or girl, I don't care—who'll be born sometime next February, maybe early March." I tapped his beer can again.

"Say what?" Hues asked. "How you know that? Man, you proposed marriage in a letter to a lady you love . . . but she ain't got the letter yet . . . and you ain't gonna get her answer for at least another month . . . but now you predicting a baby in February, March?"

"Yup."

"Uh, maybe we should wait a little bit, Buck? You feeling okay? Something happen? Something you not telling me?"

I raised my beer can again. "And my third toast is to you, Hues. I want you to be my best man in our wedding later this year in Hawaii."

Hues tapped his can against mine as an utterly confused smile spread across his face. "Man, it would be an honor to do that, Buck. Your best man? Sure! We'd have so much fun, but . . ."

I laughed at his expression and nearly choked up a swallow of beer.

Then his eyes shone brightly. "Wait, what ain't you telling me, Buck? I know you too well. You holding something back. Come on, give me the punch line! What the hell's going on?"

I laughed and tapped my beer against his again, then took a long drink.

"Okay, wait. You got some news from Jeanie, right? She pregnant with your baby, Buck? Is that it? That what this all about? She pregnant? That your big news, right?"

I nodded and laughed. Hues joined me and we toasted again, then opened new cans of beer.

"I got a long letter from her yesterday; took about three weeks to arrive," I told him. "Jeanie's pregnant, probably from our last two nights together in May. We're gonna have a baby, Hues! Can you believe it?"

Hues gripped my shoulder with his left hand while he tapped my beer can with his other hand. "I'm so happy for both of you!" he said. "Best news I've heard since I been here. And if you get married on R&R, I'll sure as hell be there, brother!"

"I hope we can pull it off in Hawaii. I sent her a long letter this morning, my proposal. But she won't get that for at least a few more weeks."

"Hey, maybe we can set up a call for you, Buck. There's a place here, I heard, where you can set up a call home on a schedule. I'll check it out. You two need to talk."

"That'd be great. We had a tentative R&R planned for Hawaii later this year. Jeanie was going to meet me there for a week. Maybe we can make that our wedding. We've been in love for a while now and have talked about getting married and having babies. Just never imagined it might happen this way!"

"Would be great, man. Hope you can make it happen. Can't wait to meet her."

"And a baby, wow! Hadn't even thought about a baby," I said. "But one with Jeanie? What could be sweeter, right?"

"Congrats to both of you . . . and the baby! May all your dreams come true. I'd love to be at your wedding. And we both know you *need* a *best* man!"

"Amen to that!"

We laughed.

"I'll start writing a special psalm for the wedding tonight," Hues said. "I'm on it!"

CHAPTER 3

—— THE CRASH ——

Late the afternoon of September 2, just ten days after Hues and I toasted Jeanie and our future wedding and baby, I received a phone call from Graves Registration. Fighting was intense around several firebases, and GR needed help evacuating some dead and wounded soldiers from firebase Bastogne. I agreed to join them after Sgt. Moretti approved the request. When I walked out of the Admin Center to meet a jeep driver for the ride to GR, Captain Randall appeared and walked toward me.

"Where you headed, Private?" he stopped and asked.

"GR, sir. They asked for help with evacuations from firebase Bastogne. They're backed up with the rains and heavy fighting. A jeep is coming to pick me up."

He stepped close to me. He was, as Tiny described him, an in-your-face type of officer whose bark was probably a lot worse than his bite. "Did I give you permission to leave work here and help GR?" he challenged me.

"No, sir. But Sergeant Moretti knows and approved it."

"Do I look like Sergeant Moretti to you?"

"No, sir."

"And who makes decisions about requests from GR? Especially when we're under a shit-heavy workload like we are right now?"

"You do, sir."

"Yes. I make those decisions. Not you. Not Sergeant Moretti. From now on, you clear every request for assistance with me. Do. You. Under. Stand?" He was close enough I could smell whiskey on his breath. I really wanted to punch him out. *Really.*

"Yes, sir. You make the decisions," I forced myself to say while I squeezed my fists tightly.

"And don't you forget it. Now, get out of here. And when you return later tonight, get back on those letters. Forget sleep tonight. Am I clear?"

"Yes, sir! No fucking sleep!"

He stared at me for a moment then walked away.

Great send-off, I thought. *Helluva leader. Brothers dying, and he's spewing his rank.*

The jeep ride and liftoff in the medical evacuation helicopter provided a break in a long day of hot, muggy, and windy rains that felt like a heavy warm shower. Hues was in the chopper, along with the pilot, Warrant Officer 1st Class Bill Perkins; Warrant Officer 2nd Class Harold Meadows; the crew chief, Vince Thompson; and the medic, Karl Davis.

"Two other medevacs been to the firebase earlier," Hues shouted in my ear. "They picked up four dead and four wounded. Heavy fighting at Bastogne and two other firebases. And the damn weather and visibility, they ain't cooperating."

As our helicopter neared the firebase, Perkins gathered information from his radio about our destination then shared it. "Here's the situation," he shouted above the engine and blade noise. "We have three deceased to evacuate—god rest their souls. They're near the normal landing zone. We also have three seriously injured to take to the hospital. One has a bad chest wound. A second lost most of his left hand and has a shoulder wound. And the third man . . . wait one . . . the third man just died. So, we'll gather four bodies and two injured."

Perkins paused briefly and quickly looked around at us. "That's more than a load for the chopper, so we have to work fast and efficient. Fighting is heavy. The rain is picking up again, and dusk is closing way too fast. Artillery on the firebase knows we're coming. A couple gunships are with us. They're our primary defense. Our secondary defense is our speed of execution. We land, load, and get back in the air as quick as we can. Got it? Let's do it."

As the chopper drew closer, we saw flashes of gunfire and artillery and a few puffs of smoke slapped by wind on the west side of the big firebase. From above the jungled area resembled a dark green sea around the cleared, muddy firebase located in the Ashau Valley. A soldier waved us in, and we saw the four bagged bodies. The two injured men were on gurneys nearby, a medic kneeling with them.

Davis shouted at Hues and me. "The two wounded first. I'll work on them. Then the four bodies. We're gonna be way overloaded in here."

Hues and I nodded, then glanced at each other, feeling the tension grow by the second as the chopper neared the pickup point where sounds of the fighting rapidly intensified.

An artillery round exploded sixty or seventy yards from our landing zone. We saw the gunships race off, firing as they attacked the apparent artillery site. Then the gunships rose, circled, and raced in firing again.

Davis, Hues, and I jumped out the side door of the medevac just as it touched the ground. More artillery hit nearby, a bit farther off target this time, though it sounded even louder and closer. We sprinted in the mud as best we could and slid to a stop near the two injured soldiers.

When we reached the men—loaded with drugs and looking dead—our world slowed down even as the actual pace picked up. We felt the rain fall hot on our skin like soft water bullets, pelting us and blurring our vision. We heard the distinct crackling sound of rifles and the thumps of mortars and artillery beyond the thumping chorus of our chopper nearby.

Davis took a quick check of the man shot in the chest, peeling back the cloth wrapping his body. He pointed to Hues and me. "He's first!" he shouted.

Hues and I carefully lifted the gurney. We fast-walked as much as we could in the slimy mud to the open chopper just yards away. We were very aware of some bullets pinging past and then the thunder of outgoing artillery fire not far away. We lifted the gurney inside the chopper, where the crew chief helped settle it. Davis climbed aboard.

We raced back to the other wounded soldier. We carefully lifted him on his gurney. Then we resumed our muddy race with the injured man to the chopper, where Davis and the crew chief helped lift him aboard.

As he was lifted, the wounded soldier with the blasted left hand and shoulder cried out, even though heavily medicated. He opened his eyes and begged me to put him out of his pain. "How the hell can my damn hand hurt so bad when it's no longer here?" his voice and eyes implored me.

"Move, move," Perkins yelled, waving us toward the four men now dressed in black body bags as Davis climbed back in the chopper to work with the wounded soldiers.

One body at a time, we moved quickly in the slippery mud and now driving rain that was mixed with the steady muffled sounds of artillery and rifle shots. Hues and I lifted the bodies onto gurneys and carried them to the medevac.

When we lifted the gurneys, Hues mumbled his prayer of thankfulness for each brother. I couldn't hear his hurried words above the noise, but I knew what Hues was saying because he'd told me. It was part of the ritual of his work.

I was struck with a sudden haunting sensation that each body we were moving contained a piece of my body. I was lifting and loading my heart, then my mind, my arms and legs, and the shadow of my soul, which weighed far more than other shadows encountered in life.

Each piece of their bodies, *my body*, was part of a bigger version of life. This was the last chapter of their lives in a book I didn't fully understand. And I wouldn't until maybe I finished my chapter by dying and being loaded on a chopper in the middle of the war amid combat sounds and heavy rains washing over us like angry waves. The sounds of life or the chorus of death? How could anyone ever know for sure?

"Last one!" Hues yelled. "Getting hot here!"

The sounds of the present moment returned fully. Artillery muffled in the distance. Gunships looping and pouring steady fire into the green sea of jungle. The distant scream of a soldier. Then another. The medic waving, screaming, beseeching us to hurry. Our chopper thumping its own drum-like music with its blades.

We lifted the fourth body, stared at the black bag and each other, then walked and slid as fast as we could through the mud to the chopper. We lifted the gurney, the medic helping, then pulled ourselves up into the medevac, where we adjusted the last gurney in the overloaded craft as it lifted off.

"We're out of here," the pilot said. "Hang on. Gonna be a hot ride for a minute or two."

The medevac rose slowly, then lifted and banked a bit toward the northwest, which the pilot must have felt was the quickest, safest air pathway above the battle below and the artillery position in the southeast. At several hundred feet the chopper travelled further to the northwest. I was taking a picture of it in my mind so I could remember it when I wrote KIA letters for the four dead soldiers on board. I wouldn't directly write about it in my letters, of course. But maybe it could somehow improve the tone or sensitivity of my words. Or maybe it was all meaningless.

Maybe a half mile from the landing zone a sudden burst of gunfire raked the overloaded chopper. Machine gun rounds or AK-47 shells tore through the chopper, which immediately began shaking then bucking up and down, ultimately sliding to the right and losing altitude. The pilot was dead, shot in the head and chest. I saw him slump down.

Pilot Meadows took control to the extent he could as he'd been shot in his right shoulder. He nursed the damaged chopper another quarter mile or so, fighting to keep it in the air though it continued sliding earthward. He was trying to fly the chopper over a small hill and out of range and view of the weapons outside the firebase. But all of us and the chopper were tilting and sliding ever faster toward the dense, darkening jungle below.

A new round of gunfire tore through the chopper, hitting radios, rupturing fuel lines, spreading debris, killing one of the injured soldiers, and riddling the deceased. The medic was hit in his head, which snapped back and then forward, chin on chest, mouth open, dead, staring at me. One of the wounded screamed until more bullets tore through the stacked bodies. Hues and I hugged the chopper floor, trying to hold on to the framework and the gurneys with the wounded, now likely dead.

The pilot was hit in another burst of fire, struggling to say "May . . . day . . . May . . ." The chopper began spinning slowly but sinking faster, sliding now to the north and out of sight of the firebase. The injured pilot leveled it just a bit before he passed out or died.

The injured crew chief grabbed the controls but lost them almost instantly when the chopper spun into some treetops and began a twisting, slashing descent to the jungle floor—tearing into trees, slowly coming apart as several bodies spilled out, then crashing on its side, nearly split in half when it finally stopped moving. My last conscious thoughts were the realization that the tip of my left ear had been brushed by a streaking bullet and my head was smashing hard against the chopper frame.

CHAPTER 4

— BENT OVER MARCH TO THE CAMP —

When I regained consciousness, I was totally disoriented. The night was dense blackness. The hot, heavy air clung like a wet fur coat. My swollen head throbbed with a rhythm matching my steadily thumping heartbeat. A misty warm rain trickled down my face, soaking. My body felt exhausted and constrained. I had no sense of time.

Several years ago, I'd had surgery on my shoulder following a car accident and they'd put me under for about an hour. Afterward I gradually passed through several stages of regaining consciousness and awareness. It was the same experience now. I slowly realized the rhythm and pressures I felt around my moving body were the arms and body of Hues. He was carrying me through the dark jungle. What was that all about? The tumbling, twisting crash flashed again in my mind. I tried and failed to put the two together. I brushed at the mosquitos in my face.

"Hues?" I whispered. "What's happening?"

Hues lowered his head near my face. "Don't talk," he whispered softly. "Chopper crashed. We alive. VC got us. Talk later."

I became aware of the assembling shape of a Viet Cong soldier moving in front of me: the faintest shadow of his back, a cone-shaped hat, and a rifle ready in his arms. I slowly twisted my head and looked back. Another VC followed close behind, the tip of his rifle just a few feet away. My brain couldn't fully process it, though I tried for another minute while I brushed at more bugs.

"We captured?" I whispered.

"Yup."

"Where we going?"

"West."

Several minutes later Hues asked softly, "Think you can walk?"

"Don't know, but think so," I whispered.

"We gotta try. We can't walk, we're dead. Killed Vince at the chopper. Wasn't dead but couldn't walk. Here we go, okay?"

"Okay."

Hues abruptly stopped walking. "Hey, my buddy, Buck, he's awake. And he's ready to walk," he said in a normal voice.

The VC behind punched Hues in the back with the butt of his rifle. "Cam mom," he hissed. "Cam mom." Or something like that. We later learned that meant "shut up."

I slipped out of Hues's arms and stood awkwardly, trying quickly to clear my aching head and regain my sense of balance. I was still a little dizzy, but my legs felt okay. The guard in front watched me closely. He suddenly pushed me hard to see if I could stay on my feet. I stumbled a little but remained standing.

"Di chuyen," the guard grunted. "Di, di." Get moving.

We pressed ahead steadily in the dark like the VC knew where they were going. They paused often to listen to the jungle's night chorus and assess the surroundings. Then they were off again, their rifles pushing and directing us. We followed what appeared to be a faint trail for several hundred yards, though I had no real sense of distance. In the darkness I could see faint shadows of towering trees and feel long grass brushing my legs. Bushes often rubbed my sides. Occasional vines caused one or both of us to stumble.

At one point we walked through ankle-deep water that felt good on my feet. We struggled up and down several low hills covered with small bushes and clusters of bamboo trees. Apart from being in the jungle, I had no sense of where we were, how long we walked, or the time. My body still ached from the crash. My mind was numb.

Maybe it's all just a bad dream. Maybe I'm lying unconscious at the crash site.

The VC eventually stopped and pushed us down on the jungle floor. They handed each of us a small rice ball to eat, followed by a small drink of water from a big canteen. The warm water tasted great but was far too little. Hues tried to hold on and drink longer, but they smashed his back with a bamboo club.

They pushed us flat on the wet ground and quickly tied our feet together with a split-bamboo thong. We wouldn't be running away tonight. But I couldn't imagine we had the energy to do so even if we tried. So, we lay side by side on the muddy jungle floor, our feet bound together. They threw a mosquito net over us. I interpreted that as a sign they wanted to keep us alive. At least for a while. The rain slowed.

Hues began to whisper one of his psalms, but the guard heard him and smashed the rifle butt in his stomach. "Cam mom!" he hissed. I put my arm around my brother's shoulder when the guard walked away.

I pushed aside thoughts that we were POWs and might die soon. I wasn't there yet in my mind. I never wanted to get there. Maybe it was all just a nightmare brought on by the helicopter crash. Maybe we still lay unconscious back at the crash site. Or maybe we'd died and were just walking into hell. Missed out on heaven.

Bathed in rain and sweat, embraced by the constant humming music of mosquitos hovering near our net, bodies filled with pain, and minds numbed from exhaustion, fear, and uncertainty, we fell into an uneasy sleep.

I returned home to friendly voices and smiling faces I missed. Or I tried to go home. Sometime during the night, Hues whispered in my ear, "We got this, brother."

They awakened us as first light crept into the jungle. The rain had stopped. The trees dripped. Heavy gray clouds covered what little sky we could see above the big bodhi trees and obscured the sun. Wet grass and towering trees constituted our world, along with the VC, four of whom surrounded us. One bent down and untied our numb feet. Then he began loosening and pulling on my shoelaces and boots.

"Hey, what the hell you doing?" I asked. "I need my boots!"

The guard slapped me hard. "Cam mom," he hissed. He slapped me hard again, knocked me on my side, and roughly jerked my boots off. Another guard also slapped Hues when he resisted. A third guard pulled his rifle up and tapped Hues's forehead, quieting him. They removed his boots.

More VC crowded close, reaching for the boots, arguing, trying them on, fighting to see who got to wear them instead of their jungle sandals. Two finally claimed them proudly and boasted to the others, who laughed.

Hues and I were left with our olive drab socks for footwear. No boots made me feel even weaker, more helpless. How could we survive with just socks or bare feet on the damn jungle floor?

They gave us another small rice ball and a drink of water. Then they delivered another nasty surprise. They forced us to stand, and two of them pulled our arms behind our backs. They wrapped our wrists tightly with split bamboo thongs. To top it off, they used more thongs to wrap our elbows tightly too. Our tied wrists and elbows already hurt, and they prevented us from standing up straight. We were hunched over awkwardly with our arms laced behind us. Utterly useless. Except as a target for beating or cursing. Or shooting.

When we moved out, we could only step slowly. My weakened sense of balance was accompanied by tremendous pressure on my thighs and ankles. Progress was difficult, to say the least. But the guards kept us moving with regular bamboo whacks to our backs, shoulders, and thighs if we slowed too much.

"Remember as much as you can about our surroundings and directions," I whispered to Hues in front of me. "We'll need it when we escape." The nearest guard whacked me hard with his club.

"Gotcha," Hues said as he twisted his neck toward me. "We'll get through this, man." He was whacked hard too.

The western side of northern South Vietnam bordering Laos was a difficult and confusing maze. The land consisted of shades of green, brown, black, and occasional yellow or orange colors painted and splashed across dense hillsides, steep slopes, and marshy swamps and woven thickly into scrub bushes and tangles of vines and vegetation. The trees overhead, thick and long-limbed, blocked most of the sky. Virtually everything on the ground beneath the trees also was invisible from above. Planes and helicopters would be unable to see much in the green sea below. We were literally submerged in a green sea of vegetation that threatened to drown us in the humidity and rainfall.

GIs who shipped to Vietnam were briefly introduced to the country's jungle trees, vegetation, and creatures in one of several re-training sessions after they landed in Nam. These "p-training" sessions, as they were called, consisted of several days of refresher classes focusing on things like rappelling, compass reading, treating injuries and basic first aid, identifying booby traps, and basic survival skills, which included information on the geography and nature of the jungle. As one instructor said, "Imagine you're lost in the jungle out there and have no idea where you are. No weapons. No food. No water. How the hell would you survive?"

I wish I'd paid more attention to the answer to that question.

The tall trees in our march were a combination of giant Fokienia trees, which reminded me of redwoods in California, and the two "big B" trees, as the instructor described them: bodhi and banyan trees. The bodhi trees bear huge, heart-shaped leaves and abundant vines. Banyans are also huge and majestic, considered "holy" trees on the one hand and "killer" trees on the other. They wrap their abundant vines around the trunks of nearby trees, eventually strangling and killing them. More importantly, the instructor said, manioc plants or bushes often grow near banyan trees, and their leaves and roots are edible and nutritious.

I learned many other jungle trees also bear fruit. These included mango trees and their green, orange, and yellow fruits. Slender papaya trees with star-shaped leaves and juicy, breast-shaped fruits filled with little black seeds. Persimmon trees bearing orange-red fruit. Medium-sized Jackfruit trees, whose fruit can be eaten raw or cooked. Star apple trees with round green and purple fruit. And peanut trees, which are low shrub plants whose nuts grow underground in pods.

I remembered bodhi trees had broad green leaves that might be used to protect bare feet or heads. We might need some of them for our feet and heads. Large teak leaves could also be used on the feet or serve as roofing shingles or tiles over shelters.

One of the most common trees was bamboo, exceptionally fast-growing, sturdy, and tough. Bamboo forests were common in the Ashau Valley and other parts of western South Vietnam. They sometimes grew so dense and thick that they were virtually impenetrable, which makes staying on a compass course difficult. Bamboo trees were used for everything in the war, from fighting clubs or bars for prison cages to logs for building dwellings, bridges, and fences to fishing poles and sharpened spears.

Recollections of this briefing played in my mind as the VC drove us hard. A faint glimpse of the sun at one point confirmed our general westward direction. Some things I identified easily in the jungle, like bamboo, the big B trees, several fruit-bearing trees, and a cluster or two of grapes. I imagined if we ever escaped we could survive on food in the jungle, though food might be the least of our concerns. Enemy soldiers, killer animals, and safe drinking water would rate higher. Okay, the odds were very damn long . . .

It took little time for us to discover in our constrained condition that the most difficult steps we took were ascending or descending the hills. And the hills in that part of western Vietnam were everywhere, one after another, endless waves of brush-covered, vine-tangled hills. With our arms tied behind our backs and bent over, we didn't have a free hand to quickly reach out and grab a limb or bush to pull ourselves up and maintain balance. Or to push down on the ground to keep us moving and prevent a fall. Given that and our overall lack of balance in other parts of our bodies, we fell all too often going up and down the hills.

The rhythm of our march battered our bodies and minds too. Take a step or two, lose balance, stumble, and fall, sometimes rolling or sliding a bit down the hill. Then, use all of your strength—*all of your strength*—especially in your burning, quivering thighs and shoulders, to struggle to roll over, climb back on your feet, and regain balance. Take another few steps and stumble and tumble again. Every fall was accompanied by at least one whack from a bamboo club. Again. Over and over. The phrase *rolling hills* took on an entirely new meaning.

Sometime later—and I had no sense of time in the heavily forested jungle with a cloudy sky above the trees—the VC took a short break. They each ate a rice ball but fed us nothing. We took a leak, which we did about every break. Two VC would untie our arms and guard us closely while we peed. Freedom for our arms, though very brief, felt wonderful. I was feeling the beginnings of diarrhea and tried to will that away. Then they gave us a small sip of water. With a bamboo whack they ordered us to move out once more. Somehow we continued to move physically. But we checked out mentally part of that afternoon in the hot and grueling march. We returned home in our heads to find some strength, as we shared later that night in whispers during heavy rain.

I caught myself softly humming "Amazing Grace," like my mother so often did. I pictured her home in our kitchen, wrapped in her favorite blue and white apron, baking bread and watching cardinals, robins, and blue birds flitting and chirping in the young maple trees in our backyard. She alternately hummed and chatted happily with the birds through the screened window over the sink as if she were talking with old friends. She had so many friends in life and nature, and she loved talking and making music with them all.

Jeanie's smiling face then filled my mind: the world's greatest smile, perfect—her big blue, blue eyes shining with lights of love, joy, and hope. More of her face came into focus: her flawless skin, the deep dimples winking at me from her cheeks, her strong chin and long blond curls spilling over her forehead and framing her perfect ears, often adorned with tiny silver rings.

Would I ever see her again? What was she doing at this very moment? Was she thinking of me? Had she received my letter and marriage proposal? And that baby inside her . . . our baby . . . it would certainly have blue eyes like the two of us, right? Boy or girl, I didn't care. I just wanted to hold that baby someday, and I wanted to hold Jeannie too. Replace the bamboo constraints on my arms with the feel and pleasure of her flesh and body, her firm, rich curves.

The present moment then returned, and as I tumbled down a small hill I wondered when would she find out I was gone, missing in action.

Later that night Hues told me where his "twisted" mind had gone as we marched.

"Back walking the streets of my church in River Rouge. Sunny but cool Saturday morning in autumn. Man, cool air was great, Buck. Saw the wind swirling, leaves curling on the ground, spinning and tumbling from trees. Remember them fall leaf colors? But the weirdest thing was, walking back home wearing the *same* tie-ups behind my back and bent over. Just like now! You believe it? Was my mind already so twisted I couldn't recognize now versus then? Here versus there? Jungle versus concrete?

"Old man Rollins, who can barely walk himself with a cane and some bad hips and knees, he walked up smiling and removed my arm ties. Hugged me big. We sat on a bench near the river. 'Would you like some coffee, Hues,' he asked?

"Rollins, one of my street parishioners, always carries coffee in his thermos. For me. With my free arms, I happily accepted the coffee—just a pinch of sugar, they all knew. We sat and shared some stories and hopes. Caught up on the lives of so many others walking the streets of our church of hopes. Who was a new grandparent? Who'd lost a loved one and was now trapped in grief? Who had moved on to another place or spent some time in jail?

"Old Rollins, he wanted a psalm. So, I sang my MoCity Psalm Number Sixty-Nine. Adapted it to the current crazy scene:

> Rescue us, Lord, from the drowning rains,
> bodies twisted in our marching despair,
> bare feet stuck in jungled misery,
> overwhelmed by pain, whispering our prayers,
> softly calling out your name, oh, Lord,
> eyes searching for your ever-shining light.
> Rescue us, Lord, we'll serve you forever.

"The music helped me, Buck. Me and Rollins. But then it quickly carried me far away from River Rouge, miles from sugar coffee and conversations, so many friends. Back over the big damn ocean. Back to the jungle. Back to marchin' with my brother. Then I got a bamboo whack. And damn, here I am again!"

Later in the day the march halted suddenly, twice. Each time a hand signal was passed down the line of VC, who quickly went to the ground, pushing Hues and me down with them. Listening to the silence in the first stop, a faint sound emerged in the distant sky, growing slowly into the sound of an approaching helicopter. Hues and I looked at each other. Was it a medevac? Or maybe a gunship looking for enemy to attack? As the sound passed over our heads in the sky high above the trees, I imagined it was more likely a Loach, a small observational helicopter scouting the landscape.

There was no way anyone in the helicopter could see us. We were lost in the green sea of jungle, hugging the ground. But what I really wondered was whether the chopper was actually looking for us? Had the Army already examined the crash site and counted and identified who was dead and who was missing? It had been less than twenty-four hours since the crash, so it wasn't likely given all the fighting in that area. Chances were, they didn't even know we were missing.

The chopper and its faint sound disappeared. The VC waited a few minutes, mosquitoes swarming around everyone, then forced us up and got us moving again.

The second sudden stop was more urgent. We'd just skirted an open, grassy area in the jungle and were slowly moving up a small, wooded slope along what seemed to be a faint trail. Hues and I were pushed down again. This time our guards pushed the noses of their rifles against our heads, clearly ready to shoot.

The VC were laying and facing the same direction, up the slope, their weapons at the ready. They were watching and listening closely. Were there soldiers over the rise? The two guards again nudged our heads with their rifles, their eyes blazing with hatred. They would shoot us if we moved or made a sound. I wanted to spit in their faces. Beat them with their own bamboo clubs.

I imagined maybe a squad or platoon of Airborne soldiers was quietly moving through the area, searching for us. Or maybe it was just a routine patrol. Or a team moving into position for an overnight ambush. I strongly sensed a presence in the jungle nearby, and when I glanced at Hues, his eyes conveyed the same sense.

At one point I was sure I heard a faint clicking sound. I thought about screaming out loudly, "Over here!"

Would they hear me? Would there be a firefight? Was there a chance for escape?

I glanced again at Hues, who was staring back at me, slightly shaking his head. I knew for sure I would be shot if I screamed. Would Hues too? If they would just kill me, not Hues, then I'd do it if it meant Hues might live and be saved. But I knew, I knew too damn well in my head and heart, we'd both be shot. And Hues's eyes again confirmed what I was thinking. The man could truly read my mind.

We lay silent for what seemed a long time. The only things moving were mosquitos and flies, an occasional breath of air. Then another faint sound resembling a muffled cough hovered in the air for a long moment. The VC guards were on full alert. Hues and I stared at each other again. Maybe it was a bigger, company-sized troop of men moving past.

Eventually, the signal passed back down the VC line: move out. We rose and, our minds numb, our quivering legs stumbling and sometimes giving out before we pushed ourselves back up again, we walked on for what seemed like an eternity before dusk fell, and we settled in the jungle for a second night.

We were almost blissful when the VC gave us each a rice ball and two small drinks of warm water. They removed the constraints on our wrists and elbows and tied up our feet again, which were cut and swollen. Our socks were badly shredded. We spent several minutes pulling leeches off our feet and ankles.

They threw a mosquito net over our bodies. My last thought was that tomorrow would be day three of our captivity. I quickly fell into an exhausted slumber that blocked everything around me, including the constant music of hundreds of humming mosquitos hovering near, waiting their turn in my bloodline.

CHAPTER 5

—— ARRIVAL AT THE CAMP ——

At sunrise they gave us another rice ball and a small drink of water. Our raw wrists and elbows were again bound tightly behind our backs. They moved us out quickly and quietly, winding their way early through a small valley lush with plants, bushes, groping vines, and scattered patches of sharp elephant grass between dense stands of pine trees.

For a while, the terrain remained more or less flat. The rain stopped. The sun occasionally broke through the clouds and sharpened my sense of direction. We were headed west, maybe a bit south. The noisy chorus of jungle sounds returned—birds, frogs, crickets, lizards, monkeys, and others I didn't recognize. Yet. The pace was faster without the frequent stumbles up and down the hills. The day warmed quickly. The air grew steadily wetter and heavier.

I tried to estimate the number of our captors. I'd counted ten that first night after the chopper crash. Yesterday I saw twelve, but I imagined one or two more were out in front of the column, alerting them to any dangers. One or two others likely trailed the pack guarding their rear and flanks. So, I estimated fourteen to sixteen Vietcong. They appeared quite confident, like they knew where they were going, though they moved cautiously. It was their home turf, right?

I wondered why they had been near the firebase and crash site in the first place. They weren't close enough to attack it, but maybe they were on their way to join the ongoing battle. Or perhaps their goal was to capture survivors from helicopter crashes like ours. Or maybe they were on their way to set an ambush for American soldiers trekking to the firebase.

All I knew was I'd never know. And in the end it didn't matter, did it? They'd captured us: we were prisoners now—their prisoners—which was underscored with every step with the tight restraints biting and cutting our wrists and elbows.

At one point we heard the faint hacking sounds of another helicopter growing louder in the distance. We were again pushed to the ground in the bushes, rifle tips pressed against our heads. Our guards gave us their killer stares again.

The chopper, another Loach, flew overhead, slowed, and hovered. It then made a sweeping turn and flew the same track over the valley and us again, flying a bit lower this time. But whatever the pilot imagined he saw he apparently didn't see again. The chopper turned and resumed flying south. When we rose, Hues gave me a frown, like he was disappointed the chopper missed us again.

After a brief wait, we moved out, more westerly again, our general direction since the crash. We encountered more hills. Hues and I worked back into that sweaty, painful rhythm: moving slowly, balancing awkwardly on our aching thighs and swollen ankles, sometimes stumbling, falling, rolling, then fighting to get back on our feet again. Over and over.

Our bodies grew filthier and more bruised. Our minds struggled to find the right balance of physical and mental numbness to bear the burden of pain—if there was such a thing as balanced numbness. I went long stretches lost in my mind. Lost track of time. The future distanced itself ever further from the present. I imagined Hues dreamed about the past and struggled with an unknown future in the same way.

When the VC finally halted again, we collapsed under the limbs of a giant bodhi tree. We tried to shake off clouds of mosquitoes hanging near us, which was difficult to do with arms and wrists bound. The best we could do was shake our heads and blow breath at the bugs, which made our lungs burn. The little things in life are sometimes huge. Like a bug-free breath of air.

Three VC gathered nearby to talk and appeared to be quietly arguing about something. When Hues and I stared at each other while they argued, it was like looking into a mirror: our sweaty faces were swollen and red from mosquito bites.

The pain in our arms, wrists, and thighs outweighed the pain of those bites. But the combination of the two, along with our cut and sore feet, triggered a few preliminary thoughts about the possibility of dying, the positives of dying, and some corresponding suicidal thoughts and strategies. Then I suddenly realized no brilliant strategies or clever tactics were required to die. All we had to do was jump up and start running. Or lay on the ground and refuse to move or walk. They'd quickly shoot us or beat us to death. Dying was so much damn easier than living like we were on the march.

Man, get hold of your damn crazy mind! Get it together!

I shook my head and tried to clear it of stupid thoughts and silly self-pity.

Through all the pain a human rainbow suddenly appeared. Just four feet away, Hues broke into a giant grin and winked. "We got this, brother, piece o' cake," he whispered. "Just a little bite o' damn hot jungle cake!"

"Just a little bite o' damn hot jungle cake!" I whispered back.

We laughed hysterically and silently as we lay together and briefly forgot our pain.

Later in the morning the VC halted near a river. It was probably a creek in the summer, but now it was chocolate brown and swollen from the relentless rains. One of the soldiers slowly explored the edge of the bank. He stepped into the water at several places but found it too deep for crossing, apparently. He then disappeared around some bushes for several minutes before returning to wave us forward to a crossing point.

We entered the brown water. A strong current pulled steadily at our legs. Downstream a green water snake weaved its way quickly across the river, disappearing into a bank of thick brush on the far side. The assigned guards grasped the bottoms of our shirts, pulling and pushing us roughly into the river, which rose to our thighs and tried to carry us away. We moved slowly. My sore feet welcomed the cooler water. The river bottom was firm with some weeds or occasional small stones underfoot.

Near the middle of the crossing, I cast a wistful look downriver. The current carried my mind to better times on the water, free of physical constraints and far richer with possibilities for the body, mind, and spirit. Roaming free on the sudden horizon of hope. I followed my memories through the water as we reached midstream . . .

I was wading and fishing for trout in the cold rivers that crisscrossed central and northern Michigan. I found myself standing in one of my favorite rivers, the majestic Pine River, flowing northwest for about ninety miles in the northwest corner of the lower peninsula before pouring itself over a dam and spilling on the other side, joining other rivers racing west to Lake Michigan.

The Pine was set within a beautiful jigsaw puzzle of pieces of nature: green pines, oaks, and maples; silver and gray rocks and boulders aligned randomly along lush banks that lodged like gray chairs in the water; high sandy bluffs and river bottoms; and the bluest sky overhead. The river was a shining, curving, sluggish then racing, falling flow of pure cold water winding its way through that dazzling nature puzzle. It touched and painted everything with breathtaking beauty and swirls, eddies, and rushing, spilling white water rapids. For me, this and other rivers were magical places filled with the music of water and the powerful air of possibilities.

I cast a fat nightcrawler into a fast-flowing current running along a sand shelf, which gave way to a ninety-degree bend left, marked with a deep hole, maybe ten feet or so, of greenish-black water, which harbored an old log just breaking the surface and no doubt hiding some trout in the darker deep water.

I let the bait sink and flow through the right edge of the deep hole, feeling it brush bottom or perhaps the log. When nothing hit I retrieved the line and bait and cast it to a slightly different spot, dead center in the current, where it moved quickly into stiller waters beyond the hole and into the bend. Nothing.

On my third cast, I spun it a bit left of the hole in slower water, letting it settle on the bottom that sloped down toward the log. Nothing happened for a moment, but then I felt a small tug on the line, which I slowly tightened. When the anticipated big hit came, I snapped the rod up high and hooked the fish.

The fight began with the fish twisting, shaking, and pulling the line, working left powerfully across the fast-moving river, bending the pole. I admired its strength and fighting spirit. On the left side of the river, the fish braked abruptly and tried to dive deeper and race downstream, but I held him steady. The fish then flashed back to the right side of the river, momentarily twisting and shaking there, trying mightily to shed the hook. But he failed, and I pulled him a few feet closer.

The fish once more zagged left across the river while I was still reeling it in slowly. At that point, now tiring rapidly, the fish gallantly broke water and soared into the air and began that most magnificent dance on his tail: six or seven twisting steps, a perfect rainbow trout dance to shed the hook. His markings shined in the sunlight, a dazzling new sunrise of incredible beauty. Exhausted but gloriously fighting all the way, he settled into my net.

I let the fish flop in the net in the water for just a moment, admiring its great beauty and strength. Then I reached into the net and clutched it firmly in my left hand. With my right hand I carefully twisted and removed the hook that was caught deeply on the left side of its mouth.

I placed the fish gently back into the cold water and watched it flash and race downstream. Moments like these were special: prayers asked and answered in nature, God's real church, where I felt closest to people and memories I loved. To rich spirits that fed my life . . .

I was hit hard on the side of my face. A guard forced my head underwater, held me there. I couldn't resist much with my arms bound behind my back. As I began to fade, I concluded dying in a river probably wasn't a bad death in my current situation, and maybe I'd go to fish heaven. My head was then jerked out of the water. I gasped for air as I was pushed and pulled toward the bank and slammed down in the mud. Hues looked at me and shook his head. His eyes asked: *What the hell you doing, man?*

Across the river the ground remained flat for a stretch, though marshy in places and crisscrossed with more brush, vines, and a few bamboo trees that closed in on us. The VC continued to move as fast as possible while Hues and I struggled with our hobbled arms and halting gaits. Later, we stopped briefly for a drink of water and some much-needed rest. We watched several VC slip away to the northwest. We had no idea what was up. We could see no sign of a trail. Lying on our sides and ignoring the wet grass and mosquitos as much as we could, we closed our eyes and dropped quickly into a brief, exhausted sleep.

We were awakened suddenly by pokes from the bamboo clubs. Up and moving again, slipping up and down lower hills now, bathing in the humid air, struggling hard to find just one more step. Then one more. And one more. We hoped this was our last day of marching, no matter what lay ahead. Our legs were shot. The bindings on our wrists and elbows were painted with blood.

In the midafternoon, according to the faint sun overhead in the clouds, the march paused again. From where we sat, Hues and I saw a faint trail heading off north into higher grass and a slightly rising stretch of ground covered by bodhi trees. The VC set up a perimeter, and two of them followed the trail up the hill. They returned fifteen or twenty minutes later, each carrying a heavy black sack over his shoulder, the same color as their black pajama-like uniforms.

We were poked with the bamboo clubs and ordered to stand. Then we were totally surprised: the constraints were removed from our wrists and elbows. We didn't know what was next, but it felt wonderful to have our hands and arms free, our backs standing straight.

The VC handed the bags to Hues and me. We each slung one over our shoulder, the way they had carried them. A faint sweet scent came from the bags. Was it fruit? Sometimes fruit was served in the mess hall at Phu Bai, but I knew nothing about fruit season in Vietnam. Hues started to look into his sack but was whacked with a bamboo club.

Was there a village nearby? Where else could the bags come from? Did they grow or harvest fruit and other food for themselves and the VC in that village? The look Hues and I shared with each other said, *Remember this place for when we escape.* I took a few mental pictures of the site, nicely different from the dense jungle as we moved out.

We marched steadily for several more hours based on the moving sun, which we could sometimes glimpse above the trees overhead and between the big clouds moving rapidly across the sky like giant kites. We halted eventually near a gently sloping hill marked by hugely rooted banyan trees on the ridge top that appeared to reach up into the heaven and out to us at the same time. The hillside was covered with hundreds of manioc plants taller than the soldiers. The plants' green leaves sagged under the weight of the rain.

We pressed ahead and began a slow walk through a lengthy stretch of swamp. The mucky bottom pulled and sucked at our feet. The water felt good, but the muck caused us to stumble a bit under the load of sacks. For the first time, we became much more aware of our surroundings because it wasn't night and we weren't constrained and bent over so badly we couldn't see much around us.

We noticed snakes in the swamp, one curled up in a tree. The VC avoided or slashed them as needed, driving them off. Hues and I recognized a few based on our p-training. Vietnam was a special and dangerous home for snakes, we'd been told, well more than one hundred species, many lethal. We saw a black and yellow mangrove snake watching us. Then a banded water snake swam lazily parallel to us for a bit, checking us out. A dangerous brown and yellow pit viper hung from a tree. Moments later, a green tree viper with red eyes crawled on a limb overhead. Nearby a copperhead rat snake five or six feet long was coiled on a weedy mound of mud.

I remembered one of the nonbattle sympathy letters I'd written to a family whose son had died from a snake bite. The soldier, nineteen years old if I remembered correctly, was bitten by a king cobra, one of the deadliest snakes in the world. He was walking in the jungle near a firebase, apparently looking for a missing weapon or helmet or something. When bitten he'd yelped, fallen trying to get away, and smashed his head against a tree, knocking himself out.

Cobra venom works fast, and when another pair of soldiers found him about thirty minutes later, he was dead. They said the cobra was curled twenty feet away, watching them, its glittering eyes challenging them. They shot him. Two other soldiers I'd heard stories about also nearly died from bites they received from the krait, sometimes called the "two-stepper" snake due to its fast-acting venom.

Many other creatures lived in the swamp too, including big Tarantula spiders and the dangerous yellow sac spider. Hues nodded toward a giant Vietnamese centipede on a vine near the path we were taking. We saw water spiders, heard tree frogs, and watched several colorful birds stalking in shallow water on long legs. Leeches were widespread, as were gangs of whining mosquitos making their faint music and searching for a quick bite of flesh to deliver malaria, yellow fever, zika virus, or other gifts.

The VC paused briefly on the other side of the swamp and gave Hues and me a swallow of water. Dusk was coming on. A light rain began to fall, adding more visibility problems to our gray, darkening world.

When we resumed the march, the VC seemed even more anxious to arrive somewhere before dark. They pushed Hues and me to a near sprint and whacked our shoulders if we slowed the pace at all. We were exhausted, the bags now feeling full of concrete blocks, the fruit just a memory.

At one point I stumbled but didn't fall, then cursed the guard who hit me. "Stop hitting us, asshole!" I said without thinking. The guard hit me hard again, this time on the side of my head. I didn't fall, but an alarm bell rang loudly in my head. If Hues hadn't been with me, I might have started fighting the guards until I escaped or they killed me.

We walked up and down several small, brush-covered hills. In the dusk, it appeared we were walking on a faint trail. Suddenly the march stopped. We all stood quietly for several minutes until word came down the line to move on. We climbed a small slope covered with waist-high grass and dotted with pine trees.

And we arrived at the camp.

It was too dark to see much as we passed a camouflaged guard post and entered a partially cleared area covered by the limbs of a towering bodhi tree, partially blocking the rain. A bamboo shack stood nearby. We passed several VC who stared at us. An older man appeared and looked closely at Hues and me then muttered something. We were led toward a bamboo cage, the door open. The structure was a rough, eight-foot square of bamboo bars placed several inches apart for walls. The bamboo roof was tighter and thatched with large leaves. The cage was not more than four or five feet high. We wouldn't be able to stand up inside.

The older VC muttered another command. The guards began pulling and unbuttoning our fatigue shirts and ordering us to take off our camo pants. Hues and I understood what was happening but weren't anxious to lose our Army clothes. We peeled to our skivvies, which were sweat-soaked, torn, and filthy from the march. Black pajama leggings and shirts were then thrown at us. Our new gear. We slipped on the black Vietnamese clothing. The leggings ran down nearly to our ankles. The sleeves of the loose shirts reached halfway between our wrists and elbows.

A small black rubber drinking cup was handed to each of us. It was meant to catch rainwater to drink, as one guard demonstrated with his cup in the rain. A piece of the fruit we'd carried also was given to us. We were then forced to bend over and enter our cage. We sat on the wooden leg and arm constraints inside and ate the fruit, a sweet and juicy mango, so delicious we licked our lips and wanted more.

Pulled back outside by the guards, we were led to a crude and stinking one-hole outhouse and directed to use it. I exploded with diarrhea, which left me feeling even weaker. They led us back to the cage, where each of us in turn was forced down and locked into wooden leg and arm constraints attached to the floor. Lying uncomfortably on our backs on the rough bamboo floor, the constraints were closed and locked just above our ankles and our wrists.

One guard threw a mosquito net over each of us before he grunted and moved out. He locked the cage door and walked away into the blackening night. He sat under a tree fifty or sixty feet from our cage. About eight feet up the tree, a crude roof or covering of bamboo and big leaves had been built to block the rain over the guard.

Was he there for the night? In any case, he was far enough away that we could whisper without being heard and then beaten. It was the highlight of our march to the camp. We could finally talk. Quietly.

Hues and I turned our heads as far as we could and looked at each other.

"Home, but not *sweet home*," I whispered. "At least we can talk in here."

Hues smiled and whispered back, "Let's go home in our dreams tonight. We'll figure tomorrow out . . . tomorrow."

"Okay, but before we sleep, tell me about the crash, Hues. What happened? You said you would, and I really want to know."

Hues faintly nodded in the gathering darkness. Then he quietly told me the story.

"Smashed my nose when we landed, Buck. Passed out for a minute. When I came to, you were out. Big time. I looked around. Saw Vince, the crew chief, with both thighs sliced bad and trapped between one edge of the split chopper half and the ground. His scream was the only sound around the chopper. There was bodies and pieces of bodies everywhere. Sick. Vince pulled himself free from the metal. But he bled big and couldn't stand. Tried a couple times. Everybody else was dead except you. Knocked out but breathing. I checked.

"Then I heard voices. Couldn't tell what they were saying. Wasn't talking English. Then I realized they was Vietnamese voices. I looked around and suddenly saw them, moving like shadows around the crash. Maybe a dozen or so. Had those cone-shaped hats. Weapons everywhere.

"They circled our chopper. Checking bodies, slitting every throat. They were all dead anyway. Just leaving a message, I guess. One come up to me and pointed his rifle in my face. He waved it at me like he wanted me to stand. So, I did. Put my hands in the air and wiped my bloody nose on my sleeve. He kept poking me with his damn rifle. I decided he wanted me to move if I could. He poked me harder with his rifle, pushed me. I stumbled but stayed on my feet. Walked a few steps away from you and the chopper pieces.

"Another soldier come close, acting like maybe he the boss. He gave a quick nod toward me, then focused on Vince. He hurt and crying, talking to himself. A VC poked him with his rifle, same way they poked me. Vince was standing but kept crying, saying 'I can't walk.' He needed something to stop the bleeding. But the damn VC slammed his rifle into Vince's back. He screamed and they pushed him more. They trying to get him walking.

"Vince screamed more, then struggled to take a step. Fell hard on his chest and face. He couldn't walk, Buck. Legs bleeding out. He couldn't walk on his own, like I'd done. And that's what they were looking for, I guess. The squad leader waved his arm, gave a sharp command. The soldier nearest Vince slit his throat because he couldn't damn walk.

"Then they start checking bodies for anything of value. Picked them over pretty good. Then slit their throats again. Why the hell they keep slitting their throats, Buck? And why didn't they slit my throat too? And then it finally come into my head. Maybe they ain't killed me because I could walk. But why? Did they want me as a prisoner? Were they going to walk me away and stick me in a prison? And where? Man, my nose was bleeding and my aching head was spinning. Couldn't think straight.

"Then another VC closed in on you. You were just eight or ten feet from me. And I suddenly put two and two together. My slow dumb head! They were gonna kill you, too, if you didn't get up and walk. Slit your throat, just like the others. So, what could I do? You were unconscious but still alive.

"And then I asked myself, *What the hell would Buck do if he was in your shoes?* And it come to me in a heartbeat: you'd pick up my ass and carry me till I come to! What other way was there? I had to carry you, convince the VC you still alive. And you'd walk when you come to.

"So, that's what I done. I raised my hands and started speaking slowly to the VC soldier who seemed the boss. I took a step toward your body. The VC leader stared at your body and pointed his rifle at me. Said something loud and harsh,

"Took another step. Stuck my arms high in the air. Then lowered my right arm slow and pointed at you. Just started talking. 'Hey, this is Buck, my buddy. He's still alive. He'll walk when he come to. Guarantee it. He's a damn good man. And he'll work his ass off for you. Until we figure out how to kill you all, which we'll be happy to do together.'

"I was pretty sure they didn't understand a word I said. So, I made my big move. 'Now, I'm gonna bend down, pick him up. Don't shoot, hear?' I bent slow, damn slow. Imagined they'd shoot or knife me any moment. But hey, least that'd be a fast death, right? No suffering? And if they wouldn't let me carry you, Buck, until you could walk? No problem. Rather die with you than live alone in hell with them.

"The VC put the tip of his rifle on the back of my head. I bent down and checked for a pulse in your neck. Still had one, faint but ticking. 'He alive,' I told the VC with the gun poking my head. Then I turned and said the same to the boss. 'He alive.'

"*Man, here goes*, I thought and leaned over. Lifted you slow. Staggered for just a moment. Nearly fell but straightened my ass up. 'We ready,' I told them. 'We ready. Buck and me, we ready for anything you got. And we ain't giving up. Ever. We in your hands now, Lord. Show us the way.'"

Hues stopped talking.

I thought about his words. Ran the story through my mind again. Saw a rifle jammed against his head. Watched him pick me up in his arms and carry me into the dark jungle. What did it all mean to me?

Everything.

"Thank you for saving my life, Hues," I whispered.

"You my brother," he whispered back. "You'd do the same. And man, I got the idea just thinking about what you'd do for me in that situation."

"I'll never leave you behind, Hues. Wherever we go, whatever we go through, we do it together, brother."

"Together. Amen."

As I fell into an exhausted sleep, I tried to imagine where we were. All I knew was we were locked in a bamboo cage without food or water somewhere in the vast, dense jungle of western South Vietnam. No address.

CHAPTER 6

—— LIFE IN THE CAGE AND CAMP ——

Two things happened the first morning in camp. We decided to count our days, and more importantly we learned the answer to our burning question: *Why are we still alive?*

We awoke as daylight filtered like faint yellow smoke through the camp. The rain had stopped. Two jungle crows talked excitedly nearby, probably in the tree where the guard still sat watching us. A human voice nearby also spoke, but we couldn't see him. He sounded angry.

"Buck," Hues whispered.

"I'm here," I said, twisting my head to the left to see him. His head was turned toward me. Our eyes met.

"Got an idea," he said.

"How to escape?"

He smiled. "Still working on that. I was thinking maybe we should count our days, how long we're prisoners."

"Okay, but why?"

"Gonna sound weird, but every day we count, we one day closer to getting out. So, we counting up the days, but we counting them down too. Make sense? Or am I already tipped over this morning?"

"Sounds good to me. And counting days also means how long we've survived, right? Maybe some hope in that? And it's a great way to track events and memories back home. Like birthdays, holidays, or other special things that happen."

"Like having a new baby." He smiled.

"Like having a baby. You got it," I said, grinning.

"Okay, here's how we do it," Hues said. "We wake up first thing in the morning. And if it's light, we stick up our thumbs. Give a thumbs-up in our wrist constraints, like this."

I watched him flick his thumb up, then I did the same.

"That's our silent way to let each other know we alive and awake when we can't talk. And to count the days, we do it first thing in daylight if we can. We whisper the number of days captured, like 'Day seven, still alive.' If we in a place we can't talk, we hold up the number of days on our fingers. Like seven is five fingers on my left hand and two fingers on my right. Make sense?"

"Sure. So, let's confirm where we are today with our new whisper and finger calendar. Our chopper was shot down late afternoon, September second, right?"

"Right."

"And we were captured on that date. Then, we spent two more days on our wonderful hike through the jungle. So, today . . . today is September fifth. The beginning of our fourth day, by my count."

"So, day four, still alive," Hues said.

I nodded. "Day four, still alive."

Our experiences the first day in camp outlined our daily routine and explained why they kept us alive. Our primary job was to gather food for the VC and some NVA soldiers nearby, as we later learned. The days varied little except for the types of food we collected and the weather, especially in monsoon season. Hours of drenching, unending sheets of rain sometimes kept us locked in our cage for twenty-four hours or longer.

Our day began when the two guards assigned to us arrived just after first light. We nicknamed them "Caveman" and "Toothpick." Caveman was a short, burly man with thick muscles and a wide, flat forehead. His angry eyes were always lit with hatred. Toothpick possessed a pencil-thin body, strong but twig-like limbs, and empty hollow eyes. They replaced the night guard under the tree.

Toothpick opened our cage and released us from our restraints, then he and Caveman led us to the outhouse. Like everything else in camp, it was constructed of bamboo poles. It was a narrow building with a rough one-hole seat, also of bamboo. Humming and buzzing bugs and insects and an overpowering filthy stench filled the air within and around the small building. As Hues said the first morning, "Wonderful way to start and end the day, ain't it! A shithole that smells shittier than shit! Good morning and good night!" Caveman cursed and bashed his back with the club, nearly knocking him down. An early reminder—no talking.

We took brief turns unless one or both of us were fighting diarrhea, which became a growing problem over time given our meager diet and long workdays. Inevitably during the walk back to our cage, Caveman and Toothpick would whack us hard on our backs or buttocks once or twice with their clubs. It was their way of confirming they were in charge of our day and our lives, reinforced by the growling, guttural sounds they often made. We understood little of the Vietnamese language, but we became experts in reading body language and interpreting tones of their blunt and angry voices. It wasn't a complex language. But it was often painful.

Back in our cage, we'd receive the first of two meals for the day, which weren't meals as we'd known them. Often a meal was just a small ball of rice or two or a small portion of rice with nuoc mam, a salty fish sauce. That bite of food and a swallow or two of water that followed was our food for the next twelve hours.

Caveman and Toothpick would then return, armed with clubs and rifles slung over their shoulders. They'd head us out to work, one guard leading us, the other following. We weren't allowed to talk and were beaten with clubs if we did. We gathered food of many types at more than a dozen locations in the area over time. Most days we worked at one or two sites.

The first morning in camp we were surprised to be led to a place we'd passed in the late afternoon the day before on our march to the camp: the bluff topped with many big banyan trees. Our walk that morning took little more than an hour, moving steadily through jungle stretches and the big swamp where we'd seen so many snakes. We moved a lot faster in daylight without our arms tied behind our backs.

Once there, one of the guards bound our wrists together with a vine and watched us while the other guard quickly scouted the bluff. When he signaled okay, our wrists were freed and we were given little shovels, really just big spoons, no more than a foot long. As directed, we knelt and used the tools to dig up roots of manioc bushes buried deep in the ground. Hundreds of them covered the hillside below the tall trees. We broke or cut the roots into chunks about six inches long and placed them in two black bags the guards gave us. After four or five four hours of digging and fighting the tough roots, we filled our bags with thirty or forty pounds of them.

The guards gave us a short break and a drink of water. They squatted about thirty feet from us and smoked cigarettes. We were dirty and sweating heavily, exhausted but glad to be off our knees and sitting in long grass near the trees. We felt a hot, wet, heavy breeze on our faces. We lay back and stared at the dark gray sky. Rain would soon reach us. It would feel good.

Hues whispered softly, "When you get a chance, break off couple pieces of root. Hide in your pockets. Not so big they show."

"Good idea," I whispered back. "Food gonna be a challenge."

"Yup. Good thing the Banyan Tree Store close by," he said and grinned.

"But . . . I don't think we should do it today, our first time here. They may be expecting us to do just that. Then enjoy beating the hell out of us when they find the roots," I said.

Hues nodded. "You may be right on."

"The second visit is another opportunity, though. And if they don't find any roots today, they may not worry about it again."

Hues reached out with his fist, and we dapped, grinning at each other about a silly root.

The guards walked over, whacked our shoulders with their clubs, and got us up and moving again. We carried the black sacks to the edge of the swamp, where they directed us to clean the manioc roots with swamp water and our hands. The cooler water felt great, though it was dirty. We washed our faces anyway.

As we prepared to leave, the guards came over and raised our arms, checking our pockets for root. Hues winked and smiled.

We made the long trek back to camp, the sacks growing heavier every step.

That evening we learned manioc roots could be cooked, eaten raw, or mixed with other food. For our dinner they brought us another rice ball and a small piece of cooked manioc root. And two drinks of water. The taste of the root was pleasant. In fact, we thought it was a delicious change. And a much longer chew than a little rice ball.

Our night guard came on duty at dusk. We'd named him Crosseye. He was an older man, thin, who appeared worn out with the war and life. His constant sad squint was the basis for his name. He appeared at our cage door with a bowl of what looked like manioc roots in some kind of sauce or stew. After checking us briefly, he returned to his tree and sat and ate his supper.

"Hope we go every week to the Banyan Tree Store," Hues whispered.

"That's two of us," I said. "So, here's a plan for some extra roots. We don't try to bring any back here until after they stop checking our pockets. Maybe they'll check us just a few times, or maybe they will forever. But we wait until they stop checking before we take a chance. What do you think?"

"Works for me, man."

And it did work out. The guards stopped checking our pockets after the third visit, so we were able to get just a little more food, which we badly needed.

Our day formally ended with Hues softly psalming a prayer as we lay locked in our restraints. I'd heard his psalms often at Ft Polk and knew a few by heart. When I'd first heard Hues psalming, I thought it was weird. Why was he praying that way? Did he honestly believe there was a Lord in heaven who'd respond to his words and psalming with a better life?

But the more I heard, the more I appreciated the music and the man. Especially now. His psalming was like soft singing with a subtle rhythm—true musical poetry. It was a graceful way to end each sweltering day and inspire a little hope for tomorrow. Our range of hopes was vast. Escape and freedom stood at the far, far end, almost invisible. At the other end and much closer was a collection of smaller hopes, like one less beating, one more rice ball, a daily piece of fruit, two bites of fish, and a cold drink of water each day. Closer and so simple, but still tauntingly beyond our reach.

If there truly was a Lord—and I still had doubts given my own experiences with a fake minister and some phony Christians I'd met over the years—Hues was the closest man to God, or his son, Jesus, I'd ever met. The truth was in manners, his voice, his eyes, his reaching out to others. His bright light that shined even on the darkest days. His psalming.

I saw his spirit occasionally in his eyes, which sometimes seemed to explode with blinding light. I also felt his spirit in his embrace, a warm smile, his soul's hug of my heart. I don't know whether my brother's spirit truly reflected the Lord's light, but I do know his spirit was with me. I felt it. I needed it. I hung on to it.

Early the evening of day ten, we crossed paths with two other Americans. Our guards were leading us to the outhouse as the other Americans were just leaving. We were totally surprised. While speaking and talking were forbidden, the two American prisoners had somehow discovered the guards did tolerate, for whatever reason, some soft singing and quiet praying when kneeling, heads bowed and hands folded together, like they were worshipping the guards. So, when we crossed paths tonight, one soldier dropped to his knees, bowed his head, and started softly singing the "On Top of Old Smokey" nursery rhyme and folk song:

> "On top of old Smokey,
> All covered in snow,
> My name is Robbie,
> The great Robbie Hart.
> I come from wheat fields
> In Livingston, Kansas."

The other American then knelt, made the sign of the cross, and prayed softly:

> "On top of old Smokey,
> I lost my true lover,
> My name is Raymond
> The great Raymond Sloan.
> I live down in Dixie,
> Bama boy from Mobile."

When we again passed them during our food patrols a few days later, Hues and I dropped to our knees and responded in kind. I softly prayed:

> "On top of old Smokey,
> All covered with snow,
> I'm Brian Kinder,
> But most call me Buck.
> From the village of Farewell,
> In the Great Lakes State."

Hues then put his hands over his heart and prayed:

> "On top of old Smokey,
> I found my true Lord.
> Jameis Jones my name is,
> But most call me Hues.

Great Lakes State boy too,
From the River they call Rouge."

Through occasional shared "prayers," along with rare, whispered conversations over the next few weeks when we worked the same area several times, we learned Robbie and Ray had served in the 327th Infantry with the 101st Airborne. They were captured during an ambush of their squad, the others killed. They'd been prisoners seven months and were planning an escape. "Ain't no such thing as long life in this camp," Ray prayed softly on his knees one day. "Get your ass out or die in your damn cage."

When they'd arrived in camp, they discovered two other Americans lived in a third cage, a bit farther west of their cage, which was a bit west from ours. One soldier, Sojung, was an Asian-American who became lost in a patrol with a platoon from the 2/502nd Infantry. He was beaten steadily and horribly, given his Asian blood, and eventually he was beaten to death in the Beatdown Ring, his arms and legs cut off.

The other soldier, DeWayne Johnson, a Black soldier from Chicago, was forced to dig a hole and bury Sojung. Johnson also was savagely beaten because he fought back in the Beatdown Ring. One night during an intense storm, he escaped camp along the river. Some of the VC pursued him that night, but the Americans never knew whether he escaped to safety, was re-captured elsewhere, or killed and left to rot in the jungle. He never returned.

Though imprisoned in a VC camp, we came to understand the camp we lived in wasn't a traditional POW camp. Rather, it was a location that was part of a pipeline for bringing NVA soldiers into the war in South Vietnam from Laos via the nearby Ho Chi Minh Trail. Hues and I, along with the other prisoners, worked long hours each day to find and gather food to feed a couple platoons of VC in the camp, as well as some of the NVA soldiers passing through who were being prepped and armed for combat.

We learned American prisoners served another purpose too: we provided sadistic entertainment for the NVA. Every two weeks or so, one of us was selected and led into a circle of NVA and VC in an area of tall grass in the camp. We called it the Beatdown Ring, which is exactly what happened in that circle. Two or three designated NVA soldiers, armed with bamboo clubs, attacked and savagely beat an unarmed American, leaving him battered and bloodied, near death, or sometimes dead in the end.

The VC guards then dragged the unconscious American back into his cage, where he lay in pain for a day or two before being forced back into food forays. And if the American didn't recover enough to perform those duties, no problem. His assigned guard simply shot him in the head in front of the other Americans, one of whom was then forced to dig a hole and bury his brother in the Beatdown Ring.

The purpose of the Ring was never explained, but Hues and I agreed on two possibilities. First, the beating was a way of stoking even more hatred for Americans. The NVA hated Americans anyway, but the beatdown was a raw and vivid forum to fan those flames of hatred before entering combat against armed American forces. Second, the beatdown demonstrated American soldiers were not supermen nor unbeatable soldiers. Rather, they were ordinary and beatable, and they could be beaten into submission in the war too, leaving Vietnam to the Vietnamese people.

Most nights, Hues and I lay on our backs with the stiff wooden restraints on our legs and arms. We couldn't move our limbs much nor lay on our sides. Sometimes, for special punishment, we were restrained at night without a mosquito net. Since the bugs were intense day and night in camp, our faces and bodies grew red and swollen. The tough part was ignoring the pain and not screaming out. If you screamed or talked loud in the cage, you were beaten and restrained even longer.

As Hues put it so eloquently one night during our fourth week in camp, "Here we are, brother, in a deep dark jungle, on a dark, dark night in the middle of nowhere, and we don't even know *where* we are! We're in a bamboo cage in the middle of the night, no stars, no moon, no light above us. Our arms and legs restrained. The cage door locked, and our bodies being consumed by blood-feeding mosquitos and feasted on by flies and gnats. Sooo, we're no longer *missing* in action, brother, we *are* the action for thousands of friendly skeeters!"

We laughed hysterically but soundlessly.

As we became aware of our surroundings through our daily food gathering or fishing treks, we sketched a mental map of camp and the surrounding area. The camp was largely invisible to any aircraft. Vines dangled from bodhi and kapok trunks and limbs throughout, rendering the camp a kind of maze, perhaps deliberately constructed. In addition to trees blocking the sky and most of the direct sun, vegetation throughout the camp made it impossible to see more than a small section of the camp from any viewpoint.

What we visualized in our heads, and somewhat confirmed in our day-to-day work and conversations with other Americans, was that our camp was a large, rough circle with a diameter of about 150 yards. The southern third of the circle included the river running east and west; at least two small VC barracks, each holding six or eight soldiers and located on the east and west edges of the camp along the river; a stretch of mango trees; and possibly two small villages a klick or two from the camp, one east and one west, near the river. We never saw the villages, but there was enough foot traffic into camp to strongly suggest them. They were likely part of the pipeline too, whether they wanted to be or not.

Three prisoner cages, each designed for two men, were located in the middle third of the camp circle we imagined. Strategically it made sense. The cages were far enough apart, with thick bushes, crepe myrtle trees, and pine trees scattered in between; prisoners in any cage could not see the other cages nor fellow prisoners except in passing in camp, at the outhouse, or in the Beatdown Ring. On rare days, we all might work in the same area to gather food or catch fish.

A mess hall of sorts, where food was prepared and the VC ate, was more or less in the middle of the circle. Our cage, and the other cage in the middle of the three, offered a small view of the mess hall.

Nearby was an aid or medical shack with several cots and some medical supplies. VC and NVA soldiers sometimes visited there.

Hues and I went there several times for treatment of bad cuts on our feet and legs, or severe fevers. After a week in the camp, we'd gone there to finally receive some black rubber sandals for our feet, which were cut, infected, and swollen from walking barefoot. We knew the only reason they gave us sandals was because they needed us to gather food.

The Beatdown Ring was located at the western edge of the camp, in the center slice of the rough circle. It was apparently easily accessible from the west, and we imagined a VC community was nearby. We weren't allowed to walk or work on the west side of camp.

The northern third of the camp circle contained at least two more VC barracks. Overall, we estimated roughly two platoons of VC, forty or fifty soldiers, and more east and west of camp. All of the buildings were constructed of bamboo with thatched roofs. Only the prisoner cages were four or five feet high. In short, there was no sky, no streets, no roads—just a few paths here and there. And vegetation in the camp was so dense in places a tiger could be lying in wait just twenty feet away, and no one would see it.

Deliberate or not, the location and layout of the camp produced confusion and depression. How could we escape safely from a place largely invisible in the jungled, dangerous countryside? We felt utterly lost in South Vietnam—somewhere near the Laotian border, somewhere with several unseen villages in the region, somewhere that was part of the NVA supply chain. Bottom line: Hues and I were simply part of that supply chain, wherever it was.

In that sense, one day Hues asked me: "When we free one day, you think we might be court-martialed for helping feed the enemy?"

Just trying to lighten the load.

Apart from the food, we enjoyed the Banyan Tree Store for its location in a more open area, slightly elevated, which provided a bigger, more panoramic view of the world versus the tight, small world in camp. We could see more sky and gaze over a spread of bamboo trees leading east, the direction to safety, which triggered thoughts of escape and good memories.

We shared memories often, though sometimes just in our minds. Most days from dawn to dusk we toiled steadily and quietly, exchanging a whispered thought on rare occasions. On hot days we might be given another drink or two, depending on the guards' attitudes. In the rainy season we caught rainwater with our black cups and drank a lot more. And we often managed to sneak a bite or two of a manioc root we were cleaning. We weren't totally starved to death, just near death.

At other sites we visited—some just a few hundred yards from camp, others much longer hikes—we gathered a variety of vegetables and fruits: sweet potatoes and their vines; greens growing wild that the guards indicated were edible; and clusters of wild grapes, bananas, and other fruits in season, which was much of the year. These included mangoes, papayas, star apples, and jackfruit. Edible vegetation was often included in soup or broth, which we rarely received.

Sometimes we spent the day gathering firewood for cooking or hoeing and weeding two big vegetable gardens on the south side of the river. And when one of the guards saw a nonpoisonous snake, he usually killed it with his club, cut off its head, and threw it to Hues or me to put in our bag.

Our "favorite" work was fishing once or twice a week when the guards led us to any number of fishing holes in the river cutting through the south side of the camp. In summer, a makeshift bridge was over the water, which could be easily moved and disassembled if aircraft were heard in the distance. We carried simple fishing poles: a seven-foot length of thin bamboo with a piece of twine or line attached and a small hook, along with a mosquito net or two to place in good holes to trap fish.

We baited the hooks with grubs or worms, then stood in the water or sat on the bank. The water cooled our scarred feet while the sun cooked us well done. Fishing also provided a brief opportunity to bathe our sore bodies—the rare, rare blessing of the feel of real water on our skin to provide some relief from the intense heat, heavy perspiration, and constant skin infections. And sometimes the guards might be seated far enough away, Hues and I could share a whispered conversation.

During the normal hot season in northern South Vietnam, roughly March to August, the river was thirty or forty feet wide and several feet deep, with some holes and bends six or eight feet deep in the log jams and pools. In monsoon season, roughly September to January, the river widened two or three times its normal size and deepened accordingly. The water moved faster then, was murkier, and frequently clustered with limbs, brush, and debris. More snakes appeared in the wet season, both in the water and on the grassy, brushy banks. It made it more dangerous to fish, but it was still far better than walking through swamps to gather food.

Carp were the most common fish we caught—black, gray, and crucian carp. A "good" fishing day would yield three or four carp, a similar number of brown and yellow catfish, and a handful of Goby and snakehead fish, which were yellow and black with light blue spots. We mostly learned the names of fish and plants from Rob and Ray, the latter who could speak some Vietnamese. Sometimes one of our guards would get excited about a big fish we caught and point to it and call it by name. Or that's what we thought.

Late afternoons we'd head back to camp. If we were fishing, we cleaned the fish first. We were given small knives or sharp pieces of bamboo and worked on the fish at gunpoint. Then we were led to the mess hall, where we left our bags with vegetables, fruits, snakes, or fish. We and the other prisoners gathered a lot of food over time, enough to feed the VC and some NVA. But no matter how much we brought to camp, we rarely received more than two rice balls a day, and maybe a bite or two of fish at night, or a piece of fruit along with a drink or two of water.

We'd sit in the cage until dusk, when the guards led us to the crude outhouse once again. When we returned to the cage we were often placed in restraints, netting tossed over us, the cage door closed and often locked with a chain. Cross-eye would arrive and replace our day guards, spending the night sitting against a nearby tree. Our cycle of daily life: boring, tedious, sometimes very painful, always hungry and thirsty. But still alive.

At dusk on day forty-four, we were forced to watch Rob get beaten mercilessly in the Ring. Two weeks earlier we'd seen Ray beaten even worse because he resisted and fought them hard. He suffered swollen, blackened eyes, a broken finger on his left hand, some badly bruised ribs, and a headache that lasted a week. He lay on the edge of death for two days in his cage. The hatred for Americans was unleashed in the NVA's jack-hammering blows with their clubs, fists, and feet in the ring. Hues and I were sickened and saddened by it. And next in line.

The following morning, Hues woke me with a whisper just before dawn. He was deeply troubled by the beating; he'd screamed twice during the night. He wanted to talk about hell. This was nothing new. We had occasional talks about the Lord and the Bible. We often disagreed. Hues wanted me to believe in the light of the Lord. I wanted Hues to understand why the light might not exist as he imagined. I argued the real light shining on us was probably evil, not good, given the prevalence of human evil and suffering throughout history.

"You ever wonder, Buck," he whispered, "if the life we living on earth is the actual hell the Bible talks about . . . supposed to come *after* life?"

"All I know is, we're living in hell right now, man. And it's here on earth. Not too worried now about hell afterlife. How much worse can it be?" I asked.

"Okay, but what if we already lived a previous life; we just don't know it? And we failed in that life to love the Lord and live his light?"

"You mean a previous life as a person on this earth, or some other planet? Or a previous life of another kind—like maybe a rock or a river? I wouldn't mind being a river," I said with another yawn and a smile.

"Not what I meant, but I get it. I love rivers too, lots of good memories about days along River Rouge. But if you were a river, think about all the crap people do to rivers. Dam 'em up and let 'em run dry. Dirty and pollute 'em every day with garbage and trash. Then oil and gas spills, you name it."

"Okay, but what did you mean when you mentioned a previous life?"

"I meant maybe we already lived life on this earth, maybe once before, or more. And we just don't remember it. But what if we did?"

"So, we tried it at least once and failed?"

"Exactly. I honestly believe we born with purpose. To do some good for each other, like the Bible says. And we can do it in so many ways every day."

"Like being a good brother and letting the other one sleep, right?" I yawned again.

"Okay, sorry, but this kept me awake last night. But brothers is a good way to look at it. Most brothers got each other's back. They give physical and moral support, share their energy, make you smile and laugh, share food and water, right? And put their life on the line for each other."

"We got each other's back," I said. "Always."

"Imagine, Buck, just imagine our world if millions of people were more like brothers and sisters. Imagine we *all* tried to make some good differences in lives of *others*, even just little ways. Wouldn't our world be far better if all people looked beyond themselves?"

"Of course, it would, man. And I wish it worked that way."

"But we know it don't," Hues said. "Most think it's impossible, a damn pipe dream. Some people are that way, but too many, no way. They think life only good if they have it *their* way. And they want to be recognized. 'Hey, look at me! I'm a king, a queen. I'm much more special than you! I got more money than you! Worship me!'"

I nodded. "Sure, I know some folks like that. Saw a lot more in TV news stories."

"You got it. And then the truly evil people who want to hurt you. Make you scream and suffer. Control you. Kill you. Watch you die while they laugh. They're the Devil's family. Think about the words: 'evil' and 'devil' share four of the same letters, right? When you add a 'd' and make the word 'devil,' you put a face on evil in the Bible with an unforgettable name."

"Hues, you've given this a lot more thought than I have."

"Okay, I'm getting to my point, Buck. Earth is a hellish place, right? Unending wars. So many horrific crimes. Huge economic differences, a few 'haves,' mostly 'have nots.' Lots of mind manipulations, all kinds. Too many just all about themselves.

"Now, there's some good and great people too, like my mom, dad, and sister, and the Reverend, and a lot of streetwalkers, and you, many other people we both know. But too many others make life on earth a literal hell."

"Can't argue with that," I whispered. "Take our own situation here as POWs, the bitter, brutal war between two nations. But the rich get richer, no matter who wins, right? They sell more guns, ammo, helicopters, tanks, even military uniforms! Do they want the war to end?"

"Exactly. So, you agree there is some hell on earth, Buck?"

"Hell yes."

"Okay, what I'm saying is, what if what we call earth and our lives on it are the hell the Bible discusses. This life is the *actual* hell! It's not something that comes *after* life on earth. It's *here*, where we live *now*, and always will be, until we live life in the light of the Lord and share his love and light with others."

"But what were we before this life in hell, then? Do you mean life starts in hell? Every new baby is born into hell? That's not much of a deal, Hues. Makes no sense."

"But it's the real deal, Buck. When we die, if we don't go to heaven, we got to come back and live life again. We don't remember it, but hell there's so much we don't remember about so many things. And we might come back in a different form—a mountain, tree, river, a critter. But we have to repeat it over and over until we get it right. Live with each other like brothers and sisters. Only then do we move on to heaven and forever life."

"So, life on earth isn't really a midpoint between heaven and hell . . ."

"Life on earth *is* hell. Period. We start out in hell. We live in hell.

Maybe live five or twenty times here until we see the light and live it in how we treat others. Just that damn simple."

"Maybe, Hues, but that ain't simple. My biggest questions about hell as you describe it are: Why the hell are we in the hellier hell we are? Are we bad people? And since I know there was beer, a lot of beer, in the hell we previously lived in, where in our current hell hole do we go to find some ice-cold beer?" I asked.

"Dig deeper at the Banyan Tree Store?"

Day by day, we lived on. Gave each other a thumbs-up salute every morning. Counted each day. Shared good memories. But most days passed too slowly. Each was a lengthy replay of the previous one, an increasingly dangerous repetition of the combination of long work hours, constant exposure to heat and humidity, too little to eat and drink, too many hard whacks from the bamboo clubs, and a veritable smorgasbord of pains that worked in reverse, feasting on our increasingly gaunt bodies.

The repetition underscored our growing need for even a single moment of beauty each day. Maybe a bright green magpie winging near, a striking pink lotus flower shining in the swamp, or a bigger-than-life silver star hanging low in the heaven. Or a genuine laugh that lifted our spirits. Or a hint, just the faintest sense of hope for a future life beyond our cage. Looming overall was an invisible, even bigger, and more dangerous cage that slowly constricted our minds in a dense jungle of haunting despair and sometimes-seductive dreams of death.

Like me, Hues was not a perfect man, nor did he claim to be. He shared small secrets about some bad things he'd done, like lying sometimes to his father and mother. Stealing things from stores on three occasions (two books, a hunting knife, and two bags of potato chips). Ignoring someone telling him directly or indirectly they needed help or hope. Killing at age fourteen the man who'd killed his father, even if it was in self-defense.

He also admitted fantasizing about young women but for whatever reason found it difficult to talk to them about his feelings. Except for the Mexican lady who'd become pregnant with another man's child. And then, of course, there was Sena, the small Korean lady with the tiny waist and huge heart whom he loved and talked about nearly every day.

Hues also possessed many fine attributes, including a vital POW survival skill—evoking laughter. He could create a smile on my face or spark me into soft or sometimes raucous laughter, whether quietly expressed in the cage or in the jungle. But controlled laughter was well worth it too. For example, we'd agreed not to talk about our constant pains; we didn't want to devote more time focusing on our pains in words as well as those in our minds and bodies. They had their own voices and spoke to us constantly.

On the other hand, it was okay to talk about pain to trigger a smile or a laugh to momentarily ease the pain. At the end of one especially hot and humid workday, for example, when we lay in our restraints wrapped in pain and bathed in sweat and our overpowering body stink, Hues put it all into a smiling, laughing perspective.

"Okay, Buck, just imagine, you back in the real world. You know, that place we used to live and call home? And it's in the hot, hot middle of the summer heat, which we used to believe was really hot, 'fore we knew what hot heat humidity really is. And you, dutifully going through your three-times-a-week, sixty-minute workout you imagine is so damn difficult and demanding 'cause it includes sprinting and running, lifting some weights, pushups, nasty calisthenics—all that and whatever more you normally do in your workout to think you've given it all you have and are one hell of a tough man.

"And at the end of that grueling session, you go into your normally air-conditioned house to shower, dry off, rub pieces of ice on your head, turn the fan on, cool down, sip cold drinks, and recover, whatever. But you suddenly discover there's no house, no AC, no shower, no water running or otherwise, no fan, no ice, no drinks of any kind, unless you capture some of your own saliva to try to swallow again, no bed to crash on, not even a cot, no pillow, not a single damn towel!

"So, imagine now, if the only thing you can do after that rugged workout you think is so damn tough is to lay your ass locked down in a bamboo cage for hours, days, weeks, or months. Smelling yourself and your buddy stinking with sweat. Growing thinner and weaker with every breath. Nothing much to eat, far too little to drink. Just imagine that and then you know what? You'd feel just like we feel! You'd be one of us, every hot and waning second of your sweat-stinking life! And then you'd begin to understand how good life was—the life you had, the one you thought was so damn tough because you had to exercise three damn times each week!"

We smiled, softly giggled, then silently laughed our asses off. We gave each other an imaginary slap with our hands since we couldn't reach out in our restraints.

CHAPTER 7

—— THE BEATDOWN RING ——

Hues was chosen for the Beatdown Ring on day sixty-three. We knew it was coming but received no advance notice. Caveman and Toothpick simply arrived at our cage at dusk, ordered us out, and marched us quickly to the ring. The rough circle of cleared ground was located on the western side of camp. Head-high elephant grass surrounded the ring, and four bodhi trees with giant limbs blocked much of the sky.

The audience was already in place: a couple squads of NVA and a similar number of VC. The old mess hall man was also there, along with the regular emcee for the event, a man who looked bizarrely like an older Ed Sullivan with slicked-back hair on his hatless head, prominent teeth, and hands clasped together behind his back in the center of the ring.

He appeared happy in the role. A huge smile broke and spread across his heavily wrinkled face when we arrived. He pointed at us, clapped his hands, and laughed like a giddy fool. No women or children were present, but we rarely saw any in camp, apart from two older ladies we sometimes glimpsed at the first-aid station or mess hall.

The audience stood, kneeled, or squatted at the edge of the long grass surrounding the circle. They were spaced several feet apart, ready to push the prisoners back into the ring should they try to exit. No prisoner could escape his regular beating every five or six weeks unless he was badly diseased or injured. All POWs were required to watch their brothers' savage beating. The rumor was that two Americans had been killed the previous year and were buried in the ring in addition to the ones we already knew about. All POWs who died in or near camp were also supposedly buried in the muddy ring. No graves were marked, but I counted six minor depressions in the ground.

On the far side of the ring, Rob and Ray sat on the ground, their guards close behind them. They slowly and simultaneously shook their heads at us. They'd strongly advised us early on not to fight too hard in the ring. There was no way we could ever win, they'd said. So, we should just throw a couple punches, get in a kick or two, and curse the damn NVA if we wished. But then fall down after the fifth or sixth vicious whack from the clubs. The NVA would club them hard when they were on the ground, but only briefly. They didn't want to kill the Americans but rather fill them with a bitter pain that would live inside them forever.

It's much, much worse in the end, Rob explained, if you fight too much. They'd truly enjoy beating you to death given the slightest opening. So, make it look good, but don't get yourself killed by fighting too hard. They knew from their own first experiences in the ring some months ago: Rob acquired three bruised ribs, and Ray broke a finger and lost part of his ear and his hearing. Both complained of ongoing headaches. Hues and I thanked them for their advice, but we agreed to fight like hell.

The two designated NVA beaters waited in the center of the ring, bamboo clubs gripped in their hands, slowly swinging them back and forth, staring at us. We could see and literally feel the temperature of hatred in their seething brown eyes. Hues spit toward them, and Caveman clubbed his back. We were off to a good start.

The emcee, whose eyes were now filled with anger, waved his hand in a circle and shouted out a harsh command of some sort. The ring of men fell silent. The emcee then went on a loud rant. We couldn't understand it, but we could see the angering effect of his words on the circle of men. Finally, in the sudden silence following the rant, Toothpick poked Hues sharply in the back with his club, directing him to the center of the ring.

"Hues, stop," I said. "You stay here. I got this today."

"Don't think I got a choice, Buck. You neither."

I turned to Caveman, tapped my right hand on my chest, and pointed to the center of the ring. "Him," I said, now pointing at Hues. "Him, no go!" I shook my head side to side, then tapped my chest again and pointed to the center of the ring. "Me fight the SOBs tonight."

Caveman growled and slammed his club on my right knee, which dropped both my knees to the ground. I climbed up, gimped a step on the bad leg, and watched Hues being pushed and led into the center of the ring. He stood face-to-face there with the NVA, just two yards away. Both were shorter and stockier than Hues, who was skinny by comparison. He suddenly stuck out his hand.

"I'm Hues, your brother. Let's be friends," he said. "We all God's children, no matter the color of our skin, right? You got that? Well, I guess not!"

Hues then surprised everyone but me. He lunged at the NVA beaters and tackled both to the ground, one in each arm. They quickly twisted out of his arms, jumped up, snarled, and cursed at Hues, clubbing him, or trying to, with every swing. Hues was skinny, hungry, and a prisoner, but also fearless. He blocked some of their blows, connected on several kicks that swept their feet from under them, and landed a hard blow with his fist on one beater's nose, who spewed blood and went into a roaring rage.

The emcee screamed at all three fighters like he wanted all of them dead. Or maybe he was just thoroughly enjoying the fight.

The beaters screamed and regrouped, then launched a ferocious attack. They didn't want to just hurt Hues now; they wanted to crush him. The action was fast, relentless. Their blows now connected, coming hard and fast in a rhythm of pain causing Hues to weaken further. Blood from his nose ran down his chin.

He reacted to each big blow with a grunt or a scream and tried to fight back. But a savage blow to his left shoulder and an even bigger blow squarely on his back caused Hues to groan loudly. He shot a quick look at me, just twenty feet away. He fell down but rolled over, slower now, and rose up bent at the waist and shaky on his legs. He launched a weak kick that bounced off one of the beater's thighs.

More quick blows followed: a hard smash on his back, then one to his right shoulder that looked like it separated the shoulder from its socket. His left forearm blocked a blow, which appeared to numb it momentarily. The calf of his right leg was whacked hard. As Hues started to fall, he stumbled and then drew on his last ounce of strength for one more big move. He turned sideways to one of the beaters and somehow snapped his right elbow sharply into the face of the attacker, knocking him to the ground like he'd been shot.

A third NVA beater jumped out of the circle of watchers and smashed his club hard on the back of Hues's head, who dropped like a rock, unconscious or dead at that point.

The three NVA then pounded his inert form. The emcee appeared to try to stop the beating, but he was shoved aside and knocked down.

Another savage shot struck Hues's head, which appeared to bounce on the ground.

I screamed at Caveman: "Stop them, they're killing him! Stop them, dammit!"

Caveman grunted and signaled me to shut up and sit down, then hit me hard on my left shoulder with his club.

I could take no more. I wouldn't let them kill my brother. No way in hell.

"Sit your ass down, Caveman!" I screamed.

Caveman swung his club again, but I blocked it and punched him hard in the face, knocked him to the ground, and jerked the club out of his hands.

Toothpick stepped in and took a big swing at me, but I saw it coming and ducked under the swing, then twisted and kicked Toothpick in the balls, dropping him to his knees.

I spun around, raised my head toward heaven and screamed, "If you're real, Lord, then help us! Help us, dammit!" I charged the three

NVA who'd paused their merciless beating to stare at me. One of them actually grinned. I went straight to him.

My physical strength was nowhere near what it had once been, given my skinny body and shrunken muscles. But my mental strength and discipline had never been greater or more focused, forged in the heat of the war and the brutality of camp life. I focused totally on killing all three of them.

I raced screaming and attacking, swinging my club so fast it was a blur. Yet, it was a controlled attack because I maintained a clear focus in one part of my brain on some defensive moves and fighting mechanics to maximize my strength. So, while my ferocious attack may have seemed out of control, I actually was in total control of my actions for at least a few moments.

I saw their three clubs moving toward me as if they were in slow motion, the world spinning slower. I could almost predict their moves. I ducked under the first swing, blocked the next swing with my club, and prepared for the third NVA, who lowered himself to kick my legs.

Still screaming, I jumped over his kick, landed, spun rapidly to the left, then backhanded one of the beaters on his head, knocking him to the ground.

Yet another NVA soldier entered the ring. He clubbed me from behind and smashed the shoulder of my arm holding the club, which fell to the ground as I hit my knees.

Another took a vicious swing at my head. I saw it coming in slow motion and partially blocked it with my other arm. I pretended to fall back down, but then spun and twisted in the air and kicked one beater in the balls, dropping him to his knees. I kicked his head hard with my heel.

My strength was fading as I heard the roar of the usually silent crowd. Yet another beater joined the fight. I saw him clubbing my brother's still body on the ground. Now clubless, I knew I had only one or maybe two more moves left, and I knew what they were.

I was then hit hard in the back. My head snapped forward, sucking my breath away. Another club smashed into my stomach, bending me over. I groaned in pain and anger as I gasped for air and fell on my knees.

Just when I felt I was all in, my spirit fired up somewhere in my mind or heart. I found enough strength to stagger up and make two sudden moves.

I lunged at the NVA beating Hues, grabbed him by the neck from behind, bent his head back, savagely punched his Adam's apple, and threw him aside.

Using my last ounce of strength, I staggered two steps toward Hues as the blows smacked my body. I threw myself over him, covering his still body. The intense fight probably lasted no more than sixty seconds, though it seemed much longer in my mind. My last conscious sensation was hugging my brother.

The following two days were mostly lost. Our minds lived somewhere in unconscious and semiconscious pain between that night and the next tomorrow we'd recognize only when it fully arrived: the present. It was elusive in our current state, meaningless.

The places we now lived in our minds would likely be forgotten or deeply buried in memory when we reentered the present. I hoped so because where we were at that time, in addition to where we would be in the present moment in the real world, might be too much collective weight for any mind to carry sanely. The Beatdown Ring was physical *and* mental.

Hues told me our stories more than a day later in the cage when I finally regained consciousness.

"Best I could tell was afternoon when I came to from wherever I was. I'd just become aware of life when a skeeter tried to fly up my nose. I waved a hand at it. Hurt so much I damn near cried. The weight of being conscious fell on me hard. I was sore everywhere, especially my chest, left shoulder, right thigh. Just felt crushed. But the biggest pain? Just trying to breathe, man. Breathing give life to pain all over my body.

"Then the beatdown come back in my head. The damn clubs, the hate in their eyes, my strength shrinking fast, getting knocked down, falling down, but stopping just short of dying. And then you were there, Buck. Fell on top and covered me up. Heard you yell in my ear, 'We got this!' Did you really say that, or did I dream it?

"Then I realized I was in the cage, but you weren't! I saw your restraints, but no Buck. Surely you were still alive, right? Or did they beat you to death when you fell on me? I tried to scream, get Cross-eye's attention, but could only whimper, barely even heard myself. Then I cried a bit and fell back to sleep, running from the pain.

"Woke sometime later and stared at your restraints. Only realized then my damn restraints weren't on me either! Lifted my head and saw Cross-eye staring at me. And about twenty feet to his right, I saw something else. A body? Looked like tips of bare feet pointing to the sky.

"Was it you? Had they killed you? But why you laying there if you were dead? Wouldn't they bury your body in the ring? Or were you alive? But why you spread there near the trail. I couldn't make no sense of it, man. Cursed my dull damn brain. My head a bucket of pain. I slowly pulled myself up, leaned back against the cage. Took some deep breaths, and I was suddenly certain I was still alive!

"When I looked out the cage then, I saw that body on the ground, and I knew it was you. Bearded face tipped back, mouth open. But why you laying there? And then I got it. They were still torturing you, Buck! You were laid out in a big X shape, wrists and ankles tied to stakes, spread-eagled for all to see, all the rain to fall on, and all the damn bugs to feed on.

"I was mad as hell. I wanted to shoot 'em all. 'Hey!' I yelled at Cross-eye. 'What the hell you doing? Buck still alive? Bring him to the damn cage so I can take care of him, asshole. Bring him here!' But Cross-eye just stared back at me. Smoked a cigarette like nothing wrong in the whole damn world.

"Maybe couple hours later they brought you to the cage. Toothpick left us three rice balls, couple bananas, and a bowl full of water. I lifted your shoulders and pulled you back, so your head was on my shoulder. I felt the pulse in your neck. Still alive! I hugged you, Buck, and cried.

"I held you until night, and over and over again I sung a special psalm for you. Sung it softly until you finally come to, like you just did now:

> Lord, your light is brighter tonight
> for my brother in my arms.
> He risked everything for me last night.
> Guide him safely back into life
> to shine his light on hearts and souls
> of hopeless others blind to your light.
> Thank you, Lord, for my brother tonight."

Maybe it was the sound of Hues softly psalming, the faint smell of food, the cooler air of the dark night, or simply the comfort of my brother's arms that tipped me back to consciousness. The one thing I remembered from my unconscious state was the feeling of weightlessness, floating in the air and basking in the soft light of a special room filled with pictures and memories. I stayed in that room, waiting for whatever and wherever came next, surrounded by memories of those I loved tethering me to life.

I opened my eyes and raised my left hand to touch Hues's face behind me.

"Alive?" I asked.

"Yes!" Hues whispered in my ear. "Alive and together, thank the Lord! And we got some food and water. Can life get any better?" He laughed.

"Wow . . ."

"Yeah, wow is right."

"Water?"

Hues filled his black cup with water from the bowl and lifted it in front of my eyes. "Just drink slowly." He tipped the cup a little and let some water spill into my mouth.

I choked then drank slowly, savoring the wonderful feel of warm water in my parched throat.

"How long, Hues?"

"Don't know for sure. Thirty hours maybe? I only came to maybe seven, eight hours ago."

"So glad . . . you made it."

"More water?"

"Please." I drank another cup of water.

"Only made it 'cause of you, Buck. I felt you on my back. I was dying from pain."

"Brothers bound . . . always. Food?"

"Rice ball or banana, man?"

"Ball, maybe."

Hues placed a rice ball in my hand. "You got it?"

"Yes, thanks."

I took a bite of the little ball in my dirty, scraped hand and chewed slowly. Simple rice in a ball. It hurt to chew. But this pain was delicious.

Hues picked up a ball and chewed it too. "Never thought this little bit of nothing would taste so good," he said. "We got one more, Buck. They're so damn generous tonight, ain't they? You eat it. You need it more than me."

"Split it. Both been to hell . . . for a day."

"For a day? You kidding, right? We're living in hell, brother, every day for months. Yesterday was just a little bit worse, a holy hellier hell!"

We laughed softly, though it hurt my chest and lungs.

"Now a banana, if you up for it?"

"Maybe later . . . more water?"

"Here it is," Hues said, lifting another cup of water and pouring it slowly.

The small bite of food, along with water and knowing we were still alive, provided a sleep-inducing narcotic for both of us. We sat quietly for a minute. Then I heard Hues snoring softly in my ear. Or maybe he was psalming. Or maybe I was listening to my own snoring. I returned to the memory room in my mind.

The sorrowful, haunting call of a loon woke me some hours later. As alert as I could be, I listened closely but heard no loons. Had I dreamed it? Did they even live in Vietnam and Asia? Lots of water here, for sure, but isn't it just too damn hot for loons? Was I back in Michigan? I sure as hell wished I was.

"You okay?" Hues asked, waking too.

"Yes. Hey, you remember a loon . . . what it sounds like?"

"A loon?"

"That bird in Michigan . . . looks kind of like a duck. Lives around rivers and lakes. Makes long, haunting sounds, like he's lost someone . . . or is lost somewhere himself?"

"Okay. Don't think I ever heard or saw one in Detroit. But I met a few one summer up north. I remember their cry in the night. Why you asking?"

"I swear I just heard one . . . but can't imagine one here."

"Didn't hear one, Buck. But maybe it's like everything else here. We live a lot of stuff in our heads that ain't really real, but we sure as hell wish they were. Maybe you just remembering a better place, dreaming."

"Okay but tell me. When you were beatdown unconscious on the ground in the ring and hours afterward . . . where'd you go? Where'd you go in your head?"

"Where'd I go? Man, nowhere! I laid on the ground, didn't move. Hurt too much to even breathe. Couldn't get up and go nowhere."

"I know your body stayed . . . but what about your head and mind—your heart? They stay on the ground too, or go someplace else . . . maybe a better place?"

"Honest, Buck, I don't remember what was in my head. I just remember getting the shit beat out me, then waking up hurting everywhere. Thinking maybe I should have died instead."

"Nothing else you remember?"

"Nothing else, least not right now. Why? Where'd you go, Buck? You visit someplace else when you were staked to the ground?"

"I built something . . . a little memory room in my mind when I hurt so much. I was all but dead . . . created this special room. Like a safe house in my mind . . . where I can go and live . . . medicine for my body and mind to ease the pain."

"A memory room? Hey, tell me more. Maybe you ain't totally tipped over like you sound right now." He laughed and hugged me.

"Like you, the pain was bad. I was unconscious but . . . somehow I was conscious of being unconscious. I know that sounds nuts."

"Well, then I'm a little nuts too. I been there, Buck. Like your mind is outside your body, floating above it, watching it. Trying to figure out what the hell to do."

"Exactly. So, I went to this corner in my mind, and I built this little room, long and narrow . . . like a school hallway. I added a door that could close and lock. Went into that little room and closed the door when the pain was too much . . . and an amazing thing happened there."

"You didn't hurt as much?"

"Yes, and then a light came on."

"Like a light you turn on and off?"

"No, like some sunlight was in that dark room . . . or maybe moonlight. It was a bright light that came on. And when I opened my eyes I saw on the walls a bunch of picture frames."

"Okay . . ."

"And I crawled up to the closest frame and imagined the face of someone I loved and missed . . . and that person's face was suddenly there, hanging like a painting in the frame. Like a real picture, Hues, my mother . . . was smiling at me. And her picture brought back memories about great moments we shared. I crawled to the next frame . . . and suddenly there was a beautiful picture of Jeanie. I just thought of her when I looked at the frame and there she was, smiling too. Her eyes were alive . . . they were with me.

"But most important in that little room . . . my pain wasn't as bad, Hues. Those pictures made me feel a little better, stronger. They made me feel like I could . . . survive. I could make it. I felt like each picture was hugging me."

I stopped talking, trapped in the memory room. Hues still held me in his arms. He hugged me. Our whispered conversation had not disturbed Cross-eye, who sat twenty yards away smoking and watching us.

"So, this memory room took away some pain," Hues said.

"Some. Dulled it."

"And made you feel like you could survive?"

"Those pictures . . . gave me hope."

"Bless the Lord," Hues said softly. "What a beautiful way to give hope to you and to me! I got a place in my mind kind of like that, Buck—my little safe room. I go there when bad shit happens. I feel safer and have good memories too. From now on, thanks to you, it's going to be my memory room."

"Do it, man. Hang your memory pictures. And maybe in the future when we're hurting bad . . . we can share trips to our memory rooms, who we saw there, rather than talk about where we hurt or how bad we feel."

"Deal," Hues said, squeezing my shoulders lightly. "We share stories, Buck, and hope. To hell with the pain." We sat quietly for a few minutes, thinking, dreaming, and hoping. Then we fell asleep again.

Hues was given one more day in the cage, then led away to gather food. I spent two more days in the cage before I resumed my daily chores. Both of us received the same "welcome back" whack from our individual guard's bamboo club, along with a loud, direct order that sounded much like a dog barking—*get your ass back to work, arf, arf, arf!*

Six weeks later, when Hues was due again in the Beatdown Ring, the VC and NVA changed the protocol. When they came to gather us early that evening, they tied our hands behind our backs with tough vine and walked us to the ring. When I sat down, Caveman put a length of chain around my throat to hold me in place. Hues entered the ring, hands tied behind his back. He fought the best he could with his legs, shoulders, and head. But he didn't last sixty seconds before he was beaten unconscious on the ground by two NVA.

Two weeks later, when I was led into the ring with my hands tied behind my back, I sprang a surprise on the two NVA soldiers. I was still reasonably nimble, and my body was skinnier than ever, so I tried it. I took three quick steps toward the NVA, stopped, and sat down quickly, pulled my legs up in front of me, slid my tied hands under my butt and over my legs, and then jumped back up. My hands were tied in front of me, a new weapon.

One NVA slammed my shoulder with his club, but I ducked another blow aimed at my head. When that soldier's body partially turned after his missed swing, I leaped behind him, quickly put my arms over his head, and applied a tight chokehold with my hands and vine. I then dropped to the ground, pulled the NVA on top of me, choked him, wrapped my legs around his body, and made it more difficult for the three NVA to club my body.

In the end, they stopped me from choking the soldier to death by pulling a knife and cutting the vine holding my wrists. They pulled me from the guard, beat me unconscious, and staked me out again for twenty-four hours near our cage. When they finally carried me to the cage, Hues said he was sure I was dead. He hadn't seen me so much as twitch since the beating.

Hues once again held me in his arms as he sat back against the cage bars. I lay through much of the night and the stormy next day. Barely alive. Lost in my head. Sometimes in the memory room, sometimes other places I couldn't recall.

Hues was put back to work the next day. I slowly regained consciousness and some strength. Eventually I described to Hues my extended visit with near-death this way: "I could see it; I could feel it. I could reach out and touch it, and it sweetly called me to join it. 'Come on, die! It ain't half as bad as the life you're living!'

"But I wasn't ready to let go of Jeanie, my baby, my family, or you, Hues. I know if I ever get closer to death than I was in those hours, I'll be dead. The amazing thing is that it truly made me realize how close, how damn close to death we all are at any moment in life."

From that point on, I was led into the ring with my wrists tied behind my back and my elbows tied, as well. I couldn't stand up straight or use my arms in any way. But I always landed a couple of good kicks, a head butt, or a bite or two before they finished me off.

We never quit fighting. It took us near death but helped us survive. Or so we believed.

CHAPTER 8

── TWENTY-FOUR HOURS OF HIGHS AND LOWS ──

Day 179 was already sweltering when they marched us to the river early in the morning. Despite an occasional heavy downpour like we'd had the night before, the summer heat was intense, day and night. The glistening blue sky was cloudless, marked only by an occasional bird soaring past. From the open riverbank we could track the sun overhead. The stretch of river that ran near the camp flowed directly from west to east as far as we could see before disappearing in a dense cluster of pine trees, coffee bushes, and giant ferns in a big curve in the distance.

From this vantage point, it was easy to understand why prisoners attempting to escape the camp would choose this river route. The modest current was headed easterly in the right direction. Simply riding a log in the river would likely be the fastest and easiest way out. Much more so than stumbling and struggling in the dark, tangled, disorienting jungle.

On the other hand, we were certain at least one village was located downriver a klick or less, with likely more beyond. You'd be much more visible too, on the river than in the jungle. So, getting away faster might also mean being recaptured faster. Or killed.

We were quietly discussing possible escapes while fishing that morning. Caveman and Toothpick sat on the riverbank thirty or forty feet from us, so we whispered softly as we stood ten feet apart in shallow water. We often talked about an escape, but we were especially concerned now because Rob and Ray, who'd spent more than a year in the camp, had given us a strong hint three days earlier that they planned to escape soon. Rob was recovering from yet another savage beatdown, and both of them were wasting away from diseases and too little to eat. When we crossed paths with Rob at the outhouse at dusk that night, he kneeled and shared his information prayer with us.

"Dearest brothers," he prayed on his knees, crossing himself and nodding at us, "just letting you know. We flying the coop soon. Downriver on a dark night. Got to get out or die here. Adios, brothers. May lady luck and each other keep you alive."

"I know why they'd come this way," Hues said, "especially if I was hurting like Rob."

"Sure, fastest way out—and easiest," I said. "But don't you think the VC know that too? For all we know, they got men stationed in places downriver. We don't know what's there."

Hues nodded. "Probably more villages that way too. I get it. But it's still a hell of lot more attractive than the damn jungle," he muttered. "Odds got to be low, if any, on surviving in a jungle escape."

"Agree, but at Phu Bai, you ever hear any stories about prisoner escapes? Don't think I did. And in the Casualty Branch and Graves Registration, wouldn't we hear those kinds of stories? They'd be shared with others, right?"

"Maybe, but don't remember hearing any stories like that," Hues said. "Only story I ever heard about an escape is the one Rob and Ray told us just after we arrived, remember?"

"What'd they say?"

"Two other Americans who'd been in camp at least a year made their getaway on a dark night down the river."

"Okay, it's coming back," I said. "And one of them just disappeared, right? Never seen again, at least back here?"

"Right. Might have survived, but not likely."

"You'd think if he escaped successfully, that'd be a story that's told a lot. Especially in training for new guys coming into country."

"But the other prisoner in their story was captured," Hues said.

"Okay, and they brought him back to camp, spread-eagled him on the ground for two or three days. And there he died, right?"

"Yup. And Ray and Rob had to carry his body to the Beatdown Ring, dig a grave, and bury him there forever. Brother's always under our feet in the ring."

"So, one died, and one might have made it to freedom," I said.

"Or likely died trying. We'll never know. Hate to think about the jungle route, but maybe it's our best bet."

"Hardest way to go, but lots more hiding places, as we well know."

"Yeah. We saw that when they marched us here. Trees, vines, swamps, hills. So many hiding places, so many places to get lost forever. Jungle's a total maze, man."

"Impossible to see where you're going or know where you are," I said.

"Or where you been. Easy to get turned around, lost. And not even know it."

"But still our best bet, right? A dark, rainy night in monsoon season?"

"That's our plan in the next monsoon season, if not before."

"Hope Ray and Rob make it out."

"Me too."

We fished half a dozen holes in the river in a stretch of one hundred yards or so. The deeper holes were often marked by logs, stumps, or sometimes brush nearby in a small bend. The water was dirty enough that we couldn't see into it. But we could feel the bottom with our feet—soft and mucky in some stretches but mostly firm with sand or gravel in other areas. We kept an eye open for snakes at all times.

Wading and fishing a river like this in Vietnam wasn't radically different from fishing a river in Michigan, I thought. Well, except for the crude stick in my hand versus my well-oiled spinning rod and reel at home. And the warm, dirty water here, quite unlike the cold, sparkling rivers in northern Michigan. And of course, catching sluggish carp or catfish versus the soaring, dancing, diving trout in Michigan. And the presence of deadly snakes here. And armed guards watching every move you made. Okay, fishing *was* radically different here. But I still enjoyed it—a great break from humid, backbreaking days toiling in the jungle.

Though it was hot, the fish were biting. We caught five black and gray carp, two of which were nearly two feet long, and eight brown and yellow catfish. It was a productive fishing day. Even the guards seemed pleased with the catch. They gave us small knives to clean the fish while they stood nearby with their rifles. When we finished cleaning the fish we put them in our black sacks, which we then hung on a branch that sagged into the river and kept the fish cooler.

Then the guards really made our day. Once a month or so, they'd let us bathe briefly in the river, and they directed us to do so this afternoon before heading back to our cage. The ten minutes we spent in the warm water felt incredibly cooling and healing on our skinny, scarred bodies, especially our sore feet and itching private parts. The river dip was one of those rare "highs" we experienced in prison life: a chance to cool down, clean up a bit, and feel more alive physically and mentally. For a few minutes. The sweat would return rapidly, along with some bamboo hits, but that brief break, that little high . . .

We were in a deep sleep in the cage later that night when I first heard it—the rare sound of a whistle. A moment later the whistle sounded again.

"Oh-oh," Hues whispered.

Cross-eye came over and peered intently into our cage. We weren't locked in our restraints, which was increasingly the case in the last two months. I guess they figured we were too weak to try to escape after so many beatdowns. Or maybe they imagined we finally believed that trying to escape meant certain death. He checked the chain wrapped tightly and locked around the cage door. He grunted some words we didn't understand, then returned to his seat beneath the tree, cradling the rifle in his arms. Ready for action.

We heard the faint sound of a third whistle, then a fourth further away.

"Must be their night," I said.

"Whistles going off not good when you're trying to escape quietly."

"When we go, won't be the river way," I said. "I'm convinced. We've just got to figure out how to get a good head start, enough time to find and get to a good hiding place."

"And sooner rather than later, Buck. We know damn well ain't no future here. We got to go while we still got some strength."

We fell back into a restless sleep, then woke abruptly when we heard two shots in the distance to the east, spaced just seconds apart. It was still dark outside our cage, but daylight couldn't be far off. We didn't speak. Thought about Rob and Ray. We hoped they were safe, but it didn't sound good.

We celebrated being alive with our thumbs-up salute first thing in the morning, followed by counting the day. On rare days, we also celebrated important things that had happened on that day in our past lives or what Hues and I hoped might be happening on that day now. Our 180th day in camp this morning was special for two reasons, one small and one huge. First, at daylight before we'd been to the outhouse and eaten our rice ball and led to work, bombs had exploded in the distance to the east. It was a wave of eight or ten explosions.

"Different sound than we heard with those shots last night," I said. "Maybe a B-52 dropping a load of bombs? Haven't heard them this close for a long time."

"They're much closer now," Hues said. "No way related to Rob and Ray."

We knew B-52s bombed along the Ho Chi Minh trail often at night. Some nights the ground shook a bit beneath us from the explosions, which we didn't always hear.

"What do you think: two, three klicks away?" I asked.

Hues nodded. "Couple miles, maybe, but I got to admit I like that sound. Means the brothers still fighting. Hope they bringing it this way."

Then Cross-eye, rather than our normal daytime guards, Caveman and Toothpick, came and checked our cage lock once again. He then disappeared toward the river.

"That's strange," I said. "Our two guards must still be looking for Rob and Ray, and now Cross-eye is gone too. Which may mean we get a day off!"

Hues grinned. "And that's perfect," he said. "Means we got the whole day to celebrate something big, a really big high!"

He held up his hands and counted the number with his fingers again. "It's day one-eight-zero: not the official day but close enough by our count. Our hundred-and-eightieth day is a very special day for you and Jeanie: a special day to celebrate the birth of your beautiful new baby! Congrats, brother! So damn happy for all three of you. Just wish you was back home with them, not stuck in the damn cage with me on this special day. Nobody . . . *nobody* deserves it more. And don't ever think you won't make it home, Buck. If I have to carry you every step of the way, you will get home to see that baby. I promise, man!"

We dapped fists, and I counted the number 180 with my fingers too.

"A hundred and eighty days and still alive," I said. "Thanks, Hues." I was filled with joy and sadness. I was celebrating something wonderful but totally missing it at the same time.

I nodded at Hues and gave him a thumbs up. "To the birth of our baby!"

The way we figured it, we'd been in captivity at least 180 days, or six months, give or take a few days we'd lost track of following the Beatdown Ring when we were too weak or tipped over mentally to count the day. If Jeanie became pregnant during my last three nights home with her, that made it roughly ninety days before my capture after the chopper crash. Do the math and that 180 plus ninety equals 270 days, the normal nine months required from fertilization to birth. So, our math suggested this day, today, was the time the baby should be born, or maybe had been, or soon would be. We'd celebrate today. The birth of our baby.

I tried to wrap my mind around that . . . our baby!

Locked in a cage thousands of miles from home, I still felt incredibly close to Jeanie and the new baby in my mind at this moment. Like I was right there in the hospital room, watching her nurse our new baby, imagining that scene, that moment when virtually everything in my and our world would be perfect, beautiful. We'd be together as three. I would never let go of that thought or image, even though I didn't have a picture for my memory room.

"So, which is it, Buck, boy or girl? You keep going back and forth," Hues said.

I smiled and shook my head. "Don't know, doesn't matter. Just come out safe, happy, all I ask. Either one will be special. And loved."

"You two ever talk about baby names? I mean before she was pregnant?"

"Don't remember ever talking baby names. Besides, maybe the baby will eventually create its own name like someone I know, Jameis Jones. You ever heard of him, Hues?"

"Yeah, I've heard of him, Brian Charles Kinder!"

We laughed and dapped fists again. Thoughts of Jeanie and a baby made it a wonderful day, a special, special high among so few in Vietnam.

After the bombing stopped earlier, the camp had grown eerily quiet. There was no one in view, no sounds of any soldiers nearby. The mosquitos, however, were as active as ever. We pulled the netting over ourselves. The bugs' soft humming was literally the only sound in camp apart from nature's regular noises in the jungle.

"Wonder what's cooking? They're always organized like clockwork," Hues said.

Then we heard gunshots and what sounded like mortars exploding. The shooting continued and sounded closer than the bombs had, but still a ways off.

"Sounds like a firefight," I said.

"I don't remember the sound of fighting this close in the six months we been here," Hues said. "We in the middle of nowhere. Two klicks off, maybe? Come get us brothers!"

A brief time later we watched a squad of VC file past, headed toward the river.

"I ever tell you the story of Sena and what she told me when she joined me one day for my street-church walk in Belanger Park?" Hues asked.

"Only twenty or thirty times, but please, Mr. Jones, tell me again."

We spent a work-free baby birthday sharing stories of people, experiences, and good memories. We needed today. We'd shared many of the stories often to feed our hopes in the bamboo cage.

Somewhere in the jungle.

Halfway around the world from the woman I loved.

And our new baby who I hadn't seen but loved anyway.

Late in the afternoon the VC returned to camp. Four of them surrounded Rob, who was carrying Ray in his arms. Toothpick and Caveman trailed the party. As they drew closer and then stopped on the worn trail in front of our cage, we could see Ray was dead. His arms and legs hung limply in Rob's arms. Looked like he'd been shot in the face and chest. His blood covered Rob's chest and arms.

Rob appeared anguished and totally exhausted. Sweat and tears smeared his face. When he saw us in our cage, he tried to say something. But a guard growled at him and hit him so hard in the back with the butt of his rifle he dropped Ray on the muddy ground and fell on him. He screamed loudly and wiped at his tears.

Two soldiers jerked him back on his feet, cursed him, pointed to Ray with their rifles. Loudly ordered him to pick Ray up. Rob struggled and finally stood again with Ray's body in his arms. The glance he gave us was straight from hell: the most anguished look I'd ever seen.

Toothpick and Caveman unlocked the door to our cage and ordered us out, using the butts of their rifles to help us scramble out on our knees. They tied our wrists and elbows behind our backs and directed us to follow Rob carrying Ray, still surrounded by four soldiers.

We ended up at the Beatdown Ring, where a dozen or so NVA stood at the edge of the circle, smoking casually in the shade, watching us.

Another soldier arrived with a shovel, which he handed to one of the four guards. Rob was directed to put Ray on the ground, and when he did so, he once again fell atop him given his exhaustion. This led to more whacks from the rifle butts until they forced him back up on his unsteady legs. He was handed the shovel and ordered to dig a hole to bury his brother on the edge of the ring.

We stood bent over and watched Rob fight to dig a hole. He was running on fumes at that point, struggling to dig and move the muddy earth aside, even as he cried steadily and talked to himself. I couldn't imagine the pain and grief he felt, and I had some firsthand experiences in those areas.

I turned to Caveman. "Cut me loose! I'll dig the grave. Cut me loose!"

I was rewarded with a whack to my legs that dropped me to my knees. Hues then tried to kick Caveman, but Toothpick beat him with his club and knocked him to the ground.

After what seemed like an hour, an exhausted, crying and bleeding Rob had dug a hole about three feet deep. He was forced to put Ray in the hole, which he awkwardly did. One of the soldiers then stomped on Ray's body to pack it deeper into the hole.

Rob tried to say a prayer over his brother, but he was beaten again, forced to stand up, given the shovel, and directed to cover Ray's body with the wet earth. Rob slowly spread the dirt over Ray, talking to him, telling him how sorry he was. How much he loved him. How much he would miss him forever.

When he finished the grave, he begged the guards to kill him too. "I'm ready to die," he gasped. "Go with my brother!"

But they weren't going to let him off that easy.

When we left the ring we walked the pathway back that ran about thirty feet in front of our cage. One of the guards left the group and returned shortly with a hammer and four bamboo stakes. We knew what was coming.

They laid Rob on the ground and pulled his body into a big "X" shape. Drove a stake in the ground near each wrist and ankle. Wrapped a thin vine around Rob's wrists and ankles. Pulled and tightened the vine until Rob screamed in agonizing pain. The sound echoed and lingered for a long time in the hot, heavy air. It was the last sound he made.

He lay staked out for two days with no food or water. His body, mind, and voice were paralyzed in pain. We could see him from our cage, a deliberate placement for sure. And we walked past him each day when we went to gather food.

We saw no movement. His eyes were always closed. He made no sounds. His mouth was partially opened and covered with hovering flies and bugs.

The image of him staked to the ground haunted us. Where he was in those last, long hours we didn't know and didn't want to know. Hues prayed often for his death.

Near the end of the second day, they cut Rob loose from the stakes.

Hues was forced to carry him to the Beatdown Ring.

I dug Rob's grave and buried him.

CHAPTER 9

—— MEMORY ROOM (1) ——

My visits to Jeanie in my memory room gradually shifted from memories to dreams and imaginings in the weeks before and after our child was born. I was sure Jeanie had delivered and kept our baby. And I was quite sure she hadn't married someone else, despite my long disappearance from her life. We'd been deeply in love the summer before I was drafted, and we talked about marriage in the new year. She once confided in me her top two priorities were marrying me and having a house full of babies to enrich our lives. If two people in the world still believed I was alive, they were my mother and Jeanie. I'd be alive in their minds, just as they lived in mine. Every day.

I was also certain, okay, ninety-five percent certain, our baby had bright blue eyes, whether a girl or a boy. Me and my father, mother, sister, and brother and Jeanie and her parents and brother—we all had blue eyes. So, our baby would have blue eyes and maybe curly blond hair just like Jeanie. I'd been a blond-haired boy until my hair turned light brown as a teenager.

In short, the baby would be beautiful—bright blue eyes and blond hair, or any other color of the human rainbow of eyes and hair. I didn't care. I just wanted to see that baby, touch it, hold it, kiss it over and over, feel its little heartbeat, see it smile. Make sure it's real.

And I wanted to see Jeanie nurse the baby. I often imagined that picture of life-giving nourishment: Jeanie nursing our baby. Was there a more loving, embracing picture to admire and hold on to in my memory room, even if it was imaginary?

I spent several minutes staring into the baby's blue eyes. Then suddenly the three of us were walking the beautiful sandy beach on Lake Michigan near the popular tourist town of South Haven, where Jeanie and I had spent some long weekends in past summers. Only we had a baby with us this trip.

Jeanie put cream on the baby to protect its skin and tied a small pink bonnet snugly around its tiny head. I carried a blanket, pillow, and a cooler with water and soda packed in ice and a dozen or so chocolate brownies wrapped in a plastic bag. The sunny day was about eighty-five degrees, but a northwest breeze made it perfectly comfortable. Only a few wispy clouds etched faintly in the northern horizon marked an otherwise clear blue sky.

Many others were there too, but the big beach gave everyone a sense of space of their own. Young children ran in and out of the water, splashing themselves and each other amidst their shrieks and screams of joy and laughter as the sun painted them golden and silver in their delightful watery party. Several elderly couples walked slowly across the sand to the edge of the water, carrying lawn chairs and then sitting in those chairs, their bare feet close enough to the lake so the gentle waves washed their toes and ankles in a soft rhythm of cool pleasure.

Seagulls soared and called to each other in their flights, making sudden dives and banking turns. Overhead a big green hot-air balloon carried several couples on a guided tour. The backdrop for the voices was the wind and the steady but distant crashing of big lake waves against a long pier on the north end of the beach.

I rubbed suntan lotion on Jeanie's back and arms, feeling her young and firm body, growing aroused. Then she returned the favor, smiling seductively as she rubbed the lotion on my shoulders, legs, and thighs. She kissed me lightly, sweetly, and flashed her most wonderful smile. Then we laid back, heads resting on a beach pillow, bodies on the blanket, and the baby now begging for a long drink of milk.

Jeanie shyly pulled her swimsuit top off her left shoulder, exposing a beautiful full breast. She pulled the baby into her arms, tucked the nipple into the baby's greedy mouth. The baby looked at Jeanie, who kissed its forehead. Jeanie then looked at me with love and a clear sense of family in her eyes. The three of us, my arm now wrapped around Jeanie, holding her and our baby, lived in that moment.

Amid the beauty of nature and joy surrounding us, from the golden sand to the white-capped waves and endless sky, our eyes locked on each other, promising everything forever.

CHAPTER 10

— SURVIVAL IN THE CAMP —

Some months after they brutally murdered Ray and Rob, the VC captured two more American soldiers. We watched them being led down the path near our cage at dusk tonight. The shirtless, sharply muscled Black men had been beaten during their trek to the camp. No surprise. One appeared to have a swollen, likely broken nose. The other bore a badly swollen eye and a bloody ear. Their backs were swollen with bruises, bare feet cut and bleeding, arms tied behind their backs at the wrists and elbows.

"Two more checking into Hotel Hell," Hues said.

"Looks too damn familiar," I said. "Want to let them know we're here?"

Hues slipped off one of his sandals and slapped it hard against our cage bars. Both prisoners glanced quickly at the sound and saw us behind the bars.

"You ain't alone, brothers. Never give up," Hues told the prisoners, who were quickly herded on.

We "formally" met them at the one-holer three nights later. As Rob and Ray had done with us, we kneeled in turn and prayed our names using the "On top of old smokey" format. They picked up quickly on our communication-praying practice. When we saw them several days later, they kneeled and prayed their names and where they were from. Wilson, the slightly taller and thinner man, was from Phoenix.

Biggs, from Memphis, was the one with the broken nose. All four of us nodded as we were led away to our cages. We imagined they were staying in the cage where Rob and Ray had lived.

Two weeks later we learned more when the four of us spent a day together digging and preparing a big new garden near two other large plots that were planted with a variety of vegetables on the south side of the river. The new garden made us wonder if more VC or NVA were coming. Or maybe we'd get more to eat?

Biggs and Wilson had completed infantry training at Fort Polk, Louisiana too. When they arrived in Nam they were assigned to the 501st infantry in the 101st Airborne Division. They were on their third patrol in the Ashau Valley, Biggs explained, when their squad was ambushed. The fight was brief but intense. When the firing stopped they found themselves surrounded by seven VC. Another soldier near them was shot in the chest but was still alive. One of the VC quickly slit his throat and ripped off his wristwatch. Biggs and Wilson were forced to their feet, hands tied behind their backs, and marched for two days in the jungle. They believed they were the only survivors.

They took their first turns in the Beatdown Ring about four and six weeks later. They fought hard. We silently cheered them on and gave them an imaginary thumbs-up since our wrists and elbows were tied behind our backs. Biggs' nose was broken again. Wilson, whom the NVA seemed to hate even more, was beaten so badly they had to carry him off. He spent two days and nights recovering enough to walk and work.

We'd been in the camp so long that time moved in a downward slide and grew less meaningful. The days, weeks, and months blended together in a kind of timeless, hopeless, futureless world of constant pain. As we discovered and repeatedly confirmed, lost time—prison life—is slow-moving time that pushes the limits of survival every day. At this slow, monotonous, continuously painful pace of life, one of the big questions we confronted daily was: how do the body and the mind adapt and survive?

We tried to become experts, but all we had to show for our expertise were our skinny, bony, sunbaked bodies shaped and marked by constant thirst, hunger, and physical abuse. Scars layered on scars from cuts, scrapes, bugs, and bites in the jungle. Bruises painted over bruises from the Beatdown Ring and daily whacks of the bamboo clubs.

Most concerning, we shared a growing thousand-yard stare that filled our sunken eyes more often as we increasingly found ourselves neither here nor there but some other place in our minds outside our bodies. I came to believe our bodies and minds survived only by divorcing each other. The body was the present moment; the mind lived increasingly in the past and a faintly imagined future. They constantly fought each other, both losing.

As we neared a year in camp, we'd about reached our physical limits. In college I weighed 200 pounds. After basic and infantry training I shipped to Vietnam at a chiseled 175 pounds. Hues had come to Vietnam at a similarly fit and muscled 165 pounds. Now, we were the "thinnest of thinny twins," as Hues described us sitting in our cage one morning during an early monsoon season downpour so heavy everything around us was invisible except for the cage bars.

"Look at us, man," Hues said, staring at himself then me as he ran his hand down his skinny arms and legs, poking his finger on what was mostly bone. "What you think? Maybe a hundred ten, hundred fifteen pounds?"

"Pretty generous," I said.

"You ever see pictures of concentration camp survivors? Like Auschwitz?"

"History class in college and in a film," I said. "Maybe some other places too."

"That's us, Buck. We are them: skin, bones, no fat, all ribs, big knees, knobby wrists, shrunken muscles, hollow eyes, sunken cheeks." He pointed to each of those on his own body. "Only thing growing is our hair and beards. And they pull and chop those off every couple months just so old barber man can join the torture party. We the thinnest of thinny twins," he said. "We two skinny brown ropes with cuts, bruises, and diseases painted on us. Red, yellow, and blue. Just like tattoos."

"Human tattoos . . . has a ring to it, Hues."

Diarrhea was a constant battle. Some nights it worked overtime, soiling us and our restraints and stinking up our already stinking cage. The guards cursed us in the mornings and forced us to clean our cage with our shirts, then wear the shitty shirts the rest of the day.

Fungus infections were often present too, on our arms, backs, groins, legs, and feet. Eight days into the camp we'd been given black rubber sandals because the jungle walks and rough climbing cut and scarred our feet so badly we could barely walk. The sandals helped protect the bottom of our feet but did little for the tops or ankles.

Bites from mosquitos and other insects, along with contaminated food and water, infected us with tropical diseases. We were convinced we suffered several times from malaria or encephalitis, or both. With his first-aid background, Hues had read up on diseases and dangers in Vietnam before he shipped overseas. The symptoms of the two diseases were similar, he said: "Big high fever, headaches, sore muscles, sick stomach, confused mind, and a weakness so big we exhausted and sometimes got no appetite."

We found that amazingly amusing! How could we never get enough to eat yet not be hungry? What kind of weird place did we inhabit where that was a fact? And the same weird situation with water: we were always thirsty, but our bodies were never dry. We were wet with sweat or rain most of the time. Only the cursed world we lived in explained the contradictions.

Summer was bad due to the unending heat and humidity, which created nonstop thirst and sweat. Only two things infrequently relieved us. Some nights a summer breeze wafted sluggishly but pleasantly through the camp. Best of all was time spent in the river water near the camp. Sometimes we were able to sit and fish with our feet in the water or standing in the water.

But monsoon season was the worst. Less sun and heat, sometimes almost cold air, which was great. But the unending rain left us wet most of the time—our clothes, skin, and hair. The roof over our cage blocked about ninety percent of the rain, which meant we were dripped on all night. Our shared secret wish was for a single towel to dry our faces. Or better, a fan for an hour each day. Or best of all, fifteen minutes with an air conditioner. Cold damn air: we dreamed of it! The two big positives during monsoon season were the small black cup we used to catch rainwater and fewer mosquitos and other bugs during heavy rain.

We found ourselves discussing more often the four antidotes we possessed to help deal with life in the prison camp. Our brotherhood was first, which had begun with the bar fight in Kentucky. It seemed so long ago given everything we'd been through, but at times we shared that memory. We also had saved each other's life. Hues had saved mine when I was unconscious after the helicopter crash. I had saved his life when I charged into the ring and fought three NVA who were beating him to death.

We expressed our brotherhood in smaller ways too, like sharing a warm smile even in pain. Hues had done that just a few days before following another visit to the ring. In my mind his smile said to me: "Yeah, I hurt like hell, I'm hungry, I'm sick of the fricking rain, but hey, you're still here, so I'm happy today!"

Or exchanging a knowing look or wink at a crucial moment. Or gently holding and feeding the other a small rice ball of rice or piece of fish when he was too diseased and weak to sit up and eat. Or Hues closing each night by softly psalming his musical words, which carried us into sleep and provided a kind of peace we couldn't find elsewhere. I never imagined his soft psalming would be so vital.

Sometimes I'd whisper stories at night about nature, which I told Hues was God's church—if there really was a God. Or I'd talk about trout fishing in cold rivers in northern Michigan. First night I did that Hues said, "Man, can we do that together sometime?"

"Of course. Love to fish with you," I responded. "You got to be there to fully feel the beauty and magic of it, man. Picture this: a beautiful morning with a faint mist floating over the river. You can hear the water's breath in the rush. You cast and catch beautiful rainbows, brookies, and browns, watch them dance on the water. At night I'll build us a campfire, grill the fish. We'll eat them and drink beers. The owls will talk to us. A lone wolf might howl, or a loon might sing his lonely one-note tune again and again. It'd be great, man. There are few places where one feels connected to the universe. That river is one. And you'd feel the Lord there too."

"Let's do it," Hues said.

"First year home. We'll do it."

We turned our heads and shared a barely visible nod in our restraints in the darkness.

Neither of us believed we could survive without the other.

Another antidote was the power of good memories to escape the present and relive the past. Maybe just for a moment—or sometimes minutes or even hours of memories that rolled like cool gentle waves—a pleasant motion and hypnotic cadence would wash the shore of the mind. Rinse the present away. Usher in a timeless pool of richer waters that soothed and cleaned the heart and mind. Refresh lingering hopes for another day in a new place with those we love. We often shared stories, hopes, and imaginings about the two ladies in our lives: Jeanie and Sena, who grew bigger in our minds though we hadn't seen them for months.

Like everyone else, I've always had memories, but that special memory room I created in my mind in Vietnam saved my life. My memories were captured in imaginary pictures of my mother, father, sister, brother, relatives, close friends, and neighbors, which I hung on the walls of that little room. Teachers who taught me so much and opened my mind. Special fishing moments, adventures, and unusual places I'd visited. And Jeanie, of course. So many pictures of us dancing, laughing, kissing, and loving. And now suddenly a new baby I could only imagine—a rich source of future memories gestating in my imagination.

Hues created his own memory room after I told him about mine. Like me, he visited it when the pain was hot and burning so he could cool off and survive. The previous night he'd shared a memory, a picture of their simple family dinner time.

"We all came together, just livin' in the moment," he said. "We had almost nothing, but we had everything sitting together around that supper table. We held hands, shared our prayers. Dad told funny stories, made us laugh and smile. And every night Mama, she wrapped up dinner with something warm she just baked—cookies, cupcakes, maybe muffins with berries, roasted nuts, whatever. You could just feel the love, Buck, around the table. See it in our eyes. Life was so simple but so good. When you *feel* the love, man, it means it's *real*."

He filled his little room with pictures too. His mother's smile as big as a billboard and her dark eyes that broadcast love. The light of his father's love locked in his eyes. The Baptist minister who took him into his home and preached about helping others. Dozens of street parishioners whose lonely lives touched his heart, as did their warm smiles and hugs. The old, crippled people in Belanger Park, whose lives brightened with his psalming. And Sena, a wonderful woman he barely knew, whose heart was bigger than her body. She told him her heart was always with him. He believed her and felt it beat like his own pulse when he needed it most.

Rare moments of unexpected beauty were another source of strength. Through all the cruelty, constant heat, and humidity; the presence of dangerous animals lurking in trees, slithering in swamps, or hiding behind bushes; and the constantly swarming, feeding clouds of bugs and mosquitos, we sometimes discovered stunning beauty.

Just two days earlier on the south side of the river we'd been fishing, a small feeder stream now reduced to a summer trickle spilled down the bank into the main river. It was like a miniwaterfall, and it caught the morning sun exactly right for a brief moment. In that magical time the trickle became a shimmering silver chain that glinted hope. Its movement and the glow and arc of its silver light bent the world and took us home to diamond rings, bracelets, weddings, and silver platters loaded with desserts or tiny cups of steaming tea. It was a beautiful chain ride from the present to the past and the possibility of a future.

But the strongest connection to that silver stream of watery light that lived vividly in our minds was another rare sight we saw the following night that perfectly reflected the silvery spillway. Despite the towering trees in and around camp, a handful of small openings provided tiny windows to the sky we could sometimes glimpse through the open walls of the cage at night. And that night the fading glow of the spreading and setting orange sun gave way to a darker sky that grew so black it appeared deep blue, and within it a tiny crescent of silvery moonlight suddenly appeared and flickered briefly. It was a perfect twin in the sky for the silvery stream that had spilled into the river at our feet the previous morning.

Hues saw it first. "Earth and heaven, they linked," he whispered.

We watched in awe as the blue-black heaven filled with stars, thousands of sparkling little teeth, heaven's smile, a moment of peace and harmony, the faintest whisper of a far bigger life beyond the cage— the possibility of freedom. We followed it into a rare peaceful sleep.

The possibility of that bigger forever life also influenced our will to live, and how we lived. Hues was a true believer despite being surrounded by the deaths of his loved ones and the difficult lives of others in his city. He came to believe in living a righteous life after his father died. He told me several times he would never forget the light that lingered and shined in his father's eyes even after he died on the street. "His spirit didn't die, man. Only his body died. His spirit is still alive and with me," he explained.

So, he tried to live righteously, which meant, in the words of his father and the reverend, he should try to make good differences in others' lives. "What finer gift can we give?" he asked me. That's what his psalming was all about: walking and talking to poor people on the streets of River Rouge and inner-city Detroit. Saying prayers over them with his psalms. Helping them smile and laugh to discover life isn't all bad even when it sure as hell seems like it.

Now, living in the camp, he said his beliefs were stronger than ever. And I saw it. Hues lived his beliefs in the camp just as he had in his street church. Closed each day with a sincere psalm. Shared his memories. Winked his eye and smiled even after a beatdown. Left a soft touch on my arm. Beamed a big smile in a dark moment . . .

In these ways Hues gradually rekindled some of my belief too, though I fought it with uncertainty. A creator? Yes. The Lord of Christianity? Not sure. And the Bible as the Lord's words? Maybe. Or maybe it was just another, more compelling form of a ruler's manifesto, artful domination and control over the minds of others.

Hues's spirit was so powerful it was visible and alive in what he said and did. I could feel it. I could always feel it, even when we were separated. If that wasn't a creator or the Lord living in Hues and shining his light . . . well, it sure as hell felt like it to me. And over those long days and nights in the cage, the light in Hues gradually spilled into my mind and heart. Our love and brotherhood, shared memory rooms, some rare moments of beauty, and his spirit helped us survive and hang on to life, such as it was.

Biggs, Wilson, and their two guards disappeared a month after we dug the vegetable garden with them. We were fishing that morning and had seen them and their guards head northeast earlier. We imagined they were going to the Banyan Tree Store or another fruit site more to the east, which we'd been to just a few times. It was located in a fairly accessible area that was filled with harsh sunlight or drenching rain, depending on the season.

Midmorning, we heard what sounded like a helicopter gunship firing at a distance in the east, followed by sounds of a heavy firefight. Not long after, Hues and I were herded back to our cage. They put us in our restraints and chain-locked the door. We stayed there until the next morning. Nobody told us anything or gave any indication about what happened that day. When Biggs and Wilson didn't return, we could only imagine they'd been killed in an ambush or by helicopter fire, along with their guards. The only good news was American troops might be closer than we imagined.

It was a special day, in a twisted way, when we awoke the next morning locked in our cage but without restraints. We gave each other our normal thumbs-up, then reached over and slapped hands.

"Big day today," Hues said. "Day four hundred, more or less."

"Day four hundred," I repeated. "Still alive and together."

We'd refused to celebrate our first year in the camp, Day 365. We shared a thumbs-up and named the number of the day but didn't celebrate the loss of a year of our lives in the jungle.

Hues shook his head in disbelief. "Never imagined living this way, even on the worst days in my former life, man."

"Me neither," I said. "Never ever imagined losing four hundred days of life locked away in a cage in a jungle thousands of miles away from my family, my girlfriend, my new baby, my friends . . . I know life is filled with surprises, but this one . . ."

"I lay here thinking this morning—we been gone more than a year now. What do you think: have our families been told about our . . . situation?" Hues asked. "Have they moved us from missing-in-action status to killed-in-action? We officially dead now?"

"Man, I don't know. Thought about it a few times."

"Okay, but when you worked in Casualty Branch, you ever deal with MIAs like us? Or just killed and wounded soldiers? Any idea what happened with MIAs?"

"I worked with KIA soldiers and wrote letters to their families," I said. "Another guy, Tiny, communicated with families about injured soldiers, serious injuries. But MIAs . . ." Then I nodded my head. "Okay, I remember seeing a folder with four or five MIA files in it. I asked Sergeant Moretti what happened with those files? Did they write MIA letters, or let the parents and family know some other way?"

"What'd he say?"

"I don't know exactly what the MIA letters said. Never saw one. But what the sergeant said about "when" was that the Army often wanted to alert the family as soon as possible, but they often waited some time before officially notifying next of kin about an MIA. Maybe three months or so? I don't remember. I do know they wanted to be sure the soldier was missing in action before sharing that news with families. Sometimes guys who went missing were deserters or guys who'd been blown up or wounded so bad we couldn't confirm their identity. Their bodies were literally blown away. And I imagine a few just disappeared in action or got left behind in an assault."

"Okay, but then how long before notifying next of kin that their soldier, who'd been declared missing in action, was now declared officially dead?" Hues asked. "I'm trying to figure out if a year is the cutoff point for telling families the sad news—your missing son is now dead. Think about the weight of that grief. At least with an MIA label, still got some hope, right?"

I nodded. "Don't know for sure. I never dealt with that and don't remember much talk about it. My guess? It varied. In our situation there might be some clear, or at least a little clear information we were directly missing in action. When our chopper crashed, soldiers would have gone fairly quickly to check and see what happened. I mean, some would have seen it or heard it, right?"

Hues thought for a minute. "They'd send out a squad or search team from the firebase to check things out . . . after fighting stopped. That might have taken some hours, even a day. Or maybe they sent a squad or a platoon from another firebase in the area. There were quite a few around."

"And when they searched they probably had documentation, you know, about which soldiers were on the flight. They would know we were on that flight, right?"

"GR would have logged that, yes," Hues said. "And when they went to the crash site they'd find those other bodies, but not ours. So, we'd officially be missing in action then, I guess."

"Right, but not reported to families yet. Maybe they'd look further in the area near the crash. Maybe they imagined we were killed and fell out of the chopper somewhere else before it crashed."

"Or maybe thought we survived the crash, crawled away to safety, and were hiding somewhere nearby. Or maybe they decided, based on a close inspection of the other bodies, we'd been captured and hauled away."

"What proof of that would there be?" I asked.

"What I'm thinking is, some bodies at that site were bagged bodies we'd loaded. Some others were injured men. Then you had the crew of four, and you and me. Remember, I watched the VC kill an injured crew member who couldn't walk. Sliced his throat. Our guys would have noticed that—sliced throats—on all the dead when they checked the site. Unless some animals got the bodies first. And when they checked the flight manifest against the bodies, they'd discover you and I were missing. Maybe we died in the crash, but we were gone. So, they might decide we're missing in action, maybe prisoners, until they prove otherwise."

"So, proof of life is the absence of our bodies, or at least the possibility that we are alive because our dead bodies aren't there?" I asked.

"Yup. So, our next of kin was notified of this possibility within a few weeks or couple months, my guess. I don't think they rush into MIA or KIA claims without some kind of evidence. So, our families likely been holding out hope for months. But now it's four hundred days later, and still no bodies, no proof of any kind we're still alive."

"So probably our families were notified of our deaths or will be soon," I said. "I can't imagine they'd wait much more than a year."

"Me neither. But a lot of the Army's always gonna be a big mystery to me."

"Hues, given your family situation, who'd you list as next of kin in the forms we signed when we headed over here?"

"Reverend Daniel Brown, Baptist Church in River Rouge, of course."

"Did Sena know that? Was she connected to Reverend Brown?"

He nodded. "I sent her the reverend's phone and address in my first letter from over here. And I left her contact information with the reverend. So, they likely know if there was a change in our status. Sena would know. And I hope she still cares."

"She does, Hues, and you've still got her heart, right?"

Hues smiled and nodded. "Big and warm as ever."

"Keep hugging that heart. My guess is she's a lot like my mom and Jeanie. They won't believe I'm dead even with an official Army letter declaring I'm dead, no longer missing. They'd want more proof than words."

"Hang on to that, man."

CHAPTER 11

— ESCAPE TRIGGER —

We reached a point near the end of our fourteenth month when we fully realized our hopes were dimming. Our thousand-yard stares were longer, more frequent. At times, our bodies and minds felt like they were shutting down. Or maybe they had shut down and we needed to fight daily to reopen them. Worst of all was the ever more frequent question we confronted: was living this kind of life really worth it?

Camp life was slowly killing us, though we continued to fight it. And we still had each other. But we spoke less at night, forgot several times to count the new day, shared fewer memories, and found smiles or laughter increasingly difficult to trigger. Our bodies were so numbed from pain, our daily bamboo whacks had become more inconvenient than painful.

Our biggest concern, however, was "tipping over" more often—acting stupid and doing and saying dumb things to the guards, a simple recipe for more beatings and less food. Somedays we both tipped over. I tipped over so far one night I only regained normal consciousness when Hues slapped my face and hissed in the dark.

"Buck, we got to keep our shit together, get out of here! We *losing* it, man. Big time. We dying slowly, and I ain't going that way. We got to fight by getting out. You with me? It's now or never. Let's do it!"

"You got it, Hues. Enough damn talk. Let's do it!"

The next day we began seriously planning our escape. We'd kicked ideas around before, but our talk was focused now. And we planned to do it soon—before the end of monsoon season. We needed the rain to wash away our tracks. And to drink. We weren't going the river route like the others who had tried and failed. We were going cross country, away from the river.

Two days later we had a breakthrough in our planning. We'd decided to leave in the middle of the night and head northeast. It would be harder for the VC to find us in the dark, although it would also be more difficult for us to know where the hell we were in the dark. But we'd been to the Banyan Tree Store many times, and that would be our target the first night. We could find it even in the dark. Maybe. During our trip there that day to gather more manioc root, Hues had made a discovery. As he was walking closely by some big banyan trees on the top of the hill, he looked down at one, then turned and nodded.

A bit later when we were digging root and could talk in whispers, he said, "I found us a hiding spot for our first night. That tree up the hill, where I nodded at you?"

"Yeah?"

"Looked like space underneath for two guys."

"I'll try to get a closer look."

Later, I got a quick glance at the space beneath the roots of that big tree as we headed back to camp. Hues was right. I would have liked a closer look, but the spot appeared promising. We'd plan for it.

Our planning accelerated even more when Toothpick and Caveman clubbed Hues hard on our walk back to camp. Hues was psalming, louder than normal, because he was getting excited about an escape. He was praying for our safety. I urged him to stop but he didn't. Now he was truly tipped over.

Caveman clubbed him once to get him to stop, but Hues continued. Then Caveman batted him really hard twice in the back, and Hues stumbled and fell. Tumbled down the little hill we were descending, rolling over on his head then flipping over and landing hard on his left ankle. He tumbled more and screamed as he jammed his left ankle again trying to stop his fall. I helped him stand and try to walk, but he took only two small steps before the pain in his ankle took over. He screamed and fell again.

I carried Hues for the rest of the trek back to camp, where the VC "doctor" rubbed some kind of gel onto his swollen and cracked or broken ankle. He then bound it tightly in black cloth that matched our black pajama leggings and shirts. Hues tried but still couldn't walk on the ankle. So, I lifted and carried him. Our desperate hour was closing in.

That night the guards accelerated our escape even more when they did the unthinkable. As we returned from the outhouse to our cage, Hues suddenly resumed psalming loudly.

"Enough, Hues," I whispered. "Don't make them madder, man. We barely hanging on. Don't need another damn beating. Or getting blown away like Rob and Ray. Stop, man!"

But Hues, whose leg and mind were wrapped in pulsating pain, though he wouldn't admit it, gave me a fierce but warm smile. "*He telling me to shout out tonight, Buck*," he whispered back. "I just living his words, man! We got to get out, we ever hope to live again. My psalms are opening the door for us. I'm psalming for *us*!"

I started to tell him our escape was coming soon. But then I saw a burst of familiar bright light in his brown eyes—the light of his spirit when it was on fire, which happened more and more. He broke into psalming again, a new and longer version of his MoCity Psalm #23:

> "We living in the valley, shadow of death,
> but fearing no man, nobody, nothing here.
> The Lord be with us day and night,
> filling our hungry hearts with love,
> saying tonight it's fight or flight,
> shining his bright light, our way out!"

Caveman and Toothpick yelled at Hues to stop, but he continued psalming in a powerful voice. The guards cursed and waved their thick clubs. Then they attacked and knocked Hues and me to the muddy ground. Hues began low crawling away, finishing his psalm in a deep voice that ended in a whisper:

> "Oh, Lord, I crawling into your light tonight,
> then my brother and my spirit, we walking home,
> into love's embrace and forever life with you!"

The guards smashed their clubs on his back and buttocks. Then they went for his head, which he tried to cover with his thin arms. They attacked his shoulders and back savagely, grunting and cursing as they swung. They clubbed his arms and head again, like they were competing to see who could hit him hardest or most often. They both won: my brother's lips stopped moving. He lay still. Unconscious or dead.

Then it happened: the cruel moment that would live forever in my mind and drive our escape. The guards knelt by Hues's head and waved over Cross-eye, who was waiting for us near the cage. Caveman roughly pulled and forced his mouth open. Cross-eye then pinched and pulled his tongue out. Held it tightly. Toothpick drew his knife, and with a quick twist of his wrist, he sliced off a piece of Hues's tongue. He held it out briefly to admire his work, then jammed it back into his bloody mouth.

I lost it. I pushed myself up, lunged, and dove on the three guards. I threw weak punches with my left fist. Reached out with my right hand and tried to find and grab the knife. I wanted to kill them. They'd beaten and tortured Hues and me repeatedly in camp. I wanted to kill all three before they killed Hues.

Caveman grabbed his club and smashed my head. Pinned me to the ground and beat me savagely on my shoulders and neck. I tried to block some of the blows with my arms, but I was too weak. Too ill. Too damn battered to put up a good fight. I cursed my weakness and cried out, "Stop it! Stop hitting my brother!"

The last thing I saw before passing out—red, red blood pooling in Hues's mouth just four feet away, then spilling over his lips in a rhythm of little hiccups. The small piece of his tongue bubbled up and out, sliding down his brown neck into the browner mud as the rain intensified.

Later in the rain and darkness in the cage, I regained consciousness and woke with a start. I was panting and sweating heavily from a frightening nightmare: *After they cut off his tongue, Caveman abruptly shot him in the head. The guards then forced me at gunpoint to carry Hues to the Beatdown Ring. Cursing them and grieving for my brother, I dug a hole in the roiling mud. The guards ripped off his black pajamas, threw them in my face, and mocked my grief. I gently laid my brother's body in the hole. Covered him with mud and prayers. They marched me back to the cage and beat me more . . .*

I quickly twisted my head to the left as far as I could in my restraints. I glanced toward Hues's restraints nearby, desperate to see him alive. In the near-total darkness, I thought I saw his black leggings, the edge of them hanging just above the ankle restraint. I looked toward where his head should be and discerned a slightly darker shadow nearby that had to be his shoulder.

Beyond that shadow was another darker shadow shaped like his head. It had to be him in the black night. I could feel his presence like I had for months in our cage. I closed my eyes. His spirit hovered close. I could feel its strength. He was alive and still with me! We'd escape and make it to safety together.

Apart from the rain, there was no sound. I hoped Hues was sleeping deeply in the soothing music of the rain rushing steadily like a little waterfall. He needed sleep. And a lot more to make it out alive. We both did. I didn't want to think about the odds. We'd vowed to escape and travel together, whether into new life or eternal death.

We'd escape in the next few nights as soon as I could plant a decoy at the river. I hoped our night would be dark and heavy with rain, just like tonight. I'd carry Hues every step, if needed. We were brothers.

We'd escape and make it back together. Maybe someday we'd laugh our asses off about our life in the cage in the jungle prison.

CHAPTER 12

—— MEMORY ROOM (2) ——

The picture I visited tonight was a photo of me and nine other Michigan teenagers selected to participate in a church team that spent a week hiking Isle Royale in the vast Lake Superior. The island was a breathtaking jewel of nature's beauty far removed from the small farm communities and grim inner-city streets where the kids in the group lived.

The narrow island stretched for fifty miles in the cold blue, big wave water. It was populated with magnificent trees of every shape and size, an assortment of small lakes and ponds, a dazzling palette of wildflowers, a rousing chorus of birds and animals, including moose and wolves, and a brand-new view of sunrise and sunset, which seemed far bigger and closer. We could almost reach out and touch the fiery pulse of the vast unending universe.

Reverend Dan led the hike. He was a large man with a melodious voice and a vast knowledge of forests and wildlife. Ruth, the choir leader in the church and also a registered nurse, hiked with the group too. The reverend shared morning and evening prayers and others when so moved. But primarily he led us to lookouts and vistas where he let the incredible beauty of that island talk to us and paint our horizons in life with bigger and brighter hopes.

Moose sometimes charged through our camp at night, triggering screams and laughter and toppling tents to our delight. The howls of wolves echoing against a full-mooned and star-lit heaven underscored the diversity of beauty and communications on earth. The vastness yet connectedness of the universe was overwhelming. As the reverend told us, "There's room for all, and a far richer life if we can learn to embrace rather than hate our differences."

The week we spent together drew us close as a family, though we were complete strangers. On Isle Royale we saw and marveled at all of the rugged beauty, the possibilities. The strength we felt inside our new family that week, our circle of laughter and prayers, the shared joy of just being on that beautiful island in the absolute middle of nowhere, together, changed our view of the world, and most importantly, who we might *be* and what we might *do*.

As Reverend Dan put it before departing the island, "Who could have created this amazing world except the Lord, or a bigger and higher spirit who then gifted it to all of us to enjoy, love, and live together in hope?"

My takeaway in the memory room, just one night after the guards sliced off Hues's tongue, was this: the world is much bigger than wherever you are on earth or in your mind. You are never truly alone no matter how lonely you feel—unless you choose to be or give up on life.

The possibilities of so many different people, the glories of so many natural things in the world around us—animals, stars, waterfalls, forests, rivers, mountains—empower us to be one with all. To reach out. To join others and help make the world a better place. That's what counted most in life: coming together, sharing hope and love, making good differences in the lives of others. Doing so could dramatically affect life for everyone. Why couldn't we make that happen or choose that path to life, rather than nurturing hatred for each other and engaging in constant wars?

Vietnam was my greatest challenge to hope. But I'd never give up. I had hope and help. And a big circle of family and friends in my memory room. And my brother in my arms. Hues and I could do it. Together.

PART TWO

—— 7 DAYS IN THE JUNGLE ——

CHAPTER 13

— DAY 1: ESCAPE —

We escaped two nights after the guards sliced Hues's tongue and one night after I planted a decoy at the river. We wanted the VC to think we'd gone the river route, so I found a small sharp piece of bamboo no more than six inches long—my bamboo knife. I used it to cut and tear off a small piece of my black pajama leggings.

When I fished that morning while Hues remained wrapped in pain and mostly unconscious in the cage, I watched for an opening when I could attach that cloth to a branch along the riverbank. At the moment the two guards appeared more engaged in their conversation than watching me, I pretended my line was snagged. I took three steps into deeper water and bent to pull my hook free. The guards still ignored me, so I pulled the piece of legging from my pocket and quickly attached it to a sharp pointed branch in the brush just a foot above the water.

Then I worked my way slowly back to my fishing spot on the bank. The decoy was nearly invisible in the brush. I hoped the VC would check the river first when they discovered we were gone. That little piece of legging might lead them east down the river while we headed northeast into the jungle. Misdirection could buy us some time, ever more precious for Hues in his current condition.

Over the past few weeks, we'd focused our planning on guard routines, restraints in our cage, weather patterns, and mental maps of places we worked daily around the camp. We also revisited our dimming recollections of the two-day march after the medevac crash more than a year before. We remembered few specific details about that trek beyond the bent-over pain. The general geography had included several big swamps, endless series of hills, three or four rivers, mazes of dense brush and trapping vines, and maybe a small village or two.

Due to many sleep-interrupted nights brought on by mosquitos, pain, and hunger, we learned Cross-eye's night guard routines: simple and consistent. Each night after we were placed in our cage, sometimes with restraints on our legs and arms and the cage door chained, other nights with no restraints or locks, we watched Cross-eye literally march to the guard tree. He sat down, his back against the tree, and stared at us. He was always armed with his club and an AK-47 rifle he propped against the tree.

Every hour or so, he rose and stretched, twisted his upper body side to side to loosen his stiffness, then bent at the waist and stretched several more times, flinging his arms up toward the sky and then back down, touching the ground. Standing, he'd light a cigarette and smoke it slowly, cupping it with his free hand to hide most of the light. When finished, he'd stub the butt out and shred it on the ground. He would then resume sitting against the tree, staring at the cage. Perhaps he relived his fantasies, or imagined a future without war, or simply nurtured his hatred for Americans, which he displayed daily with his angry words and abrupt beatings.

In the middle of the night, which I estimated was between midnight and one in the morning, Cross-eye would rise again, stretch, and walk to the small mess hall building about forty yards from the tree. Sometimes faint voices could be heard there. The regular night sounds were a steady chorus of crickets, birds, lizards, frogs, and other creatures, an eerie yet hypnotic music especially enjoyable when you were lying in pain. Counting by seconds, I determined the guard's break lasted roughly twenty minutes, maybe a bit longer in heavy rain. No one else observed us during that time. Another guard may have been stationed nearby or on the perimeter, but we never saw one.

Upon his return, Cross-eye would stop at the tree and stare intently at our cage for a moment. If he saw or sensed something of concern, he'd walk over and take a closer look, check the chain on the cage, and give us an evil stare along with a muttered curse. His pattern of sitting, stretching, and smoking then continued for four or five more hours until daylight filtered into the camp. On rare occasions his head would drop as he nodded off, just briefly.

We built our escape plan on these observations and the weather patterns. In monsoon season when the rain was especially heavy, or if it was storming, the VC relaxed their vigilance a bit. Confinement in the cage appeared less a concern. We often weren't restrained, nor the cage door chained on stormy nights. And that was the case for the two nights right after Hues was beaten and lost part of his tongue. If we'd been restrained or chained, escape would have been impossible. We felt rare luck might be on our side. We needed it.

I remembered a discussion Hues and I had shared about these guard observations and patterns in the days following the deaths of Rob and Ray some months earlier. Our thinking then was the guards were a bit lax with locking our cages because they hoped we might try to escape, or they believed any escape was likely to end with death anyway.

"Maybe they think, hey, where the hell would these stupid prisoners go?" Hues said, warming to the topic. "They got no idea even where they are, right? So, how would they know where to go? Besides, they too weak, got no food and no water, 'cept for rain. And they'd never leave in the dark of night, especially when it's pouring rain, right? They'd get lost for sure at night. Or the jungle cats, or a damn big snake, they'd get 'em and eat 'em. Good night and good-bye!"

I smiled at Hues. "I once heard a soldier say about POWs—maybe it was my bad-ass sergeant in infantry training, I don't recall—but he said it's easy for prisoners to escape and just as easy to die. The hardest part is surviving every day, just fighting to stay alive. So why in the world would you try to escape if you were just going to die anyway?"

"Which means we need to escape when they least expect it," Hues said. "And head in the direction they think we'd never go, right?"

I nodded. "Dead center of a dark night, heavy rain, when the guard doesn't restrain us or lock the cage, and then walks off to eat. That's our window. Gives us twenty minutes to get as far away as possible in the darkness."

Hues stuck his fist out. We dapped.

"And if lady luck is really on our side, Cross-eye won't closely check our cage after he eats. That'd give us a four, five-hour head start," I said.

Hues nodded. "We'll figure out the day-by-day stuff on the road," he said. "Better to escape and die trying, than waste away here till we're less than two little rice balls."

We executed our plan in the middle of the night. I'd fallen asleep but was awakened by what sounded like a gurgling grunt from Hues. He was always alert and sensitive to his surroundings, even wrapped in pain as he was now. I glanced at his faint shadow in the dark night as wind blew warm rain into our cage. We were both wet, nothing unusual. Then I heard the gurgling sound again and looked in the direction of Cross-eye, who was taking a final toke on his cigarette before walking off to the mess hut.

"We're going," I whispered above the steady noise of the rain. "Got to cover at least two hundred steps in the next half hour to clear the camp and have a chance." I'd counted steps from our cage to the brushy perimeter of the camp during the return from our last visit to the Banyan Tree Store.

As soon as the guard disappeared into the mess hut, I rolled and pushed myself to a sitting position. Then I slowly opened the unlocked cage door, which squeaked softly, a sound quickly lost in thunder rumbling through the camp like a noisy freight train.

I removed one of the mosquito nets in our cage, rolled and wrapped it around my neck, and tied it with the corner ribbons. We'd use the netting for sleeping in the buggy jungle and maybe for walking in the night. I packed my small bamboo knife for cutting and peeling leeches from our skin and my black plastic drinking cup, which we'd share. I put the cup in the left pocket of my black pajama bottoms. The bamboo knife went in my right pocket. Apart from the cup, the bamboo knife, the netting, our black pajama leggings and shirts, and our worn sandals, we had only each other. We were loaded.

"Let's do it," I said, closing my eyes briefly and trying to envision our first night's walk. The Banyan Tree Store was our goal before daylight. I grasped his arms in his black shirt and carefully pulled, lifted, and guided him over the restraints on the floor. On my knees I eased him slowly out the door. I then closed the door and took what I hoped was my last look at the cage.

The night was black except for a faint finger of light in the mess hut and a sudden jagged silver lightning bolt that ripped the sky in the northeast, the direction we were headed. I bent and lifted Hues in his black shirt and leggings. I felt his weight without taking a step, as well as the hope and strength of his spirit wrapped in my arms. No way I could make the long walk home alone. I needed Hues and his spirit. Every step.

"We're going home," I whispered in his ear. "You be *my* ears and early warning system. I'm your legs."

I took that first step, shifted Hues in my arms slightly, and took the second step, then the third. We needed about one hundred steps to get beyond the cage area, then one hundred more to arrive at the edge of the jungle. One step at a time we moved slowly out of the camp and merged like two slim shadows into the darker jungle, no light except in our minds and heart.

We planned to travel northeast, back in the direction of the firebases we remembered in that part of the country: Brick, Granite, and Bastogne, among others we couldn't remember. For the first day, and likely the second, we'd move only at night. We'd discussed this at length, but I wasn't yet convinced we could survive the night walks. I knew nights provided the best cover for us from the VC, NVA, and farmers and villagers in the area. Plus, the value of escaping in monsoon season was the heavy rains would erase our tracks and make it harder if not impossible for enemy soldiers to track us. At least early on.

I also knew and was already concerned that it would be incredibly difficult to stay true to a directional course in dark nights in a jungle maze dense with trees, trapping vines, and impenetrable brush and bushes; a long series of rising and descending hills; and stretches of mucky, slippery swamp. Add to those problems the ever-present dangers of prowling tigers and leopards; cobras, giant constrictors, venomous kraits, and other deadly snakes; and lethal giant centipedes and scorpions. The catalog of dangers meant the deck was stacked against us. But we were out and moving, playing the hand dealt us. The odds be damned.

The sun, moon, and stars would be our directional signals when we could see them through the forest roof. We'd find food somewhere to eat and use the drinking cup to catch rainwater to slake our thirst. Above all, we'd rely on my sense of direction and Hues's powerful sense of imminent danger to escape successfully. "Simple enough, right?" I whispered in his ear. I sensed him grinning.

Inside our dark, rainy world, I continued my slow, halting steps. My arms were already aching, and my shoulders were numb from carrying Hues. The rugged vines kept trying to tangle my feet and trip me. It was impossible to avoid them in the darkness. Hues was asleep or unconscious in my arms. We were soaked and dripping, not even a hat to guard our eyes from the downpour. Eventually, we'd pass some teak trees with their big, thick leaves, and I'd use the leaves to make hats like I had several times when we were gathering food in bad weather. Unless the darkness and rain hid the trees from sight.

I paused briefly after every other step, listened carefully for a second or two. Was the night noisy enough, or was it too quiet—that dangerous lack of sound which often signaled trouble? Any strange smells? How would I know in the pouring rain? How much time did it take to collect one hundred steps? At two hundred steps I halted well outside the camp perimeter. We'd made it this far, which likely meant Cross-eye hadn't checked our cage after his midnight meal. We'd hear whistles if he discovered us gone. Or maybe we wouldn't in the rain.

My uncertainty about how far I could carry Hues rose with each step. I stopped and set him down, then sat near him, my arm around his shoulder. "Cleared the camp," I whispered. "Don't think they know we're gone. Hope they don't until daylight."

We huddled for several minutes in the rain. My sense of time was already lost, and I knew my sense of direction would be a constant struggle. My goal was to take one hundred steps between stops, so I could slow my breathing and thumping heart. One hundred steps here equaled about 200-250 feet in a normal place, I figured. But in the jungle, carrying Hues in my arms, a normal step was shorter and slower. Nothing normal about it.

I estimated I needed at least twenty cycles of one hundred steps, more or less straight ahead, which was largely impossible, to equate to a mile, or about twelve cycles to cover a kilometer. How long would it take? Did my slow stepping and subsequent pausing require ten minutes per cycle? Twenty? More? I had no damn idea, and I didn't really want to know. If I tried to measure it out, or arrive at some figure of time, I might just give up because it was too slow, too long, too much time, too hard to do, and I was too weak. And then the two of us would most likely be dead.

One hundred steps later I sat down breathing heavily with Hues in my arms. I counted to one hundred in my mind before I rose and struggled ahead one hundred more steps. I was exhausted and not yet even in deep jungle, the swamps, or climbing hills. One hundred more steps and I collapsed in the tall elephant grass, hidden from sight.

At that moment so early in our escape, I found myself considering giving up and returning to the camp. I already felt lost and weak. We could go back and take a beating but still be alive, I reasoned. Or maybe I should leave Hues behind and race ahead much faster. Hues was going to die anyway. Just a matter of time, right? He knew that. I knew that. How could I ever carry my brother hour after hour, day after day, forever and forever into the blinding darkness of our journey, which was already a confusing and utterly oppressing maze? How in hell could I do that? It was a totally crazy idea—there was no safe escape. I was too weak in my body *and* mind.

I was suddenly seized by a strange and powerful sensation. Though I held Hues with my left arm around his shoulder and hugged him tightly, the situation now felt totally reversed: Hues was embracing me, hugging me close, and whispering in his gurgling voice in my ear, "With you brother . . . every . . . step."

Tears filled my eyes. I hugged Hues fiercely. "Together," I whispered. I felt a pulse of new energy in my legs and then a bigger surge in my shoulders and arms, like I'd just received an injection of raw energy. Or maybe the sudden surge had grown out of my self-anger and loathing. I mentally cursed my weakness, my self-doubts, my half-assed second-guessing. Barely out of camp and already quitting. *What a sorry piece of shit!*

I stood and gathered Hues in my arms.

One step at a time, I told myself. *Just one damn step more, that's all. Quit bitching! Listen carefully. Look for movement. Be a damn soldier. Follow your plan and trust yourself and your brother. You can make it if you believe you can.*

Another step. Was that so damn hard to remember? How could I have been thinking about quitting when we'd barely begun? The night was still marked by heavy rain and darkness. Lightning continued to flare in the northeast. Some light returned in my mind too. The memory map of our escape plan came into focus once more. One more step . . .

Our goal tonight was the Banyan Tree Store, which we imagined was roughly a mile northeast of the camp. We'd gathered eighty to one hundred pounds of manioc roots there at least once a week and carried them to the camp. Now we hoped to find food there for ourselves and, more importantly, a safe place to sleep, thanks to the banyan's giant roots.

We'd spend daylight sleeping beneath the roots, protected from the rain and hidden from sight unless one was crawling along on the ground peering under the roots and logs. If everything went according to plan, we'd be safe with some food nearby. We'd been there so often, I believed I could walk there blindfolded, which is more or less what I was doing.

I completed another one hundred steps, sat and rested, then caught some rain in the cup. I leaned Hues back against my chest and poured water slowly into his mouth, which he left open after swallowing. I refilled the cup and poured more water into his open mouth, which he then closed. He was drinking. A good sign.

I caught another cup and drank it. The rainwater tasted so refreshing. I caught and drank two more cups, then returned the cup to my pocket. I sat a bit longer, sketching a mental azimuth of the route to the banyan trees.

Soon we'd enter a tough stretch of forest—thick stands of three-needled pines, brushwood, impenetrable bamboo stands, weeds, and clumps of grasses and ferns. I recalled a slightly longer way around the worst of the bamboo but wasn't sure I could find it in the dark. After that, I remembered a faint trail through sharp and cutting elephant grass dotted with bushes and crepe myrtle trees that led to a swampy stretch of land, likely flooded and deeper now.

The swamp concerned me because it meant a stretch where I probably couldn't lay or sit Hues down. It would take all my strength to clear the swamp with the muck trying to pull me down. Then, coming out of the swamp, the land would begin to rise. Eventually the banyans would appear like giant sentinels near the top, a bit of a climb up a hill. We needed to be near the towering trees at first light so we could see them.

I hefted Hues and resumed walking, pausing briefly after every other step. Though my muscles were exhausted, I felt new strength in them after my breaks. When we'd made our way around several bamboo stands, I found a three-foot length of a tree branch broken off with a sharp point at one end, which I nearly stepped on. I figured out a way to carry the stick under my right arm and across Hues's thighs.

"We got a weapon now," I whispered to Hues, then laughed. "Better than just our good looks, right?" I sensed Hues rolling his eyes at my silliness. "Yup, I'm tipped over again," I told him. "Got a problem with that?"

As we finished walking the elephant grass and closed in on the swamp, after having turned around lost in the tall grass twice, I took another break. I was dripping with sweat and rain and weakened from exhaustion and pain in my shoulders and back. We were sharing another drink of rain when I noticed what appeared to be a pair of eyes at the edge of the grass nearby: two yellow dots, flickers of yellow light that shone brightly for an instant in a brief burst of lightning. I tensed as the eyes disappeared, then reappeared, closer now and more in front of us.

I carefully set Hues on the wet ground and slowly rose with the pointed bamboo shaft gripped tightly in my right hand. I took one step toward the eyes, which I was convinced were those of a cat—a tiger or jaguar—inching closer. I slowly waved the stick in my hand high overhead to make myself bigger.

"You want us, come get us," I said in a clear, steady voice. "My brother and me, we not backing off. So, make your move, or get the hell out of our way." I waved the stick again and repeated my words. The big cat, or whatever it was, just watched me. I knew I was no match for the cat, even if I wasn't weak and worn out. If that was a tiger or jaguar looking at us and then suddenly decided to attack, well, we'd be killed. Yet, living on the edge of death daily in the camp as we had for the past year, I felt unafraid, ready for anything.

During our brief stand-off, I glanced at Hues, still lying there in what was now a lighter rain. When I turned back, the eyes had disappeared. That concerned me even more. I blinked my own eyes several times to clear them, but the cat's eyes didn't return. I waited a moment, then waved the stick in the air and walked a slow circle twice around Hues, marking our territory. But the cat was gone, at least for now.

I gave Hues more water and lifted him. Had I just imagined the eyes? In my current state of mind, I might have. I could have tipped over because I was exhausted. Lost in the jungle at the edge of a big swamp.

We made it through that swamp only because I discovered, by

accident, several logs extending somewhat flat about a foot above the water, which was thigh deep. I bumped into the first log and nearly fell when I began my fifth set of one hundred steps in the gloomy swamp. I staggered then parked one butt cheek on the log, which allowed me to get some of the weight off my shaking legs which the swamp tried to trap every damn step.

I hugged Hues and waited for my breathing and pounding heart to slow a bit. Just a few hours into the escape and I was feeling empty again. I gulped air in short painful bites, each one cutting my chest like a knife. My lungs were hot and heavy, like two bags of heated air that choked me when I inhaled. How long would we last? Self-doubt was getting its second wind.

"Not in great hiking shape, man," I gasped, trying to laugh but choking instead. I looked at Hues, his head resting on my shoulder. "You still with me, man?" His mouth appeared to move, but there was no sound. His eyes were closed. I leaned my own face close to his and eventually thought I felt his faint breath on my cheek.

I awoke suddenly when his eyes flashed with light for a brief moment, giving me the wonderful grin I remembered—so fast, full of light, illuminating everything around me. A flash of lightning then lit the swamp sky before zigzagging rapidly west. Just follow the lightning, I thought. So, I did. Two hundred more steps. The night sounds tracked us closely.

When we rested again on another log, I struggled to keep my eyes open. The rain slowed to a light drizzle accompanied by a cloud of hungry mosquitos.

"We can't win for losing," I told Hues.

With one hand, I peeled the mosquito netting from around my neck and wrestled it awkwardly over our heads, blocking some of the hungry, humming bugs.

We sat for a few more seconds, or maybe a minute or two, when I felt myself slipping off the log, awakening abruptly as I was nodding off.

"Ready, brother?" Once again I thought I saw a brief light flare in his eyes. "Lost count of the steps, so starting over," I said. "Don't be shy about helping me count, hear?"

I rose from the log and stumbled one step ahead, then another. My feet moved slowly against the water. I stopped and listened to the night. Sometimes I felt fish or other critters bump or glide around my legs. I ignored them. I had no control of them. I hugged Hues tightly.

Another step, then pause. Listen. Again and again. The intensity of rain increased once more. The mosquitos thinned. Given a choice between rain or the bugs, I'd take the water every time. Hell, we could drink water and wash our faces at the same time. *Talk about the good life!*

Part of my mind drifted briefly to another dark night at a different place two years earlier. I remembered a night sky I'd seen with Jeanie, where the blackness overhead seemed more like a dark blue ocean upended and suspended overhead. The stars filling that sky glittered like teeth, forming a vast, curving smile, beautiful and sparkling—heaven's big, magnificent, humanly unmatchable grin. That picture in my mind was a virtual clone of the night sky Hues and I had seen from our cage the day after we saw the miniwaterfall when we were fishing.

For a few steps with Hues in my arms, and under a leaden black sky filled with rain and empty of stars, I felt the same sense of awe and peace I'd felt with Jeanie that night; a rich harmony linked us, the earth, and the vast universe. Maybe linkages in life counted most.

Inside that brief memory lingered a whisper of possibility. And then, within that whisper in my mind emerged a new sound, the faint brassy voice of a trumpet, announcing the music of hope—Louie Armstrong and "What a Wonderful World"! I listened to the music in my mind as I waded water, amazed once again at the incredible power of the mind to be anywhere, anytime, reflecting and processing anything and everything. Or doing nothing but remembering good times, a form of coping and hoping. Here we were in the middle of the swamp in the middle of a dark jungle, we knew not where, and I was listening to Satchmo sing and play his song in my mind, drawing strength and hope from that incredible memory music.

I paused and gazed down at Hues, finding the same gift of hope in his shining eyes, which were magically looking right back at me and through me into the heaven above. Did he hear the music too? Was he sitting with Satchmo?

And so, I took another step, paused, scanned the wet darkness that was our world now, hugged my brother, and took one more step. And another.

When we finally cleared the swamp, soaking and chilled though the night was heavy and humid, we sat and rested. I caught more rainwater and spilled it slowly into Hues's mouth, then drank two cups myself.

"We need to wait for first light," I told Hues. "See if we're remotely close to the Banyan Tree Store." I gave Hues another drink and listened to the steady jungle chorus surrounding us. I drank another cup of warm delicious water. I sat back against a tree, holding Hues. Needed sleep.

I woke with a start, no idea if I'd slept two minutes or an hour. Night was beginning to fade. I peered into the distance and felt a big smile spread across my face.

"We close," I whispered to Hues, pointing to the big banyan trees slowly emerging in the gray light on the hill to our left. "Within a hundred yards or so," I said. "Pretty good night's work for two lost POWs. Even blindfolded, we're still pretty damn good!"

We began the slow uphill climb as the sky lightened. I stopped counting steps, struggling with his weight, and trying not to tumble on the muddy hillside. I recalled the many stumbles and tumbles we'd taken up and down hills, hands tied behind our backs, on the long march to the camp after our capture.

The rain stopped briefly again. Nearby a pair of hooded pittas, vivid green birds with black heads, squawked like they were directing us through traffic. "Under the roots, under the roots," they seemed to chatter. We passed a papaya tree and a cluster of manioc bushes, food for later, after some much-needed rest. At the base of the banyan tree Hues had identified for a hiding spot, the gap and space beneath the roots beckoned us. Perfect. I laid Hues on his side, inspected the space, killed two spiders, then slowly pushed and tucked his thin, wet body into the snug place and laid mosquito netting over him.

I walked to a four-foot log nearby and slid it near the open space in front of our hiding place. Then I dropped exhausted to my knees, slid back next to Hues, and pulled the log near the opening, largely blocking the entrance.

We were now hidden from sight and protected from the rain, which suddenly resumed showering softly and steadily, covering our tracks and erasing our presence in the visible world.

In my mind I heard Hues psalming MoCity #36, his voice a blend of gurgling whispers near my ear. This was another psalm I knew. And so, it was early morning, the end of our first day of escape. His words fit our flight:

> Lord, your kindness so near, so dear this morning,
> for your two sons who are brothers here,
> seeking refuge in the shadow of your shelter.
> Your Light provides forever hope
> to escape sweltering despair, the Devil's lair.
> Embrace us Lord, bathe us in your Light,
> make us invisible to all save you, day and night.

My last conscious sensation was Hues's arm hugging my shoulder. *We got this, man.*

CHAPTER 14

—— DAY 2: BAMBOO NIGHTMARE ——

I woke suddenly when Hues tapped my shoulder. Once. Danger in front? In our last two days in camp, we'd agreed to a silent danger code. I'd seen his awareness operate in our training and in the camp. His sense of danger and awareness of our surroundings were crucial to our safety, and that was still the case despite Hues not being able to walk or talk now. So, we'd decided that Hues would tap my back or shoulder once if danger lay in front of us; twice if the danger was behind us; three times for danger on our right; and four times for danger to our left.

I was on full alert beneath the banyan roots. A bird called out anxiously as it flew somewhere nearby, followed by an answering call from another bird farther away, and a third faint call in the distance. I felt and heard the warm, moist, hushing breath of a steady wind. I noticed the ground around the log near our entrance was unmarked, washed clean from the rain as we hoped. For the moment, the rain had stopped. The sky was clouded with shades of gray from what little I could see from my vantage point hidden in the roots. It looked and felt like a "normal" monsoon morning between storms.

Then I heard it—a human voice quietly speaking, the words indistinct.

"Thank you, Hues," I whispered.

I pushed my right cheek flat on the mud and strained to see more.

My view was partially blocked by the log, but then I saw them: two human legs in black pajama bottoms, from the knees down to the brown feet in black rubber sandals. He stood about thirty feet in front of us, facing down the hill. The man spoke several more words, but I couldn't understand them.

Suddenly I heard a second voice, louder and much closer, from a man literally standing on top of us. I froze. I couldn't be sure, but the voice sounded like Caveman, who grunted angrily when he spoke. I translated his words loosely into "no one here," or maybe "no sign of the assholes," but I was guessing and hoping. The quiet voices of the two men, along with the relaxed body posture of the one man I could see, suggested they were unaware of our presence.

For several minutes the two VC, and maybe others out of sight, stood on the ridge among the banyan trees and manioc plants and silently observed the jungle below. No working POWs appeared. I couldn't imagine any other reason for the VC to be here, except searching for us.

They quietly departed. I watched the pair of feet and legs in front of me turn and head back in the direction of the POW camp. Their voices disappeared. I remained confident the VC first focused their search efforts on the river. But finding nothing there, apart from a small piece of black legging caught on a stick near the water, the search teams were then likely dispatched to check other POW work sites, like this one. This was the only site—and the farthest from camp—located in the northeast, the direction we needed to go.

"Gone," I whispered to Hues. "Rain stopped for now. Feels like late afternoon. We'll give it more time. Then eat some root. Head out at dusk. You up for more?"

I imagined the soft sigh I heard near my ear was Hue's affirmative response.

"I'll take that as a yes."

We fell back to sleep.

After they cut off his tongue, I hastily devised a simple but crude plan to feed Hues. I hadn't seen what happened right after they cut his tongue because I was unconscious. But I believed they heated a knife and seared it to stop the bleeding. What remained was utterly painful and useless for talking or chewing food. He couldn't tell me so in clear words, but his gurgling-like sounds and the memories of his bright brown eyes highlighting his words, communicated with an exclamation point.

I chewed his food for him now.

I crawled out of our hiding place, rose slowly on my knees, and did a thorough 360 of the land around us. Saw nothing concerning. A long-tailed Zebra dove flew near and cooed softly as it passed us, welcoming or cautioning us. Dusk was coming on. I dug some manioc roots with my hands and bamboo knife from a bush nearby and cleaned them as best I could with my wet shirt and leggings. I pulled and helped Hues out of our hiding space, then carried him to the base of a banyan tree nearby. I sat and pulled him back against my chest, holding him in my arms.

I bit off a piece of the manioc root and chewed it slowly and methodically, steadily converting the rather good-tasting root to a thick ball of paste in my mouth. When the ball was ready to swallow, I used my own tongue to roll and push the paste ball into my right hand, which I then used to gently guide the manioc paste ball into his open mouth.

Again, I thought of all the possible germs from my mouth and hands I might transmit to Hues. But a few germs between brothers were the least of our concerns here in the jungle. With his head tilted back against my shoulder, Hues worked slowly to swallow the paste ball. I gently massaged his neck and throat and whispered my support: "That's it, brother . . . nice and slow . . . easy on the swallow . . . you got it . . . good man. . . . We need this . . . for the big walk tonight. . . . Okay, great . . . you did it!

"Care for another delicious manioc meatball? Sorry, it's the only choice on our menu tonight." I closed my eyes, laughed, and hugged Hues.

I ate some root then prepared another manioc meatball and helped

Hues swallow. We fed a bit longer, then drank rainwater gathered from the light shower now spilling steadily from the darkening heaven. I tried to prepare mentally for another tough night of humping through the jungle.

Since we'd traveled to this banyan tree site at least once a week, I had a fairly keen sense of direction last night. But tonight, the territory was all new. The directional challenge would be far bigger. I'd need my antenna working well, along with Hues guarding my back.

We sat and watched the sky blacken slowly as light rain continued, then drank another cup of rainwater. It was time to go.

My steps downhill in the gathering darkness were deliberately slow to avoid a spill and tumble down the wet slope. Hues seemed to weigh even less tonight, or maybe I just felt a little stronger after a deep sleep and some food. He also looked thinner as I glanced closely at him—so skinny and gaunt he looked fragile. Only his eyes looked the same when they were open, filled with bright light despite the pain he was suffering.

When is the last time I saw his eyes open? Was it just last night?

I wished to hell he could talk. I needed his voice, the deep music of his laughter.

We reentered the jungle at the bottom of the hill, confident we were headed in the right direction, at least for the moment. I resumed counting steps. One step, two steps, stop. I shifted Hues a bit in my arms as I listened to the gathering night and its normal chorus of sounds. We slowly completed one hundred steps surrounded by jungle music, then briefly stopped. Piece o' cake, right?

I poured rainwater in Hues's mouth, then drank a cup and wiped my brow, already bathed in sweat. Nothing seemed off, and I felt certain the VC had returned to camp. One step at a time, then another step, pause and listen.

The painful rhythm of our slow walk resumed quickly. We brushed through some sharp elephant grass taller than I was, making us more invisible and blinder in the night. That grass gave way to some oil grass which had a distinctive sweet smell I loved. We then stumbled and dodged vines in the dark, which was becoming an art, the so-called art of luck. We worked our way slowly around several mango trees and some dense brush—all with no clear sense of direction, no vision much beyond the next step.

I hoped for lightning to illuminate our surroundings, if only briefly. Or a faint trail to follow, though that might be deadly. The bottom line was becoming clear: we needed to *see* more in this damn jungle, which we hadn't seen before walking this way! We needed to start walking days, tomorrow. It was a tough trade-off: us seeing better versus them seeing us better.

We were far enough from camp the VC weren't likely looking for us out here. On the other hand, they may have alerted others to be on the lookout for us. There were certainly others in the area: more VC, more NVA, more villages and villagers. And maybe some GIs too. Moving in daylight might prevent us from stumbling blindly into a village, or enemy troops, or GIs on ambush who'd shoot us in an instant because of our black pajamas.

"We go in daylight after tonight," I whispered in his ear.

My sandaled feet grew numb again from pain and several cuts around my ankles. I needed to find some big teak or kapok leaves tomorrow and try to bind and protect my ankles. I didn't want my feet to give out before we were safe.

Just one more step, then another. I thought I heard Hues softly humming me on. We hit a good rhythm as I followed the cadence of the humming, real or imagined.

Sometime later, after another hour or more, around four hundred steps or so—I'd again forgotten the exact count—we worked our way around what appeared to be a small square of dense bamboo forest, maybe thirty by thirty feet. It seemed so perfectly square in the occasional lightning and to the touch of my hand that I wondered if it had been planted and cultivated to keep its perfect shape.

I admired it as we rested a moment, then wondered: Was there something important in the middle of it? Was this a great big bamboo safe? They used the wood for everything else, so why not a safe? Or was it a big bamboo prison cage for GIs or a symbolic mortuary for POWs?

And why was this perfect jungle architecture, a dense square of bamboo, suddenly appearing here in the middle of the jungle? Was somebody just having fun, playing a trick, and trying to make something simple appear more significant in the middle of nowhere?

I shook my head to clear it, then tried to remember if we'd passed this square on our march to camp after we were captured. I couldn't imagine I'd ever forget such a perfect square of bamboo in daylight, but we were so exhausted that last day and bent over with our wrists and elbows bound behind our backs, we might have passed close without even seeing it. That was a more comforting thought than the alternative: we were already lost tonight.

Hues slept or was unconscious more often tonight. He desperately needed help, but none was available until we found safety at a firebase or with a group of American soldiers. Or maybe we'd luck out and a helicopter taxi would miraculously arrive to take us back to the hospital at Phu Bai. I shook my head. *Keep it together, man!*

I tried to increase our pace but couldn't. It remained a sluggish step after step in elephant grass, broken here and there with bamboo clusters that felt like walls when I bumped into them. More challenging was a sudden slope down or up the side of a small hill. It was hard, blind, extremely slow work. I stumbled and fell to my knees too often. My mind increasingly wandered to nonjungle places.

The rain grew heavier. Waves of thunder echoed loudly in the distance like bombs exploding. Lightning flashed like warning lights—danger everywhere. The jungle was putting on quite a show. Again, I tried to recall other places we'd passed on our march from the crash site. It was a brutal march for two days and nights, all of it seeming to have happened years ago.

No, it seemed like yesterday it happened, but a century ago. I shook my head. That made no sense. Tipped over again. I was totally soaked, hungry, and filled with pain but overall, I just felt old, incredibly old for my twenty-four years. At what point did the mind take over the body? Or did it work the other way around?

Get over the self-pity shit. Your brother is hurting far more than you. Get your shit together and quit tipping over! Focus on the damn jungle.

I then recalled a series of low but steeply wooded hills we'd climbed the first morning of our march, made even more difficult with our wrists and elbows tied. I'd never forget that experience. But would I remember those hills if we walked into them again? Must be thousands of hills in Vietnam, so probably not, I concluded. And certainly not at night. Yet another reason to walk in daylight.

Memory of the endless hills also triggered a memory of a small but swollen river we'd crossed, one of several, apart from some swamps we waded. I might remember that river, and it would be a great sign we were headed in the right direction. And if Hues and I crossed more than a couple of rivers on our way home now? I wasn't ready to go there yet . . .

We also had passed a small village, as I recalled. We imagined a small village because we'd heard a dog bark in the distance. And following a short break in the march, two VC suddenly appeared from the direction of the sound. They carried two bags of food—mangos that Hues and I ended up carrying the rest of the way. But which came first during that march—the river or the village?

Back to counting steps, I whispered them softly so Hues would know we were making progress too. I wondered again how he really felt since he couldn't tell me. And that carried me back to that still raw place in my mind, reliving that moment just four nights before when Caveman and Toothpick had beat Hues for psalming too loudly. Then Cross-eye joined them. They cut off part of Hues's tongue. And here we are tonight. He can't walk or talk. I'm lost in the jungle.

To escape that memory, I stopped and sat in the wet grass. I hugged Hues and focused on the memory of his laughter and the light that spilled out of his eyes when he was laughing—laughing so hard like it was his most natural thing to do. Maybe only second to breathing. I nodded off for a few minutes, sitting in the rain and listening to Hues laughing and psalming.

Eventually, I rose and moved on, counting our steps strictly, though I paid less and less attention to the direction we were going. Increasingly my movements simply talked to me and described the environment around me. I mean, how weird is that?

This is a big damn bush. I didn't see it coming.

Where'd this hill come from?

And all these damn vines! A guy could get dizzy trying to dance around them in the dark!

Why am I now standing in water?

Where the hell am I?

Aware I was growing goofier and more confused and whispering a lot more to myself, I changed my step-counting routine to try to stay more focused. I began counting my steps down from one hundred rather than up to one hundred: step ninety-nine, ninety-eight, ninety-seven, and so forth. All the same but different, right? It helped a bit, and I focused more on our direction and landscape as much as I could see in the dark night. I was relying big time on my instincts.

At some point during the night a sudden awareness struck me hard, like a club in the face: the cage in the prison camp we'd worked so hard to escape was only one tiny part of a much bigger prison—the vast jungle itself that spread for miles in all directions. I loved the outdoors and hiking, fishing, camping, exploring. I'd grown up close to nature. But this huge, unending jungle, especially at night, was totally overwhelming, frighteningly confining, and utterly confusing in its dense invisibility and haunting sounds and shadows.

On one hand, that was not news; I'd lived and survived more than a year in the jungles in Vietnam, in the camp. On the other hand, with Hues, the two of us were really alone in this incredible maze. And to top it off, we were totally unarmed in a world where men and animals of all types were hunting us as prey.

The jungle was the real prison, an all-encompassing giant green cell so big it was like a huge planet of its own, one that radiated waves of alternating pain and numbness. Inflated fear. Muted the voice of hope. Teemed with threatening prisonmates of every shape and size who hungered for our blood and lives.

I felt leeches sucking blood on my right knee. It was nothing new, but it felt like a lot of leeches. I bent and set Hues on the ground, then pulled the bamboo knife from my pocket and reached down with my left hand and felt seven smooth and fattening leeches. With the knife in my right hand, I carefully cut and scraped each of the leeches off my knee. It was a struggle in the dark. I then plucked some small pieces that remained. Tempted to eat them. That was my own blood, right? I didn't.

We moved another eighty steps and came upon what looked like a small creek. I decided to wade it—pluses and minuses like every choice in that big prison. The creek quickly turned into a series of mucky sinkholes, which nevertheless were less difficult to negotiate than the dense jungle brush and vines. I didn't recall this series of mucky sinkholes, but why should I?

Five minutes into the creek walk, I realized the price for this easier path: dozens more leeches sucking on my legs and feet. I said to hell with them and pressed on, stubbornly counting one hundred more steps before stopping to rest.

Propping Hues against a tree along the bank, I gathered some large teak leaves nearby and carried them to the tree and Hues. I stacked and arranged the big leaves over the lower limbs of the tree and around Hues and me, reducing just a little the rainfall on our exhausted bodies. I caught rainwater with my cup and drank deeply, enjoying the pleasure of the warm moisture sliding sweetly on my dry tongue and down my throat. I shared three cups with Hues, whose nodding head and imagined gurgled words indicated his delight with the water too.

I then cut and scraped dozens of leeches from my ankles and legs and removed six leeches from Hues's battered left ankle and leg. I couldn't see the leeches in the dark, but I could feel them and remove them, or most of them.

As I settled back for a moment of rest, two aircraft passed overhead in a now lighter rainfall. Their sounds were muffled, but I imagined they were probably C-130 transport helicopters moving equipment or troops. Or perhaps I just imagined the choppers. Leaning back against the tree and beneath the big wet teak leaves covering us, I put my arm around my brother's shoulder and took a short nap.

Later we found ourselves in a large stretch of swamp, which I didn't recall wading on our hike to the camp. Again, there was no place for me to sit with Hues, so I just staggered on in the darkness. My sandaled feet and ankles were cut and scraped, but they actually enjoyed the sucking mucky bottom. No other part of me did. I was amazed my arms could still hold Hues and I could maintain balance. I'd never felt more exhausted or weaker than right at that moment.

I found myself talking aloud to Hues, whispering how much I loved Jeanie and the unseen baby. Then I thanked Hues for all he'd done to help me survive and break out of the camp. I stopped for a moment and stood in the light rain and the swamp water, just below my knees. I hugged Hues and cried briefly.

"You're the reason I'm still alive," I whispered to him. "I'd never make it on this damn dark journey without you, man. Thanks for hanging with me, Hues. We got this!"

We cleared the swamp. I had no idea what time it was, where we were, or how long we'd walked. Three hours? Six hours? Was it nearing dawn? I found a small stretch of flat ground under a trio of tall papaya trees, which helped break the rainfall. I laid Hues down, then stretched out to rest my aching body for just a minute and decided we needed to eat.

I pulled the last of the manioc root out of my pocket and washed it in the rain. I pulled Hues up again, resting his head on my shoulder. I slowly chewed a bite into a soft pulpy ball, which I fed to Hues and helped him swallow. He wanted no more. I ate two bites for myself, followed by small drinks of rainwater for both of us.

I must have fallen asleep again because I found himself suddenly opening my eyes and sitting up, next to Hues, and momentarily confused.

I'd been dreaming about my father and his long workdays, his strength and discipline. He was a lunch-bucket worker who gave it his all every day and always came home with a smile. I needed his strength.

Had Hues awakened me? I peered around in the darkness and confirmed we were still living our nightmare, lost in the jungle. Yet, I had the powerful sensation that Hues had awakened me and whispered in my ear, "Time to move on, brother. We ain't there yet." I started to ask Hues if he said that, but he seemed peacefully asleep, so I didn't wake him.

I lifted him and found the most comfortable spot in my arms to carry him, then resumed our journey. I hadn't gone far when I lost track of counting steps, so I started over, counting them up again. One step, two steps. Stop and listen. Three steps, four steps. Just a normal stroll on a swampy, rainy night.

One more step.

I was getting back into the rhythm, gaining more strength and conviction, moving on with my brother, walking home to be with my girlfriend and our baby, my family; moving on to create and live a real life back in the real world outside this damn unending jungle.

And then my heart stopped. I let out an agonizing cry and dropped to my knees, hugging Hues tightly in my arms. No way this could be happening, no damn way! Tears filled my eyes.

"No, Lord, no, no, no!" I cried. "Don't let this happen! Where the hell are you, Lord? Where the hell are you when we really need you, dammit?"

Just feet in front of us, hauntingly visible in several flashes of lightning, stood one corner of that distinctly perfect square of bamboo trees we'd passed several hours earlier. I was certain there weren't dozens of perfect squares of bamboo in the jungle, which meant we'd marched for what seemed like endless hours, one agonizing step after another, in a big, ragged circle in the jungle.

We'd gone from nowhere back to nowhere, lost in the night, no sense of direction, standing again at the squared edge of despair. That dense bamboo wall might be some form of jungle voodoo. Or maybe it was a planted square of trees in memory of others who'd died walking in endless circles in the jungle too. I was sure I heard it laughing as I stood on the edge of the abyss of life-ending despair.

As I cried and begged my brother's forgiveness, I found a spot nearby under a teak tree where we were partially protected from the steady rain. I set Hues on the wet ground, then sat near him, sweating but shivering, and hugged him tightly. "I'm so sorry, man, I've let you down," I whispered repeatedly in his ear.

I finally pulled the mosquito netting over us, then held Hues in my arms. "Don't know how long I can keep going," I whispered. "Got to find a miracle somewhere tomorrow, get back on track. And we got to see, so we walk in daylight."

Above my own tired breathing, I heard Hues psalming his end-of-day prayer: MoCity Psalm #69. His gargled words were faint, so faint in the rain, yet they lingered, humming softly, like the music of the mosquitos gathered and circling our netting.

> Rescue us, Lord, from the drowning rains,
> feet tangled in jungled vines of misery,
> overwhelmed by pain, whispering our prayers.
> Softly calling out your name, oh, Lord,
> eyes searching your ever shining Light,
> the sound of your voice, directions home.
> Rescue us, Lord. We will praise you forever.

CHAPTER 15

—— MEMORY ROOM (3) ——

The picture of my father, then in his late forties, depicted him in his dark blue work pants and shirt, a Detroit Tiger baseball hat tilted to the right on his head, and a worn black lunch bucket dangling in his left hand. He'd just returned home in his red pickup truck from a long day of work in new homes. The small hand wave and smile on his face were enigmatic. He was much more difficult to read, far less open with his emotions and feelings than my mother, who wore hers vividly in her blue eyes and robust words.

That image captured my father on the day he shared one of life's most important lessons. I was athletic and strong, played football and wrestled in high school. And in the spring of my fifteenth year, I was trying out for the high school track team. I could run a fast quarter mile, but what I really wanted to do was become a pole vaulter and soar like a bird over the bar.

My father helped me construct a vaulting pit filled with sawdust to break my landing. I then dug holes for the two poles that would hold the crossbar, a bamboo fishing pole. My high school coach provided a vaulting pole for practice.

I started vaulting at a height of five feet. When that became routine, I moved the bar to six feet high. After a few days of practice, I was clearing that height too. But for a week now I'd failed to clear seven feet, inevitably knocking the bar down before I could lift my body over it. I felt clumsy and awkward.

When my father came home from work late that afternoon, he parked his pick-up in the driveway, grabbed his lunch bucket, and walked into the backyard to watch me vault. I tried and failed twice to soar over the seven-foot mark. After the second attempt, my father walked over and set his lunch bucket on the ground.

"Giving you trouble?" he asked, nodding at the crossbar set again at seven feet.

"Can't seem to get over it," I said. "I think my sprint and form are okay. But I can't pull my body high enough. I'm starting to think, maybe I can't do it."

"Can I see the pole?" my father asked, reaching for it.

I handed it to him. For a moment he held and rubbed the pole, then looked down its long length, shining in the late afternoon sunlight.

"Like many things we do in life, Brian, pole vaulting is as much in our heads and hearts as in our muscles," he said.

Then my father, nearly fifty years old, dressed in work clothes and heavy brown work boots, the baseball hat on his head, lifted the pole skyward, hunched his shoulders, and began to jog slowly toward the crossbar, looking pretty silly.

He increased his jogging speed to a sprint, closed in on the bar, planted the pole firmly in the vaulting box, swung and pulled his body up, and soared smoothly, beautifully over the seven-foot bar, like a bird swooping easily over a low hedge. He landed perfectly on his feet in the sawdust pit, hat still on his head.

I was stunned.

"Dad, that's great! How'd you do that? You been secretly practicing?"

We laughed.

Dragging the vaulting pole in his hand, he walked over and looked me in the eyes. "Never let anyone or anything convince you, Brian, there's something you cannot do. Never." He handed the pole to me, gathered his lunch box, and walked toward the house.

I held the pole while in my mind I watched him fly over the bar again. Smooth as a bird. My old man.

I hefted the pole and sprinted toward the vaulting box, planted the pole, pulled, and then soared so very awkwardly and clumsily, like a bird with only one wing, but *over* the seven-foot bar. I'd done it!

I turned toward my father, now standing near the back door of the house. He gave me a smile and a thumbs-up salute. I smiled and returned the salute.

Never give up.

CHAPTER 16

—— DAY 3: VIETNAMESE SPIRITS ——

Hues likely saved our lives this morning.

I awoke to three sharp taps on my back—*danger on our right side*. I listened to the sounds, which blended into a normal morning chorus of bird chirps and warbles, frogs croaking, insects' softly buzzing, wind whispering, and a gathering of monkeys chattering in the distance like they were engaged in a big, testy political rally. A large red-breasted parakeet watched us from a low limb nearby. Rain dripped slowly from the leaves overhead, though it wasn't raining now. Nothing unusual. I raised my head and looked to the right, where the threat was quite visible.

A thick python, mottled in browns and golds, lay about thirty feet from us. With its eyes open and head raised about a foot off the ground, the big snake watched us intensely, maybe trying to determine whether we were one meal or two given how skinny we were. I scanned the area in front of us, then to the left, seeing no other threats for the moment, though I couldn't see far into the noisy jungle.

"Thanks, Hues," I whispered. "Guess we won't do breakfast here because . . . we might *be* breakfast!"

I heard Hues laughing softly, a reassuring sound I knew well. I rose to my knees and checked our gear. The drinking cup was still in my left pocket. The bamboo knife was in my right pocket, along with a small piece of manioc root. The mosquito netting was draped over and tucked beneath us.

I removed the netting, rolled it up, and slowly tied it around my neck, keeping my eyes on the snake, which had crawled several feet closer. Despite the netting, I felt a handful of black leeches clinging to my right ankle. Hues had several in the same area. They would have to wait.

I gathered Hues in my arms and stood, wavering a bit under his weight and sensing again his body was growing lighter. I know I wasn't growing stronger, so Hues must be losing weight. If Hues could talk, he'd probably say something about his weight like, "It's the Lord responding to my psalm last night, man, calling for more strength. He with us, man!"

The python raised its head a bit more, moving it slowly and hypnotically side to side, almost like a wave of hello or a slow goodbye. I knew most snakes wouldn't chase you unless you tried to run. Well, running with Hues in my arms wasn't an option, so I backed up and walked slowly away from the snake, one short step at a time. I counted ten steps, stopped, and looked back over my shoulder. The snake appeared not to have moved, though it still watched us. I took five more steps; the snake's head still waved hypnotically, side to side, but it hadn't come closer.

We set off in what I imagined was still early morning. We hadn't slept long, maybe three or four hours, but it felt like a deep sleep. I needed it physically and mentally to recover from my wasted, walking-in-a-great-big-circle routine yesterday. I was still angry with myself, but that was yesterday. Today we were moving on and making up for lost time. I resumed counting steps, then paused and listened, shifting Hues's weight a bit.

I stopped after the first hundred steps, which seemed to go fast though we were moving slowly. For the moment we were out of the dense jungle and moving through some pine trees and a few crepe myrtles. A thick cluster of coffee bushes lay beyond the pines. It was nice to be able to see where we were walking. I had a far bigger and better picture of the landscape. I still believed that escaping and moving in the darkness helped us survive that crucial first night by keeping us invisible. But it also made progress far slower and more difficult. And produced the angry agony of last night.

The morning also offered some welcome signs in the rain-free sky. Through breaks in the limbs overhead, I could see streaks of blue sky among the puffy gray clouds that looked like thick berets. Most importantly, I saw some of the sun behind the clouds in the eastern sky, showing us the way to go to have a chance to make it home.

"See the sun, Hues? We can see our way home," I whispered happily in his ear.

His closed eyes seemed to glow a little, maybe with the light of hope or just the sunlight on his face. I felt better and took my bearing from the sun, steering us a bit more north than east, ensuring we wouldn't encounter again that perfectly shaped and haunting bamboo square.

We took a brief break in the warming day. A yellow-crowned woodpecker croaked as it flew by. *Follow me*, it seemed to sing. I set Hues down and worked on the leeches with my bamboo knife. I squeezed, pinched, then cut and scraped their fat bodies off. This left bloody marks, and who knows what else, on our skin. Leeches, like flies, ants, and mosquitos, were constant companions in Vietnam, and maybe more dangerous. They also were easier to remove in daylight than in a black night. We shared the small manioc root and moved on.

The jungle suddenly thickened again, so much so I often couldn't see more than a few feet ahead. Other times I could see twenty, thirty feet, and when we climbed hills, sometimes much further. If the brush forced us a bit left, or north, then my mind and body corrected back to the right, or south, when we could, or vice versa if I were fully alert.

The direction was branded in my mind. The trick was I had to think about it all the time, yet not overdo it, or I'd begin to lose confidence in my natural sense of direction. If that happened, I imagined we'd become utterly lost and die in a jungle maze. Our bodies would disappear quickly, I knew, courtesy of the many creatures who'd feed on us. Just some of our bigger bones would remain, eventually covered by mud and water, steadily decomposing. We'd lie buried somewhere forever in the same constantly changing jungle. I reached a dead end in my brain when I asked myself: *Will I still have a sense of direction in death?*

I shook my head. Why was I thinking that way? Was it just part of losing my mind, a natural companion to losing my strength? Or was I simply getting an early start on the day to tipping over again? At the next rest stop I removed some small red ants that bit my ankles and feet with fire in their tiny mouths. I started to clean Hues's feet, then realized they hadn't been on the ground in the ant patch we walked through.

Hues appeared to be sleeping. He slept or was unconscious more and more often, and he seemed to grow thinner by the hour. He was literally a bag of long bones covered tightly in shiny brown skin that reminded me of the wet, sunlit, sandy beaches along Lake Michigan. Did he weigh even ninety pounds today? And without his tongue and rich, robust voice, he seemed even smaller, a shadow of himself. The good news: he was lighter to carry. The bad news: he was closer to death. Was everything in life a tough trade-off?

I decided to look seriously today for some big teak leaves to wrap around my feet and ankles to reduce bug bites and leeches. And I'd use some of the same leaves for our heads to cover and camouflage us and reduce the rain in our eyes that blocked our vision. We'd done that several times in camp when we worked in heavy sun. The big leaf protection worked pretty well when we tied them with small vines. Those were all around us.

I moved on, stopping often to balance his body in my arms. My movement consisted of three overlapping phases of observations and actions. First, I'd glance ahead to find a directional marker—maybe a tree, a particular bush, a small hill, or some rocks—and I'd move slowly toward the marker. Then I'd locate another marker, or a tangle of vines to avoid, or a dark bush that provided some shade, or a rare pool of sunlight that reached the ground. Hues and I were a battered, slow-moving but constantly sensing team machine. I was the physical senses; Hues was the sixth sense.

In the second phase, I focused on nearby ground and vegetation.

After I took two steps, I'd pause and scan the ground immediately in front of and beside me for six to eight feet, if possible. I looked for vines, traps, or snares of any kind, snakes, and clusters of red ants or leeches, threats in any form. Then I'd raise my sightline from the ground to the vegetation and landscape around us, quickly evaluating bushes, trees, grassy stretches, swamps or mudholes, rising and descending hillsides, physical structures of any kind that might present dangers, or provide possible hiding places, should we suddenly need one.

In the third phase, I quickly scanned the sky if it wasn't totally blocked by trees, hoping to see a helicopter, a possible ride home. Or maybe just a simple colorful bird like a green magpie in the sunlight which highlighted its beauty and provided a mini burst of joy and hope. In short, my job while carrying Hues, was to pick a directional target to guide us. Scan for danger or possible hiding places on the ground and in vegetation. And check the sky as possible to reinforce direction and possibly see some signs of hope.

Lost in deep thoughts, yet staying focused on direction, I was startled when Hues tapped my shoulder once—*danger in front of us?* I sat quickly in the wet, waist-deep jungle grass that lined the base of a low-rising ridge on our right side that would likely take us up and out of the wetland. The natural chorus of noises in the jungle had stopped—a moment of dangerous silence. I put my finger to my lips, nodded slowly at Hues. Then I closed my eyes, which improved my hearing and sense of smell.

A vast range of sounds inhabit the jungle at various times. The rare but life-threatening growls of tigers and leopards, and occasionally a bear or wild boar. A band of shrieking monkeys, squealing pigs, mooing cattle, barking dogs, or singing birds of diverse colors. The hoots of owls and croaks of frogs. The sighs, whispers, and howls of the wind. The voices, laughter, yells, cries, and screams of people. Insect legs rubbing together, and sometimes the frightening sounds of weapons loading and locking, shootings and explosions, bombs blasting.

Smells in the jungle were many too, depending on the location, presence of people, and level of combat. The smells of jungle combat even hours after a fight might include cordite from gunshots and gun powder, napalm, gasoline, grease, blood, and the stench of dying and death, which linger sadly forever in the mind. The smells of burning bushes, brush and trees, and the combat stink of soldiers, a smell worn like a coat by every soldier.

Noncombat smells were a mix of fetid water, rotting or flowering vegetation; decomposing animals, birds of all kinds, snakes, mice, fish, and frogs; and the constant stink of humans living and sweating in the jungle. Inside or close to villages, or sometimes troops nearby, the sharp smell of nuoc mam, a fish oil used with rice and other foods, filled the air and pierced the nostrils. And of course, there was salty sweat, wet clothes, urine, excrement, vomit, and even . . . *cigarette smoke?*

Was that what had captured Hues's attention and led him to tap my shoulder? The faint scent seemed to curl and spill over the low ridge nearby as we'd moved parallel to it in waist-high grass. The smell of cigarette smoke was real. It filtered into our noses and settled in. I pressed my fingers to my lips and nodded thanks to Hues for the alert. Pulling him onto my back as we lay in the grass, I low crawled slowly through the tall grass to a cluster of peanut bushes behind which we could hide, listen, and sniff the air.

The cigarette smoke was not strong, but it lingered, a slight wind blowing it our way. At one point I was certain I also heard whispering voices, perhaps soldiers taking a break or leaving an ambush site where they'd spent their night. We lay behind the bushes for what seemed a long time after the voices and scent disappeared.

I carried Hues up the little ridge for a better look. Near the top, I set him down and low crawled the last few yards, then peeked over the top. I saw nothing but a short stretch of flat ground partially covered with several logs and some more peanut bushes. The land then descended to a ravine or small valley and back up to another ridge. In fact, it looked like a series of small ridges covered with trees descending in the distance, rolling east like waves of jungle. I found slight indentations in the soft earth atop the ridge—boots or sandals, maybe. Some of the grass appeared flattened in places. No cigarette butts or other evidence of humans was visible.

Had we simply imagined the cigarette smoke and faint voices, which was certainly possible? If they were real, were they enemies lying in wait for Hues and me? Had they been sent out by the camp to trap us if we made it this far? Or were we close to the village I vaguely remembered, where we were given the two black bags of mangoes we'd carried to camp? Or the most remote possibility: did the voices and smoke belong to American soldiers out on patrol or departing an ambush site they'd used for the night? Had we missed an opportunity for escape?

We continued moving slowly but steadily, heading more south than east, circling a village that may or may not exist outside my mind. I was taking no chances. I often thought about the keys to a successful escape: be ultraquiet and wary, take no stupid risks, find something to eat to keep up strength, drink no bad water, and most importantly, believe you could do it, one step at a time. No matter how weak or hungry you were, no matter the volume of the pain, or the weight of the wet hot weather, if you convinced your mind you could always take one more step, then you'd never stop moving. You could always take one . . . more . . . step and know that one more was always there in your mind, body, and soul.

Between two of the rolling hills covered with pine trees, we found ourselves back in swamp land, and we worked our way through the mucky, knee-high, filthy black water that sucked hard on my feet and legs. I was increasingly amazed we had survived the long swamp walk in the dark the first night. In daylight I could see once again the dangers that surrounded us as we waded.

Colorful green and yellow snakes wound their way across the sluggish water. Other bigger and more venomous snakes curled in trees or hung from limbs, silently observing us and awaiting their chance. Some giant centipedes and a pair of scorpions itching to sting were just feet away. And nature's booby traps were everywhere in the guise of dangling, strangling vines and sharp stumps or limbs that would pierce your body if you fell.

How had we safely crossed that dark, dangerous, and deadly swamp alive, walking and carrying my brother and blinded to everything so close by, just a step or a bite away from death? How could we have done it without the help, guidance, and blessing of the Lord or a superior being? Or was it Hues? Had his strong soul and spirit carried us through? That seemed most likely. In any case, it had to be more than hours of luck, right?

Hell, if I had any luck I wouldn't have been drafted in the first place. Nor sent to war in Vietnam. And certainly not captured and now living the glorious life of a POW on the run! If that was luck, I wanted no more of it. Give me blindness in a black swamp, my brother in my arms, and one more step.

Later that afternoon as my body wore down, I tipped over completely. Life and the present moment rearranged themselves, probably due to my exhaustion. I wasn't sure how long I'd been walking around in a daze in the jungle maze, quietly talking with Hues.

He'd magically regained his tongue and his legs, walking and talking beside me, carrying a radio softly playing Detroit rhythm and blues, and snapping his fingers to the beat. We were headed out to meet some of his parishioners walking near the Rouge River. A trio of violet cuckoos fluttered around us like they loved the music, dancing with their wings.

And Sena, his beautiful girlfriend, the little Korean lady with the huge heart, was walking with us too! Hues introduced us. I smiled at her; she was beautiful with huge dimples and shining brown eyes filled with joy and hope. She smiled back and winked as she held Hues's hand. Her smile filled her face and the air around us. They laughed like two school kids, and I laughed with them. It was so damn good to be home, walking and talking, listening to rhythm and blues on the radio. Natural life. Simple daily life. So incredibly beautiful.

Then Hues was suddenly back, tongueless in my arms. Sena was gone. No birds. No music except jungle noise. We were working our way blindly through sharp elephant grass, back in the jungle maze. Somewhere. And it all fell down on me again: day three on the long road home.

I groaned and gasped air in short, painful inhales, my lungs burning and fighting me. They were saying slow down, man, slow down or your heart's going to stop. You'll fall on your head or ass. Your brother will die, and you too, if you don't slow down and get it together, man! That sounded like Hues talking in my head, but he was sleeping peacefully in my arms.

In my dazed state, I wondered if my diseases were competing again. I'd met them repeatedly in the camp and learned about them from Hues. Right now, I felt like dengue fever had returned, which I knew all too well—high temp, throbbing head, muscles gone flat with aches, no strength.

Then diarrhea took over again, for real. I set Hues down, turned and squatted and let it run, or tried to. I kept squeezing my butt cheeks, though little was there but a burning trickle, noise, air, and a hungry pain. Nothing but a hand to try to clean and dry myself.

Or was it encephalitis? I felt the fever, headaches, confusion, nausea, and real vomiting. But there was little in my belly. I felt really hungry but had no appetite. Most of all, I was fighting to hang on to my mind, which was now outside my body and floating high in the trees, waiting for the sun to rise, or set, I didn't know which. I did know we needed food and water. Real soon.

I collapsed near the base of a big bodhi tree, its heart-shaped leaves calling out to me like my mother did when I was little. "Time for dinner, Brian! Come get it!" Three pink and white lotus flowers grew near my feet. Bamboo thickets were not far away, and a faint trail ran just to the east through the grass. We'd already discussed and decided we'd follow that trail later, maybe at sunset, though my sense of direction at the moment wasn't great. And then I couldn't remember if Hues and I had actually discussed the trail or not.

In the late afternoon sun, I fell asleep, my right arm stretched out and holding Hues by the shoulder. Or maybe Hues was holding my shoulder.

The mosquitos awoke us. I'd forgotten to spread the netting. Then I remembered we were taking a short nap, not a night's sleep. I didn't need to spread the damn net! Our bodies were covered with numerous new bites, and several leeches had found our feet and ankles, their little black bodies bloated with our blood.

But what surprised us, stunned us far more than the bites and leeches when we awoke was the presence of an old Vietnamese woman, a conical hat on her head and a sad smile on her face. She stood just ten or twelve feet away, a bag over her shoulder, staring at us.

How long had she been watching us? Why hadn't I heard her approach? Had she alerted the VC or NVA? What was in her sack? She must have walked that faint trail running near the tree. We were likely close to a village and didn't know it. We also didn't know whether it was a friendly village, which was unlikely in this part of the country.

Without thinking it through, and unarmed in any case, I simply sat up, nodded, and said politely, "Hi. How are you, Grand Mama-San?"

She continued to stare at me, unblinking. Her worn face was a jigsaw puzzle of wrinkles, sunspots blended in. Living in the jungle in a war, she might be fifty or sixty years old, or younger. Or much older. I couldn't tell. The hot sun, unending rains, war tensions, and the presence of sudden death aged everyone more quickly and deeply.

I was strangely drawn to her. If she really wanted us killed, all she had to do was holler or scream, and the villagers would come running and quickly end our lives. But she didn't scream, or wave her arms, or do anything but stare. I tried to imagine what she might be thinking and what she saw when she looked at us—two Americans, prisoners in black pajamas, faces red and bitten, ankles and feet cut and leech-infested. Bodies rail thin and rib-showing skinny, looking hungry, lost, crazy-eyed, near the end.

Then she shared an even bigger surprise than her quiet presence.

She took another step closer. I rose to meet her. I saw tears form in her sad brown eyes. She reached into her black sack and withdrew a pair of thick manioc roots. She stepped closer and extended her hand holding the roots. She nodded at me. Twice. And now I could see in her eyes the light of her spirit.

I was deeply touched by her gesture. I reached out and took the roots from her hand, then bowed slowly and said softly, "Thank you, ma'am. Thank you so much for this food. Bless you and your family. I'm so sorry about this damn war."

The old woman stared at me just a bit longer, her sad eyes still dampened with tears but bright with her light. She pointed a finger at herself, turned and pointed the finger northwest. She turned back facing me, pointed at me, then pointed toward the east where several giant kapok trees stood. I took that to mean her village was in one direction, and we should go in the opposite direction.

Once more she nodded, turned, and quickly walked away along the trail, headed back toward the village. Then a dog barked, and I saw it run toward her. She said something loudly. The dog stopped. She reached into her bag and pulled out another piece of manioc root. She threw it side-arm in the direction of the village. The dog chased after it, picked it up, and ran off.

She turned and glanced quickly at us, nodded again, then turned and headed toward some bushes in the direction the dog had gone.

I felt tears in my eyes. Here was this older woman, living through the pain of war in her home country. Maybe she'd lost a son. A brother. A husband. Or other family members and friends. Her country had been in and out of war for nearly half a century. Vietnam had been home for so long now to bombings, fighting, dying, the blood of hatred flowing like monsoon rainfalls and swamping their lives. Over and over again.

There were certainly good reasons for some Vietnamese to hate Americans. But this elderly woman had just reached out to help us. She'd let her heart and the light of her spirit speak in her eyes when she looked at me, gave me food, and pointed me in a safer direction.

Her spirit was so strong it touched others too, even the enemy, despite her own great needs and the ever-present threat of death and destruction in the raging war around her.

I watched her disappear in the tall grass and bushes, then looked at Hues, whose eyes were filled with his spirit too.

I cleaned the leeches off our feet. We were exhausted and ready to eat, but we needed to move on east, put some distance between us and the village. Two sharp barks from a dog in the distance underscored that urgency. It might be a friendly village, but I didn't want to chance it for us or bring down greater harm to the villagers.

For several hundred yards we traveled parallel to the faint trail through tall grass and around some bamboo clusters so we wouldn't be so visible to others. We worked our way around an area filled with dozens of haunting skeletons of dead trees, likely a site once heavily bombed. Only some flame vines with bright orange flowers and a rare orchid tree with pink flowers, gave life to the scene. There was always a future.

Just beyond those trees, as we moved back into jungled hills and ravines, the rain resumed. I stopped and washed the manioc roots in the rain, then sat and leaned against a tree. I pulled Hues back to me, his head resting on my shoulder. I quickly caught a small cup of rain and poured it into his mouth. He gurgled his thanks. I caught and poured another cup in his mouth. Then I drank two cups too. Our first water in nearly a day.

We completed two hundred more steps, part way up a long, low hill where we stopped under a large banyan tree that partially blocked the rain. I chewed a piece of the newly gifted manioc root into a pulpy ball, which I placed into Hues's mouth. Together we consumed the two roots, which largely filled our shrunken stomachs. I thanked the lady and her spirit once more.

I spread the netting, helping Hues lay on it. Then I laid down too, pulling the netting over and around us. The rain stopped. A faint light from a mostly cloud-obscured moon touched everything around us with a hint, a promise of a silver beauty of a night ahead to celebrate another day of life. The chorus of familiar night sounds resumed, embracing us.

We were exhausted. Hues's soft, gurgling voice whispered MoCity Psalm #107. Carried me quickly into sleep:

> We wander in the wilderness of war,
> walking circles, no road home clearly marked,
> our bodies and minds painful, hungry, thirsty.
> We approach the crowded gates of death in distress.
> Rescue us, Lord, fill this darkness with light
> and the spirits of others who give with their hearts.
> We will sow your kindness over all we meet.

CHAPTER 17

—— MEMORY ROOM (4) ——

The brief glimpse of the heart and spirit reflected in Grand Mama-San's eyes that afternoon reappeared in my memory room that night in a picture highlighting Jeanie's face and smile. My feelings for her went far beyond her overall beauty, framed by the long blond curls spilling down her back and shoulders and accented by big dimples in her cheeks.

The first time I met her I was stunned by her blue, blue eyes so filled with light reflecting and portraying her rich heart and big life spirit. Her eyes were, as Shakespeare wrote, "the window to her soul." That's exactly what I'd seen in the eyes of the older Vietnamese lady too: her soul, her life spirit.

I discovered the spirit in Jeanie's eyes in our first meeting and dance. The light in her eyes said brightly to me: *I am filled with love. We might have a great life together. What do you think?* And I hoped my eyes were saying in response: *I think so too. Shall we try?* I hoped so because I was already hooked. But could her eyes really reveal that much with just a quick look?

I'd dated other young ladies and gone steady a couple of times. But the light was different in Jeanie's eyes, much brighter from literally the first moment we met, much different from other young ladies I knew. And it was especially bright in our first dance, first kiss, first love.

We discovered we had much in common. We'd grown up in poor

families in small Michigan communities. We were students at Western Michigan University. I was a senior majoring in English who wanted to teach and write; she was a junior majoring in art and history who wanted to paint and teach. We both loved the outdoors: she loved hiking, and I loved wading and fishing rivers. We both dreamed of being artists. And raising a big family.

We met at a dance at a popular student bar in Kalamazoo. I was there alone, having stopped by after finishing a class project to have a beer. She was there with several friends, one of whom knew me. When she saw me she waved me over and introduced me to Jeanie. Her eyes had immediately captivated me.

"Is Buck your real name?" she asked.

"No. It's an abbreviation for my full name: Brian Charles Kinder," I said. "Kind of a nickname."

"Does anyone call you Brian?"

"My family. Pretty much everybody else calls me Buck."

"I'd like to call you Brian too, if that's okay?"

"Sure. Of course."

"Brian?"

"Yes?"

"Would you like to dance?"

"With you? Sure!"

We embraced in a lengthy slow dance, our bodies moving closely with each other, feeling the first tantalizing possibility of hunger for more than dancing, an overall powerful pull of physical attraction. But even stronger was the pull of that persistent light in her blue eyes. We never stopped staring into each other's eyes during that long first dance. Not once. Like our eyes were hypnotized by and magnetized to each other's.

The growing light in her eyes drew me in and radiated warmth and a rich spirit. And at the edge of the light was a horizon of hope, the dawning possibility of a bright future together that would be . . . beyond wonderful.

We danced our joy of each other for another hour until the dancing ended. We held each other for a minute and agreed on a date one week later. Her eyes then came with me home and everywhere else I'd gone since that night. I had only to close my own eyes to summon them.

She was with me right then, there in the jungle. Her spirit hugged me. Her eyes glowed.

That sense of spirit is what had flared in Grand Mama-San's brief teary-eyed smile, a quick glimpse of soul light. She was with us only a brief moment but gave us something to eat, a bite of hope, and a peek at her soul.

That soul light lived in my mind. It helped light the darkest time in Vietnam—our journey home.

A glint of hope is a wonderful gift.

CHAPTER 18

—— DAY 4: TANGLES AND TUNNELS ——

A big bird woke me when it shrieked loudly and circled repeatedly overhead—like it was his job to wake all in this part of the jungle. A chorus of mosquitos hummed at the net. Several small stones and sharp twigs pinched my right hip. But the biggest pain was in my head. I'd been dreaming of Hues again—his tongue floating in the mud. The image was never far away in my mind. I twisted to check on him; he was still with me. His eyes were closed. I couldn't see or hear him breathing. I squeezed his wrist to check for a pulse. After a moment I thought I felt a faint flicker. Then another long moment, another flicker.

In the early light he was ultrathin. The biggest part of his body now was his swollen fractured ankle. I couldn't imagine bearing that pain on top of the weightless but excruciating pain of a missing tongue. At the same time, when I looked at him I saw and felt his spirit, a strong, steady wave. A religious "expert" once told me you can't see someone's spirit because spirits are invisible. My answer to that? Total BS! I saw and felt the spirit in the eyes of the old woman who had reached out to us yesterday. I'd seen it in Jeanie's eyes many times. And at this very moment Hues's spirit hovered around me, wrapping me in a soft gentle light.

I hugged him, bathed in the glow. Closed my eyes. Felt its strength, like a pulse. Lived in the moment as long as I dared. The deepest part of our beings was connected through his spirit. He was the reason we faced our uncertain future with some hope. Our bodies screamed, "No more!" But his spirit and our linked hearts spoke above that noise: "We got this!"

I lifted my arms from his shoulders and took a sweeping look around our sleeping area. I saw little in the immediate vicinity apart from a pair of black and red broadbill birds that watched us from a yellow mimosa tree nearby. My best guess was we'd camped about a kilometer beyond the trees where we'd seen Grand Mama-San. We were now at the edge of what appeared to be a dense, hilly jungle that led northeast. An overcast sky blocked the sun and its directional signal. No matter. I knew the hills were the right direction, though I wasn't eager to begin climbing them.

I cut several fat leeches off Hues's ankles, then discovered a handful of cuts on my own left ankle, already darkening and swelling. Had I done that yesterday when I was low crawling up the hill where we smelled smoke? Or was it when I was fighting through some dense brush early last evening? I couldn't remember damaging my ankle, but it hurt like hell. And so did a rib or two on the right side of my body.

I grabbed several banyan leaves nearby and dabbed and tried to clean dried blood on my ankle, which was difficult without water. I wrapped several leaves around my ankle and heel, then slid my sandal over the foot. The front crossing strips held well, the ankle straps less so. The fit was awkward at best but might provide some protection, a bigger need than comfort. We needed to find some water, even swamp water today, to clean my ankle and other cuts. And rainwater to drink. My throat kept reminding me we'd gone too long without water.

Hues remained silent with eyes closed as I lifted and settled him in my arms.

"Sorry, no food or water," I whispered. "Top of the list today. Keep your eyes open for a McDonalds!"

Our progress was slow and difficult but steady for the first few hours. We worked our way gradually up then down several small hillsides, taking two steps then pausing, listening, and looking carefully. We then went through a stretch of scrub brush, skeletons of more dead and blasted trees, and some chest-high reeds growing on mucky ground that rustled softly as we pushed through. The jungle grew increasingly dense. More and more I had to adjust Hues's body and reach out quickly to grab a tree trunk or limb to pull us forward or slow us to prevent falls.

As the morning wore on we climbed and descended two more hills slightly higher and thicker with jungle, still headed in the right direction. I suddenly realized I had stopped counting steps . . . somewhere. When had that happened? I shook my head and decided not to worry. All that really mattered was to keep on stepping, right?

Overhead the trees still blocked most of the sky. No sunlight appeared, and the sky I could see was dark gray and heavy. Maybe a late monsoon season downpour was coming our way. I hoped so. The jungle was filled with normal sounds, but they seemed muted, like they were in mourning. The vegetation steadily grew denser. It became difficult to see more than a few feet ahead in the bushes, trees, and vines that pressed us more tightly on all sides.

Partway up a third hill, not long after we'd passed a beautiful rose myrtle bush that seemed totally out of place, I began to fear the vines hanging from trees, reaching out from bushes, and lying coiled and ready on the ground. I feared them almost as much as the snakes, two of which I'd avoided this morning. One was a deadly krait, which stared at me with evil eyes and whose bite was fast and fatal. The vines, which ranged from finger-thick to wrist-sized, literally sprang out and tried to grab my foot, an arm or shoulder, even my neck. They tugged a bit, tried to pull me down, sideways, or straight up. A constant threat.

The jungle grew denser the higher we climbed, which struck me as the opposite of what it should be. Some steps I now took without seeing ahead more than a foot. I was bent over carrying Hues, so I didn't have a free hand even for a second to push away a vine or hold back some big leaves, or a branch, in order to take just one more damn step.

And then I realized it was no longer just one more step, which was difficult enough. Now the action movement included a number of steps and body adjustments I had to complete just to take an actual step forward: I twisted and pushed my left hip or side against a thick bush; lowered my head to a level with Hues's head and swung my right arm holding his legs back just a bit; then bent and lifted that foot and stabbed it forward to feel for a safe place to put it down; and finally, I planted that foot. That was the new "one more step."

I was drenched in sweat and growing steadily weaker from fighting the brush. The ever-closing vegetation, and my inability to see virtually anything in front of me except the brush in my face, also affected my mind, fed my panic. I knew every step was more difficult for Hues too, constantly being twisted and jerked around. His eyes remained closed. I hoped he was dreaming of Sena and a beautiful walk along the river. Or laughing and talking with his circle of psalming friends and a tongue in his mouth. Anywhere but here.

I was stunned once more by the incredible size and density of the jungle. It was vast, sprawling, utterly overwhelming—so big I often felt like I was trapped on a planet named Jungle in a distant, dark galaxy.

Yet, it was right in our faces too. The numerous vines, branches, bushes, and sharp grasses grabbed, slapped, bit, and sliced our bodies. Dozens of bugs, insects, reptiles, birds, and exotic predators surrounded us while leeches, ants, ticks, spiders, and infections held on tenaciously for the ride. I could hear, smell, and touch many things in the jungle, but see little beyond the foliage in my face, save for ever-present shadows sliding and shifting around us day and night but difficult to discern.

Were those shadows stalking animals or enemies? The spirits of others lost in the war who were still trapped in the dense foliage and struggling to find their way home? Or were they a parade of good memories following and trying to catch up with us to provide some relief from the dark, daunting present?

Even in daylight the darkness in the dense foliage was so enveloping it was the nightmare. You didn't dream it and wake up to escape it; rather, you lived in the nightmare and hoped to escape it in deep sleep. The sun radiated light, but the jungle spread a dense, dangerous, sticky inkiness far beyond darkness—an unforgiving, blinding, and sweltering weight that bent you toward hopelessness. The easiest thing to do was give in and die, and there were so many ways to go, most close at hand, many sudden and quick. What was the difference between one more or one less day of life?

I suddenly found myself sitting in the thick vegetation, exhausted. I must have fallen or sat down, maybe ended up sleeping for a minute or two. But I couldn't remember a thing about how I got where I was. *Had I tipped over big time?*

Hues was still in my arms. A nasty centipede and a large spider crawled on his left shoulder and arm. I pulled and batted them off, cursed them. Then I felt a swarm of red ants biting and stinging my left ankle. I drew Hues close, freed my right hand momentarily, then thrust and rubbed it around my ankle. I killed some of the ants, but my hand was bitten in the process. Almost instantly more ants were at my ankle. I wanted to scream!

Drawing from my waning strength, galloping heart, and my brother's spirit, I forced my way up, wobbled a moment, stumbled two steps back, teetered on the edge of giving up, then bowed my head and whispered: "For Hues, please!"

I dropped to my knees, closed my eyes, hugged Hues tightly. My breathing gradually slowed. My dizzy mind magically stopped spinning and then revealed the exact maze in which we were trapped. His mind suddenly joined mine, and together we read the maze like a map. We nodded at each other. It was clear: only one way to the top of the monster hill—straight ahead. His eyes then screamed at me: *Get mad and charge like a bull! Bust a gut and give every damn ounce of what you got, man! Full speed ahead! Kick some ass, brother!*

I pushed back on my feet, growled twice, and bulled ahead.

Trapped momentarily by a grasping brown vine, I twisted roughly away.

Stumbled then regained my balance, nearly dropping Hues in the mud.

Ducked under a small limb that dug sharply like a fork at my right eye.

Grabbed a bigger limb to prevent tumbling backward, cut my wrists.

Pulled Hues close as I spun away from more dense brush trying to trap us.

Twisted out of the grasp of two more thick, hungry, strangling vines.

Stepped and fought through a mucky sink hole eagerly sucking my left foot down.

Slipped again but awkwardly, somehow mystically regained my balance.

Dropped Hues's feet, shot my right hand forward to clutch a small tree to pull us up.

Gathered his legs back in my right arm and began *one more step* all over again.

Continued my desperate turning, twisting, lunging, pushing, ducking, pulling, charging.

Stumbled ahead in my rocking, awkward, dizzying dance for what seemed like hours.

I was frantic and cared not if a cliff or river lay ahead, a dozen deadly booby traps, or an army of enemies pointing their damn weapons at us. We desperately needed more open space because the jungle was closing in, squeezing, choking us, trying to wrap us and trap us forever in its oppressive, suffocating vegetation so it could add our bodies and bones to its food chain.

The first good thing of the day then happened. I plunged blindly out of my lunging charge and fell into a small open space, just grass at our knees, much like a "normal" clearing back home. I twisted when we went down so we'd land on my back and not on Hues. The open space was surrounded by dead brush and small trees that had been cut down and pushed to the edge of the clearing. It might have served as a temporary landing zone for a helicopter to drop off or pick up soldiers, one hastily cleared in a hot combat zone. Several big, bright yellow flowers in a clump of heliconia plants greeted us. Maybe the prettiest flowers I'd ever seen.

I set Hues down, then lay on the grass beside him, breathing deeply, laughing hysterically, and crying and rejoicing simultaneously.

"Man, oh man," I panted, "that was so damn close, Hues . . . just about out of my fucking mind! So closed in . . . had to break out in the clear. Didn't care if we walked off a cliff . . . fell into an ocean . . . landed in the enemy's camp. That desperate!"

I waved my arm around. "And what did we find? We found some space, man . . . some empty space in this damn dense jungle!"

We lay in the open space for a few minutes, forgetting the war, throwing caution to the wind, enjoying the freedom of space, and resting to regain some strength.

Then the second good thing happened. The dark sky overhead, which now appeared as a quilt of many gray and black shades, suddenly opened up and dumped rain on us.

"Let's celebrate with a big drink of water!" I yelled in the rain.

Hues seemed more alert and gave me a big smile.

My imagination flickered then burst briefly into life. I stood and pulled Hues up on his one good foot, holding him and helping him balance. Side by side, our arms around each other's shoulders, we closed our eyes, tipped our heads back, opened our mouths, and drank water from the big faucet in the sky. We drank until we gagged on too much water.

The rain washed our filthy stinking bodies. I closed my eyes, and in my mind I watched us rub and wash our faces. Our shaggy beards and hair. Our skinny bodies. Our cut and swollen feet. We nodded and agreed a shower had never felt better.

My body and mind felt so refreshed I did a little dance, a jig in the rain, shuffling my feet back and forth, grinning like a totally tipped-over fool. I heard Hues laughing, a sound I missed so much. So damn much.

I pulled the black cup out of my pajama pocket, filled it with rain, and gave it to Hues, who toasted me and passed the cup back.

"Should we try to carry a cup of water with us in the jungle?" I asked, laughing.

Hues gave me a look I so well remembered, one that said: "Man, you're tipped over so much you're totally frigging nuts!"

I was! And I loved it, luxuriating in the driving rain rather than trying to hide from it and stay dry. Our bodies needed water, inside and outside. The rain gave us some brief physical and mental freedom. So near death, but never more alive than in that moment.

We drank more water on the hilltop than we had for days, or so it seemed. I'd learned the joys of life range from the big, beautiful, and overwhelming to much smaller, even tiny gifts like a single drink of water, a smile, a warm nod or a grin, laughter, living totally in the moment.

Freedom was still far away, but for a few minutes we played like children in the rain, cooled down, cleaned up, and felt almost normal and sane. We played until the rain stopped as suddenly as it had begun. The black clouds and dark sky began to dissipate, and some blue sky and sunshine quickly wedged their way in. I finally confirmed our direction: northeast.

I wrung out my black pajamas and put them back on, wrapped the netting around my neck, and bent and picked up Hues. Time for some steps.

We'd heard and read stories about underground tunnels the VC and NVA had constructed in Vietnam, especially around and northwest of Saigon, some of which were constructed years earlier during the French war. Now there were many more tunnels in other areas in the country, including the hilly, wooded areas west of Phu Bai and Camp Eagle. The tunnels were difficult to construct to ensure they would endure in the rainy jungled areas. They served many purposes for the enemies and provided little but danger for the Americans and their allies.

Tunnel facts and stories were part of our training in the US and refresher training on the ground in Vietnam. In the Casualty Branch, I learned more about "tunnel rats," the American soldiers who were designated to crawl into discovered tunnels and investigate them. I'd written one sympathy letter to a mother and father whose son died in an explosion in one of his tunnel searches. I couldn't imagine the great courage possessed by tunnel rats.

Early in our tour in Vietnam, Hues and I had sat in a bar on the base and shared beers with a tunnel rat who'd survived and was headed home. The quiet young soldier shared a few chilling stories, but what we most remembered was his "thousand-yard stare:" his dead eyes, empty of light, looked through us and beyond us, locked on serious memories he wanted to forget forever but couldn't.

The tunnels served many purposes. They hid the VC and NVA soldiers. They served as supply and communication routes for moving soldiers unseen across the war zone; some tunnels went on for miles. They provided living quarters and stay-over spots for the NVA. Some larger tunnel networks included small underground hospitals to treat the wounded, along with storage space for food and weapons. And they were used to launch troops into battle, prepare ambushes, or set booby traps and trip wires.

In short, tunnels were a primary way for the VC and NVA to try to counter the greater strength of America's better-armed soldiers, its helicopters, the firepower of its heavy artillery, and other tactical and strategic advantages. To help deal with tunnels some American soldiers became tunnel specialists, or tunnel rats, whose job it was to help find and clear tunnels.

Often armed with only a flashlight and small hand pistol, the "rat" slid into the tunnel, most of which were small, narrow, and extremely claustrophobic. Below ground the dark tunnels were also home to snakes, leeches, spiders, giant centipedes, and other deadly dangers including booby traps, trip wires, and explosives.

The tunnels were difficult to locate in the jungle, though there were hundreds of them in the countryside. Entrances, often only slightly larger than the width of a small Vietnamese soldier, were camouflaged with leaves, bushes, limbs, or other natural-looking covers that would easily blend in with nature. In villages, the entrances might be covered with sacks of rice or other foods, pots and pans, clothing, and so forth.

When discovering a tunnel, the rat might simply on command drop a grenade into the entrance to blow it up. Or, more often, he entered and inspected the tunnel to locate any food, weapons, explosives, booby traps, or enemy intelligence documents. They might then explode the tunnel or rig up an explosive device to take out some enemy when they next entered the hole. Sometimes they'd stake out the tunnel site, hoping to catch soldiers going in and out.

Hues and I had never seen an actual tunnel until today. We were moving slowly in midafternoon, not sure we were headed in the right direction, approaching yet another low hill, the vegetation thickening again, when Hues tapped me once on the back, danger ahead! I momentarily ignored it, thinking his arm had just slipped off my shoulder. But then Hues tapped again, harder.

I stopped and dropped to my knees, Hues still in my arms. I scanned the area in front of us. Several bushes grew on our left side, and two medium-sized mangrove trees were on our right. The line I was walking was a narrowing stretch of sweet-smelling knee-high oil grass, not quite a pathway, but close to it, with some softball-sized stones mixed in. At the end of the grass stood another round bush, which looked dried out and partially dead or dying.

Beyond the brush the ground once again began to rise slowly to a semiflat level that was a few feet above the surrounding ground. A trail so faint it I might have imagined it ran along the hillside, which rose steadily and was increasingly covered with trees and dense foliage. The top of the hill, roughly fifty yards high, was one of the smaller hills we'd climbed today.

I continued to scan and listen but saw or heard nothing unusual. I was about to tell Hues there was nothing when I saw something maybe fifteen feet ahead. It looked like a black string, or a very straight, thin stick that was six or eight feet long. I looked over my shoulders, saw nothing, so I laid Hues in the grass and low crawled toward the stick or string. As I edged closer, I could see it more clearly: it wasn't a stick or a string, but rather a thin black wire. When I got within two feet of the wire, I realized I was looking at a trip wire.

At each end of the wire was a muddy-looking, odd-shaped "rock," which I could see close up were actually cans, like coke cans. Inside each was a grenade. The VC or NVA had wired this faint trail with grenades inside the cans. They'd removed the safety pins on the grenades, then put them in the cans to hold down the striker lever. The trip wire was tied to each grenade. When the wire was tripped, the grenades were jerked out of the cans and quickly exploded. Whoever tripped the wire would be dead, and likely anyone close to them.

I was within a foot of one of the cans, struck again by how much it was made to look like other rocks in the area, tan and greyish. Had they actually painted the cans? We'd come within a few steps of dying but stopped just in time thanks to Hues and his early warning system.

"Thanks, brother," I whispered as I low crawled back to him. "A tripwire and grenades in a couple cans. Camouflaged pretty well. And deadly as hell. Why in the world is it out here in the middle of nowhere?" Hues gave me a nod, then closed his eyes again. I sat near him and held his head in my hands for a moment, then rested it on my lap. We'd take a short break then move on further before night fell.

I tried to nap but couldn't shake the question: why was the trip wire here in what appeared to be the middle of nowhere? Was there a camp nearby? Was the trip wire an early warning system? Was it just a random placement, one of others in the area? If so, I'd have to be on special alert. But there had to be more to it. I decided to explore further. I lay the netting over Hues's still form, rose, and returned to the trip wire.

I listened to the normal jungle chorus as I crawled. Just a bit less noisy here than in the dense vegetation. Nothing unusual on the ground I could see. I moved toward the round bush near the end of the path. The bush appeared normal on the side facing me, but as I crawled around it, I noticed the back was not as green. It was more dried out at the bottom where several small limbs lay on the ground, along with a handful of bigger leaves, which also were dried out. My eyes tracked from the bush toward the hillside. The ground was covered with some vines, a handful of yellow heliconia flowers that appeared slightly sunken, and three pine-like trees.

Now on my hands and knees, I carefully moved the limbs and leaves aside. As I did so, I noticed what looked like the edge of a hole. My hand froze, as did the image of the hole in my mind: *a tunnel?* Was I playing around at the opening of a tunnel in daylight? I gently pulled the limbs and leaves a little farther away from the opening: it was a hole, a damn tunnel! I wasn't going there! I carefully slid the limbs and big leaves back into place as I had found them.

I was low crawling toward Hues when I heard gunshots in the direction we were planning to go, maybe a klick or more in the distance. Hard to tell but the shots sounded close. Then grenades exploded, several mortars and machine gun fire began barking, dominating the sounds of the fight until a helicopter gunship roared overhead and opened fire. As the fighting continued, I gathered Hues and the netting and headed back in the direction from which we'd come, back into jungle cover where we found a thick teak tree to hide behind.

The fighting lasted about fifteen minutes, then stopped as abruptly as it began. A small burst of shots closed it off, along with the sound of a helicopter fading away, echoing in the distance. I only realized the sounds of the jungle around me had ceased when the chorus suddenly resumed.

I changed direction for the rest of the day, which meant little more than two, maybe three hours of daylight. If we continued as planned, we'd be heading east toward the fighting, which might increase our chances of being seen. It was a coin flip whether American or Vietnamese soldiers would see us first, but it didn't matter. We'd be killed or recaptured since we wore black pajamas, a target for the Americans to shoot at.

I whispered all this in Hues's ears as I carried him. I realized I was counting steps again. "We're going a bit more north than planned," I said. "At least I think we're going north unless I'm totally turned around. Won't know until tomorrow if the sun appears. Hope it does."

I noticed his eyes were open now, watching me and maybe nodding. Or maybe that was just the way his head moved when I walked. I tried to remember how he'd nodded his head back in the cage and the camp. It just felt like he was nodding right now, I decided.

He's still with me.

We moved through more rugged jungle and discovered a faint trail. I was concerned about walking *any* trail because that meant others had walked the same steps and might be nearby. It might lead us into a village, or worse, an ambush. But it was far more practical than fighting the thick brush and vines on both sides of the path. My strength was just about sapped for the day, and I wanted to put more distance between us and the fighting we'd heard earlier.

The trail suddenly ended in a small area filled with blinding elephant grass taller than our heads. We sat and rested in a small, open area. Listened to the jungle. Smelled the air. Sensed nothing wrong or out of place. The sun broke through for a moment and confirmed our direction. It made it hotter, but the tall grass kept us somewhat shaded and a bit cooler. Two banded kingfishers suddenly swooped by and quickly disappeared, their colors lingering. Time to move.

I lost track of time and stopped counting steps again. We moved beyond the long grass and worked our way around some thick coffee bushes, then fought through another stretch of dense jungle. I was startled to come upon a small curving river headed more northeast, I imagined. We followed it cautiously.

A moderate rainfall began. I paused and worked my black cup out of my pocket. We hadn't had water since our rain dance midmorning. I sat with Hues in my arms and gave him two drinks of water. Then I drank three cups, gave Hues another, and a final one for myself.

We resumed our walk, and a Holiday Inn magically appeared across the river. I smirked at myself and my increasingly twisted mind. Two abandoned shacks on stilts stood along the riverbank. They'd been partially destroyed by grenades, rifle fire, or other explosives. The roofs were gone from both of the roughly ten-foot square shacks, as well as most of the walls. Flooring in one of the structures was mostly intact, however, and there appeared to be dry space beneath that flooring, maybe four or five feet high. That was enough room for Hues and me to lay and sleep, out of the rain.

We crossed the waist-deep river. The mucky bottom was slippery, but the water felt great on my feet and legs. I nearly fell twice before reaching the dry space beneath the shack flooring. I laid Hues on the riverbank, several feet above the water, then climbed out and checked the space beneath the shack flooring. It was perfect for our simple needs. We'd be close to the river, a bit of a concern regarding snakes, other river water life, and possible enemy movements. But we'd be largely invisible in the night. In the morning we'd find a log to ride down the river.

Uh, no, dummy! Quit the thought! Down river would take us back toward the camp.

I shook my head again to clear it. We had no food. I was exhausted and feverish, so I was ready for sleep after the long day. It was nearly dark. But no sooner had we settled in than two muffled explosions nearby put us back on edge. Grenades exploding in the river? That would account for the muffled sound. Maybe a hundred yards away? Impossible to estimate the distance. We huddled under the flooring for several minutes. I watched the river curling toward us. We heard no more explosions, and no sounds at all beyond the normal night sounds.

I then saw what appeared to be a large leaf, a piece of weed, or maybe even a fish floating on the river toward us. I sat up then crawled to the edge of the water, watching the river closely for enemy. It *was* a fish. And then a second fish floated down the river too. I grabbed the closest fish, which looked like a yellow catfish. The second fish was beyond my reach, as was a third one that floated by across the river. I didn't want to go after them because I wasn't sure I could actually reach them given the current. And I didn't want to move farther from Hues, nor be in the water if enemy soldiers were coming this way.

The fish in my hand was dead but intact, which supported my first thought about the explosions. There was a good chance someone, or a group, had deliberately thrown grenades into the river to stun and kill fish for food. We'd seen that done several times in the river running near the camp. The fish hadn't been hitting for several days at those times, so the guards threw a grenade or two in the water. The muffled explosions were similar to what I'd heard tonight. We'd watch and collect the fish that were killed and floated to the surface.

I watched the river for several more moments but saw or heard nothing. At the edge of the water near our sleeping space, I used my bamboo knife to roughly cut off the yellow catfish's head and tail. Then I worked in the growing darkness to slice and gut the fish as best I could with my make-do knife. It was awkward work. I rinsed and cleaned my knife again in the water. Then I used it to cut and tear the fish into smaller pieces, peeling the skin and scales to the extent I could, which wasn't a lot.

I bit off a small piece of the raw fish with my teeth, felt for bones with my tongue, pulled out as many of those as I could, then cautiously chewed the raw fish and a few soft, smaller bones into a pulpy ball in my mouth. I swallowed it slowly to taste and feel how it went down my throat. If I hadn't been starving for more than a year, I might have puked up the mess. But I was starving. We hadn't eaten more than a few roots in the last four days. So, the fish tasted . . . delicious. It brought tears to my eyes. Something as simple as a mouthful of raw fish.

I picked out the larger bones in another mouthful, chewed it into a soft ball, leaned Hues back against my shoulder, fed him the fish, and helped him swallow. I imagined I saw the bright light in his eyes and a smile spread across his gaunt face.

"Just like a five-star restaurant, ain't it, Hues? Nothing beats the fish special tonight!"

We ate quickly. Our bellies were far from full, but our hearts and minds felt better, as well as our bodies. A light rainfall began. I caught more water for of us to drink.

The combination of the fish and the music of the light rainfall carried us both to a deep sleep. We were invisible in the starless night beneath the shack flooring.

The last thing I felt was Hues's arm tightly hugging my shoulder. Amidst the rain, either Hues or the jungle's evening choir sang MoCity Psalm #3:

> You are a forever shield for us, Lord.
> Your glory lifts high our heads, warms our hearts.
> Tonight, we lay down near the river and sleep,
> the sleep of the deep, sustained by you.
> We fear not the myriad enemy troops
> encircling and set against us.
> You are our light, our everything tonight.

CHAPTER 19

— DAY 5: THE COSTS OF WAR —

Noise of the helicopter increased as it flew directly over us, heading south. The flooring overhead blocked much of my view, but the chopper sounded too heavy for a small scout helicopter. Maybe it was a medevac ship carrying or picking up dead or wounded soldiers. Or a bigger helicopter with a load of grunts headed out on a mission. The noise faded quickly to familiar jungle sounds, except for what sounded like a falling limb nearby. That caught my attention for a moment in the cooler but still humid air.

When I sat up I felt light-headed and fevered, same as yesterday morning. It made me feel tipsier, unbalanced. My mind seemed even more fragmented if that was possible. Maybe it was a fever. I'd noticed some black streaks in my urine yesterday. Last thing I needed was a fever and an active disease.

A small slice of blue sky appeared in the southeast through the limbs hanging near the little river. It was the first partially blue-sky morning I remembered during our escape, but my memory wasn't great. A hint of yellow-orange was there too, needle-thin but nevertheless promising. I longed for a big rising sun to guide us, and a brief downpour to quench our thirst.

My big hope that day was to find some sign of a firebase, or any kind of indicator one might be near. A dozen or more were scattered in this region of the country, or used to be, as I recalled from maps lining our walls in the Casualty Branch. I tried to picture where Hues and I might be located right now on those maps in my head. Then I realized it was wasted time and energy to even think about it. We were lost in the here-and-now jungle without a clue where we were. All we knew for sure is that it was morning.

How in hell could a map help?

My broken thoughts turned to how we'd approach a firebase if we found one. The best plan for a "safe" reunion with our brothers probably required us to wait until dawn the morning after we arrived near the firebase. Then I'd set Hues down just inside the wood line. Peel off my black pajama shirt to reveal the hair on my chest. Raise my hands and arms in the air. Walk slowly into the open area at the bottom of the firebase. Wave my arms and carefully present myself to the soldiers at the top of the hill. And hope like hell they wouldn't shoot me.

They'd be able to see me clearly at a distance through binoculars or rifle sights. I was banking on the hair on my chest and my beard to make it work. Few Asian soldiers have hair on their chests or beards of any kind, let alone long black ones like Hues and I wore. Okay, it was still risky that way, but safer than trying to turn ourselves over to our soldiers in the jungle. I knew how trigger-happy soldiers were, and given the black pajamas Hues and I wore, well . . .

Caution remained the keyword this morning. Caution in everything, I reminded myself and shook my fuzzy, hot head to try and clear it. The more easterly we went, the more the jungle appeared to open up, though dense tracts still marked the area. We were increasingly visible targets.

When I lifted the mosquito net, the left side of my face where the net had lain was puffy and itching from mosquito bites. I turned and looked at Hues. He lay silent with his eyes closed. Had he moved from nearly dead at the end of yesterday to clearly dead this morning? So little of him remained. Apart from the time we spent on the hill yesterday drinking and bathing in the rain, his eyes were open far less often.

Was he in a deeper sleep or resting in a new zone of unconsciousness? I hope he found one and was dreaming of good things in the past or imagining them in the future. He was probably with Sena, enjoying her big heart. He was confident she'd be in Detroit waiting for him. As he'd told me many times, "Our two spirits are intertwined and will be forever." Whether that was true didn't matter because it fed his hope.

I thought I heard Hues gurgle as he tried to whisper something. But his eyes remained closed. He hadn't moved.

"Got you, brother," I whispered in his ear. "New day, more steps. Gonna make it damn soon. Today or tomorrow. We got this."

I cut and picked leeches off our lower legs. We both bore dozens of new mosquito bites, nothing unusual. They'd been on and in our blood for months. The netting helped but wasn't perfect. When I pulled it over us at night, I tried to hook the top of it to a limb or branch, a nearby weed or clump of taller grass, so the netting rested not on our skin but rather several inches above us, thus preventing more bites.

But that seldom held overnight due to our movements or the weather. So, we ended up each morning with fresh bites. What the netting did best was keep most leeches, grubs, spiders, centipedes, and many other small jungle creatures from feeding on us. Most of the time.

I sat Hues up and leaned him back against my chest, hugging him for a few moments as daylight crept in. I watched the river flowing by just a few feet from our luxury hotel room. The water looked clearer this morning. It moved with a soft, hushing sound. Hypnotic. For a few moments, my mind rode the current and drifted home. I hugged Jeannie while she nursed our baby. Mom kissed my cheek and hummed. My dad laughed at something on the radio. We weren't in the jungle . . .

Get up and get moving!

"No food or water this morning," I whispered. "We'll find some. Just need another little downpour so we can drink, play, dance in the rain again, right?" I laughed and thought I saw Hues share a small smile.

Later, I realized I was counting steps again, which I was sure I'd stopped doing yesterday deliberately. It was meaningless to count steps. I always went as far as I could before stopping to briefly rest. Maybe that was twenty or thirty steps, if I was moving up a steep incline, or a hundred and fifty steps or more on flatter ground. On the other hand, I was quite sure counting steps helped me focus on the mission.

The geography around us was changing. The jungle we'd fought our way through for several days remained difficult to navigate, but the vegetation was gradually thinning. In some stretches I could see twenty or thirty feet ahead, or even more from a slope.

"And the vines are fewer and less hungry," I whispered to Hues. Then I realized I'd been whispering all this geography and stepping-stuff crap to him while walking.

The hills grew less steep. More open areas in between jungled stretches presented greater dangers. At the Air Force Bar in Phu Bai, Hues and I had once talked with a helicopter door gunner who was headed home. He was a little drunk and talked softly but angrily about how much he hated the war, the VC, the NVA, the heat, the stink, the rain, the goddamn jungle, every damn thing in the war.

He described what he called the dangerous "chicken pox" landscape—rolling hills or flat ground that lay open like exposed human skin but was marked here and there with "jungle blisters" or "pox:" patches of dense jungle and forest.

The gunner warned us: "I flew few—damn few—flights where we didn't draw fire from the goddamn VC or NVA hiding in those jungle blisters. Be damn careful in chicken pox country. Them open spaces? Just damn big traps. They'll kill you if you're not damn careful, maybe even if you are."

"We're in chicken pox country," I whispered. "Open spaces ahead of us surrounded by jungle. We'll stay in the wood line. We're headed northeast."

I imagined Hues raising his fist and grinning, so in my mind I dapped his fist. And that imaginary gesture reminded me we hadn't counted our days or given each other a thumbs-up salute for . . . I don't know how long.

"Keep an eye open for food, any kind," I reminded him. "Poke my shoulder if you see some, anything. Don't have to be McDonalds!"

We moved cautiously just inside the jungle line, circling the open spaces as possible. I was drenched in sweat, bugs filled the air, and I spent too much time in my memory room, even though I knew I shouldn't. But I was lost in Jeanie's blue eyes at the moment. Feeling her round, firm buttocks, curves of pure hunger and delight, gripping her hips, desperate for more of her.

I stumbled and nearly fell, which would have sent Hues rolling and bouncing down the hill, breaking his other ankle or even his neck.

Get it together, asshole!

Just inside the pine tree line we carefully descended a long, sloping hill dotted with some yellow mimosa trees and a few papayas. I saw some big fruit hanging on a papaya tree, but it was at least twenty feet off the ground. No way I had the strength to shinny up that tree. The land opened up some more. We kept moving, more southerly now. It wasn't the way we wanted to go, but I wasn't ready to reclimb the steep hill to our north. We'd rest at the bottom of this hill, see where we were.

I feared running into a village as more were likely in the area. More farmland and rice paddies could appear at any moment. More villages and more villagers, along with more enemy soldiers increased our odds for being seen and captured. Could it be on our own terms?

Get a life, man!

I must have stopped to rest in some long grass and bushes part way down a hill, because that's where I woke sometime later. I didn't recall sitting down with Hues, but here we were. Hues must have slept too, because he was yawning, just like he had so many times in our cage upon awakening. I was usually the first to wake, so I often saw Hues like he was now. He gave me a smile, just like I remembered. He pointed to his throat, which I interpreted as asking for some water and food.

"Soon as we can, man. Let's go find some," I said.

In the trees just ahead, monkeys chattered and played. I lifted Hues and stepped off, down the hill, brushing some bush limbs aside and stepping around some peanut bushes and over a series of thick vines before entering the grove of trees near the bottom. Just a few steps in, we saw a river about fifty feet in front of us. The brown water ran silently.

Was this the river we'd crossed when they led us to the camp all those months ago? I remembered crossing one river at the height of monsoon season. The water was deeper and faster. It had taken some time to find a safe place to ford the river. Then I recalled the worst part of the crossing: one of the VC had hit me hard and held my head underwater to the point I started to drown. Hues told me later I'd stopped walking and just stared down at the water. Probably fishing in your head, he'd said. He knew me pretty well.

This morning we'd cool our feet and legs in the mucky water, and probably catch some leeches too. That was an okay trade-off for my exhausted legs and bruised feet.

"We're crossing the river," I whispered.

Several entry points were too deep or slippery, but I found a firmer foothold where the water rose nearly to my waist. I lifted Hues so only his feet and calves dragged in the cooler water. I concentrated on one cautious step at a time, scanning the fast-moving water for snakes.

Fishing in Michigan flashed in my mind yet again. The river water there would be much colder and clearer. The fast current would ripple around rocks worn smooth as glass over the centuries, then spill into white water as the speed increased before stalling into a bend and creating a circling backwater. A perfect place for trout . . .

Man, get it together!

I'd have slapped myself if I wasn't carrying Hues.

On the far side of the river, I laid him in some waist-high grass near three intertwined bushes. We'd be hidden for a few minutes while I cut and picked leeches off my legs and caught my breath. Hunger and especially thirst were catching up with us. I was close to drinking some river water, though I knew that'd be deadly. I remembered several long stretches in the camp without water when we were being punished. Thirst rendered the mind crazier than drinking too much booze. No hangover, just a desperate hot spot in your head that burned and pushed you to kill for one drink of water.

We followed the curving river, staying close enough to the bank to keep some cover. I paused often to scan the ground and trees around us. I shared my thoughts in whispers with Hues about finding a big log and trying to float the river to gain ground much faster and less painful. I saw Hues shaking his head, no. And he was right. It was a foolish idea, too risky in daylight.

How many damn times had that dumb idea popped in my mind?

Once more I heard a helicopter in the distance, closing in on us. I took a quick glance around to see if there was any open area where I could stand and wave them down.

Hey, we already covered that damn ground—standing in the open in black pajamas, waving like a fool!

I knelt with Hues in my arms and listened to the growing, teasing sound of escape. The Loach soared across the sky directly above us. What I wouldn't give for a ride home, a drink of water, and a big juicy burger.

We moved on. I realized I was counting steps again, sweating and smiling crazily at my own craziness. The games ran endlessly in my mind, which now wandered far faster than my feet walked. I was on the edge . . . of something. Too much . . . or not enough . . . in my mind.

"Not giving in, Hues," I whispered. "Tap my shoulder if you see or smell food."

Another group of monkeys chattered in the trees ahead of us near the river, which curved close again. I gazed at it, still wanting a drink. Then I became aware the monkeys had suddenly gone silent. My sense of awareness sharpened. Something ahead of us talked to my mind and body. I stopped. Hues gave me a weak single tap on my back, confirming possible danger ahead.

I dropped to my knees and scanned the immediate area—clusters of waist-high grass blowing in the soft breeze, a number of bushes, several bigger papaya trees, some dangling vines, a dozen or so ferns clumped here and there, and a patch of elephant grass. Three thick bushes about ten yards to my left provided a good hiding place. I low crawled slowly to the bushes with Hues on my back.

I laid him in the grass and low-crawled around the bushes, checking for snakes or other dangers. It was nearly dark beneath the bushes, perfect. I returned to Hues and pulled him under the bushes, pushing and tucking him back into the dark area. I then flattened and positioned myself, so I had a small looking glass through the branches of the brush to the river and several broad trees on the far bank.

We waited for several minutes, our bodies sweating, bugs hanging close, monkeys still silent. The whole area was suddenly quieter—a kind of great, pregnant pause with everyone and everything collectively holding its breath, waiting for whatever came next. Hues must have opened his eyes because a faint light appeared in the darkness around us. I squeezed his arm.

Then I saw it, rising and moving forward in slow motion through the grass toward the river—a rounded dark green pith helmet, the kind worn by the NVA.

Hues tapped my back again, more urgent now.

The soldier carried a rifle pointed in the direction of the river. He moved the barrel of the rifle slowly from left to right and back again as he closed on the river. The soldier, helmet, and rifle blended almost perfectly into the background of jungle greens, browns, and blacks. I shut my eyes and counted, one complete beat and reopened my eyes. The soldier was momentarily invisible, then came faintly back into view as he crossed the river smoothly and quickly like he'd done it a thousand times before. He disappeared into the jungle.

This was likely the first NVA to cross the river, or they'd have seen us. I continued to stare at the crossing point and watched a second pith helmet rise into view, then a camouflage shirt and rifle in the soldier's arms, just like the previous one. He crossed the river quickly and faded into the jungle. I wondered if any of them were the NVA we'd seen over the months in the Beatdown Ring.

Hues tapped my back twice, hard: danger behind us. I froze and listened closely. Heard nothing unusual. The monkeys remained silent. It dawned on me there might be flanker guards, who typically worked at the sides of a column, checking for danger and providing protection. In this case, it would mean a flanker might be awfully close to our hiding spot, either moving slowly to cross the river, too, or hiding and watching for anyone approaching.

I turned my body just a little so I could still see a piece of the crossing area as well as some of the flanking area to our west. I sensed a presence but saw or heard nothing. The jungle noise remained subdued. Out of the corner of my eye, I watched another NVA cross the river.

Hues tapped my back twice again; danger to our rear and right remained, or was even greater. I turned to see more of the flanking area, while losing sight of the soldiers crossing the river. I closed my eyes, straining to listen. I sensed it was even quieter.

I slowly pulled my legs up, bending my knees until they were near my stomach. Using my right hand and arm, I slowly pushed my coiled body up onto my knees. The position was painful, but I was as ready as could be if the enemy came close. I'd launch myself from the balls of my feet, push forward with my legs, and charge or jump or dive to meet and fight any enemy who came near. Yeah, it was probably certain death, but Hues and I had agreed we'd die fighting rather than surrender or be recaptured.

For what seemed a long time I remained in that position. My legs cramped in pain. Nothing happened. At some point I turned to check the soldiers crossing the river. I watched one more. I'd seen three soldiers but imagined at least twelve or fifteen, maybe more.

The next NVA I saw stopped at the edge of the river. Unlike the previous ones, he turned and took a slow 180-degree look back. Scanned the direction he'd come from and both sides of the riverbank, including the cover where we were hiding. Satisfied with what he saw and didn't see, he waded the river and disappeared into the jungle.

We waited silently until I breathed easier and my leg cramps ended. The NVA had come from more or less from the same direction we planned to move this afternoon. Our timing was so close, just seconds, literally, from stepping into the NVA's arms. Then dying by gunshot, a knife, or a grenade, since we were unarmed. More likely they'd stab us or break our necks. Better to kill us quietly and move on.

I lay on my side and hugged Hues for a moment, realizing yet again how close we were to death at any moment in the jungle prison. We couldn't see far ahead in the maze we wandered. Humans and animal killers could be anywhere at any time. Our sense of direction was uncertain, and our skinny, distressed bodies were ever weaker. Our odds of survival grew ever smaller. The jungle chorus returned.

I awakened abruptly, still hugging Hues, then remembered where we were.

Drifted off again! Get off your ass and keep moving!

I released Hues then rose on my knees and peered through my small opening facing the river where the NVA had crossed: ten minutes ago? An hour? Not a clue.

In utter amazement I watched another NVA cross the river in essentially the same place. More of them, my God! Was I imagining this? Was I trapped in a nightmare or totally tipped over? Was an entire company of enemy soldiers headed south? Where the hell were they going? I'd just been a minute from getting Hues up and moving on. We'd just missed another damn death call.

Twelve helmets crossed the river this time, though there may have been more I didn't see. It was the unending puzzle of war in the jungle: where were they, how many were they, and how were they armed? I could only imagine they were heading toward a battle somewhere south. Or maybe they were headed to a village for food and ammunition or other supplies. All I knew was we needed to wait before moving on. We had to decide whether to continue our current path north—the same path the NVA were moving on, headed south.

I don't know how long we stayed under the bushes that afternoon before we moved on. We'd seen no more soldiers or anything else when we were sleeping under the leaves. I only realized I'd fallen asleep again when I woke up and discovered the mosquito net was wrapped around us. I vaguely remembered pulling it over us but had no idea when or why. The sunlight and partial blue sky suggested it was midafternoon. We'd covered too little ground today because of the enemy and my own crazy mind.

I'd slept but felt weaker. The pain was so pervasive and constant my entire being felt numb. I was a skinny blob of numbness increasingly difficult to keep moving and stay focused. A call for a long, forever sleep was a seductive voice that found its way into my head.

"Follow me," the voice whispered, now closer and bigger. "Follow me into sleep, and your pain will disappear forever."

And then I heard another voice, no, a chorus of familiar competing sounds and voices, which included my father's words, my mother's soft humming, and Jeanie's blue eyes expressing her explicit command: "Get up. Get out of the jungle. Come home to me and your baby! Get off your butt, Brian!"

Then a soft whisper that sounded like "brother" brushed my ear like a faint breeze of love. I turned to Hues. His eyes were closed, but each socket was lit by a tiny, faint but steady light. Two stars in the galaxy of my mind. Still with me.

We moved on while I struggled again with just giving up. Later, we suddenly came upon a small creek less than five feet wide. We followed it down a low hill and discovered an unexpected surprise at the bottom: a tiny waterfall or spillway no more than two feet high. It glistened with silver light even under the trees overhead and a partly clouded sky.

The spilling water was the most marvelous musical soft noise: a melodious hush accompanied by a faint mist floating like transparent smoke in the muggy air. It was a beautiful sensory moment even in our exhausted state—one of those powerful encounters that lives forever in the mind.

We sat and stared, watching and listening to the soft visual musical magic in the midst of the jungle prison. I could literally feel the music. I imagined Jeanie and our baby, and my family and friends, along with Sena and Reverend Brown in River Rouge, had orchestrated this magical mystical moment just for us. Express air-mailed it. Flooded our dark lives with the light of their love and the song of their spirits reflected in the hypnotic whisper of the beautiful spillway. My load lightened. A small rush of new energy stirred hope.

"Soul food," I whispered to Hues as I lifted him in my arms. "Sweet, sweet soul food."

We headed more easterly than previously planned to stay further from the NVA's route to the river. We fought our way through more tough bushes and sharp elephant grass, then approached another jungle pox, one side of which skirted the river again. I was sure it was the same one we'd watched the NVA cross earlier in the afternoon. We moved parallel to the river, fifty yards from it, as it curved more northerly too.

At one point we ascended a gently sloping hill covered with grass and semidense brush and vines. I bulled my way through and was exhausted and growing desperate again. A cluster of giant bodhi trees, partially destroyed, covered the top of the slope, and from there the landscape suddenly opened up. I stared at a stretch of several hundred yards along the river. What had once been a village surrounded by rice paddies and farmland was now a wasteland.

A dozen or more bomb craters dominated the scene. The destruction was breathtaking even as nature was starting to reclaim it. The craters were greening slowly. The area would likely be green again in a year or two, much of the destruction grown over with vegetation. The people and buildings, however, were unlikely to return unless the war ended. Or a generation passed. Or maybe never.

I once read a story in the military newspaper *Stars and Stripes* that described the extensive bombing campaign conducted by the US military in South Vietnam. The campaign sought to destroy rural villages and communities where NVA and VC were documented or suspected of hiding and being supplied with food and weapons.

The targeted villages and surrounding rice paddies were extensively bombed and often sprayed with Agent Orange, a deadly chemical mix with dioxin, to destroy homes, food crops, and forest cover. Hundreds of villages were obliterated. Some stretches in the country were literally no-man's land—homes, buildings, rice paddies, vegetation, trees, animals, people all gone. Only desolation and memories remained.

We moved to a spot on the slope that overlooked the land and provided some cover. I set Hues down beneath some low limbs, then sat behind him and held his head back against my shoulder. We stared at the destruction spread before us, the land littered with blasted branches and shattered, scattered pieces of bamboo. Bomb craters marked what once had been village houses. Fenced-in areas for grazing animals like sheep, goats, and pigs. Placid rice paddies terraced down to the water. Numerous trees providing shade, kindling, and wood for cooking. Hundreds of people of all ages working, playing, talking, laughing, sleeping, loving, praying. Gone. All gone.

Except for two things I observed and reflected on.

First, one partial building remained, almost directly below us, a kind of "ghost house," a skeleton of a former home. Pieces of the frame remained intact: half of two walls standing about four feet high, part of the flooring, along with a portion of three or four steps leading into the house, and one small corner of what had been a thatched roof.

Suddenly a bird flew near us, marked by a bright orange beak and glossy black body. It went straight to that thatched roof corner where it froze for a moment, then hopped around and pecked its beak briefly, hoping to find food. Then it lifted off, soared, then descended and swooped low across the brown river, hidden quickly by the jungle on the far side.

I let my imagination run and watched in my mind the ghost house slowly reassemble and become whole again: solidly built bamboo walls, a small home with a kitchen in the center, several sleeping rooms, and maybe a special worship room for prayers or sharing memories of loved ones. Several generations of Vietnamese families often lived together.

No running water or electricity. The inside walls were thin boards. The roof was likely bamboo thatching. The three or four steps leading up into the house were set a few feet above potential flooding and to help keep creatures out. A bright red flowering plant sat on each step.

The land around consisted of a series of rice paddies, bounded on the south side by the river where the villagers could catch fish, bathe, cool off. I could hear some children singing and laughing in the shade now creeping along the riverbank. In the village some animals were likely fenced in—chickens or ducks, a pig, a milk cow.

Maybe three hundred or four hundred people consisting of three or four generations lived in the village: a self-sufficient place in a beautiful location in the jungle. They likely didn't care who won the war as long as they were left alone to continue their pastoral lives.

The second thing I noticed looked like a small cemetery on the north side of the former village, where the hills began to rise. One side was marked by a low stone wall, what was left of it. Scattered pieces of wood that might have been grave markers or crosses rested on the soil. All that remained were skeletons of people below ground who once lived in what was once a village.

Survivors of the bombings were gone, living somewhere else now, maybe a new and smaller village or a bigger village with relatives. The mind-numbing physical costs of the bombings were huge and long-lasting—the destroyed homes and rice paddies, the cemetery, those who died in the bombings or from Agent Orange, those uprooted and relocated forever.

The mental and emotional costs for individuals and families were also enormous and longer-lasting. What had once been no longer was, and never would be again. The physical scars of war may eventually heal or fade, but mental scars, the layers upon layers of scars on the brain, never heal. They are carried to the grave and live forever in the skull, some believe. Their grief, sadness, tears, lost dreams, shattered memories, hopes for themselves and others were dashed and smashed like waves on the rocks—the costs of war.

Such a simple four-word description of complex and extraordinary human loss. All that was left of the village was some vegetation regrowing on the outer edges and some patches of green that dotted the wasteland.

In our religious discussions, Hues and I often ended at the same point: we couldn't agree. I'd sincerely declare my belief in a creator or a higher power, just like Hues. But then I'd conclude with my biggest, thorniest issue: what about evil and the Devil? How could the Lord's world include both Jesus and the Devil? As Hues argued, and many others preached and believed, human life on earth was a contest for souls between the Lord and the Devil. The Lord had given man the choice to make: good or evil. And the Lord was winning, they argued.

I totally disagreed. In my view the Devil was absolutely kicking ass because the one thing, maybe the only thing men had been great at forever was killing other men, women, and children. Human history was a long record of war after war playing over and over, the repetitious killing of others, the relentless desire to control and conquer the minds and spirits of others in the name of some religion, economic interests, pure hatred, or burning and burgeoning egos.

Where in hell was the Lord? And how could we genuinely believe in the Bible? His book was written, translated, and edited over many centuries by dozens of men, each with his own beliefs, shaped by political and personal economic wants and desires, or covertly directed by others. Each with his fervent belief in his own righteousness. How could that be *His* book?

Could life on earth ever be improved for most, if not all, if the Devil won each day in killing, conquering, and controlling? Hell no, I said. Hues argued that there's no hope for anyone seeking eternal life unless they live with and believe in the Lord. Life on earth might be the eternal hell, which was starkly depicted in the landscape before us, but life is always, everywhere, about how we live and treat others. That's how we make it to heaven, Hues said.

We'd spent fourteen months in hell. We had little during that time but each other and our memories, faith, and hopes. But looking out now over the disappeared village, it hit me hard like a bamboo club bashing my head. I realized *our* months of suffering were nothing: the tiniest of tiny ant hills literally invisible in the dark, looming shadow of a vast range of craggy, towering mountains of loss, pain, despair, and grief we saw and felt in front of us. So many largely innocent victims of war who just wanted to farm. Live simply day to day. Practice their religion. Take care of family and loved ones. Laugh and celebrate special times together. Be remembered and honored in death.

The Vietnamese people had been in unending wars for nearly a half century. Their losses of every kind—physical, emotional, mental, spiritual—were far, far beyond our comprehension.

Darkness was no more than an hour off. We needed to find a safer place for the night. I didn't want to go back to the river, nor walk through the shattered village in daylight, so I decided to go a bit further down the hill and then follow what appeared to be a more level area that skirted the village and led eventually into more trees and jungle in the east. Maybe we'd find something to eat. I'd given up on rainfall or water to drink today.

Hues appeared fast asleep when I gathered him in my arms. Progress down the slight but rough slope was slow and cautious but steady. We were surrounded by enough ferns, bushes, and scattered bamboo trees it would be difficult to see us, especially given our slow pace and the gathering dusk. But it also made it more difficult for me to see.

The jungle was quietly noisy with normal sounds, but maybe the late-day heat made it that way. Maybe the damn jungle was tired. I tried to remember what the jungle had sounded like on the other late afternoons we'd traveled, but I couldn't remember. More and more, I remembered less and less. I eventually sat down with Hues in my arms, my back against a tree, resting for just a moment to gather enough strength to press on.

I awoke at the sound of distant artillery, six muffled explosions. The sounds came from the northeast, the direction we were moving. More artillery rounds exploded.

The sounds excited me because chances were good the artillery firing those rounds was located at an American firebase, which I still believed provided our best chance to make it out alive. I estimated the sounds were at least several klicks away. More importantly, I had a fix on a possible location, which I imprinted in my head. Up and down four or five more hills? Could we find our way there tomorrow? I couldn't imagine lasting more than a few days. And not that long without water.

I rose with Hues and continued down the slope, walking a fairly flat stretch of tall grasses, scattered peanut bushes, and skinny, sentinel-like bamboo trees. I wanted to skirt the shattered village before dark, and I'd visually identified several night locations for us from higher up the hill. But we only made it part way when my dreams of food and water were brought to life. Well, sort of.

We walked directly into a small patch of wild green grapes growing at the northern edge of the destroyed village, likely once cultivated by the villagers. They were marked by some bright orange flame vine winding through them, highlighting their presence.

I found a good place for us to spend the night about fifty yards beyond the grapes, a brushy hiding space in a stretch of ferns beneath the thick limbs and big leaves of two heliconia trees. I laid Hues down and covered him with the net.

"Going for some sweet supper and wine," I whispered. I couldn't see any expression on his face, but I imagined his eyes were smiling at my dumb statement.

I returned to the grapes and picked and chewed five on the spot. In my mind they were tasty and juicy. I thought it was an odd time of the year for fresh grapes, but I had no idea of the grape-growing season in Vietnam. Perhaps they grew all year, various kinds? Or was it possible I was just imagining the grapes, like I'd imagined some other things today?

The sweet juice wasn't as wet as a cupful of water, but it definitely helped ease my thirst. A tiny bit. I spit out some seeds and swallowed others, unconcerned about eating them. They possessed some nutrition, right? Anything from the seeds was more than we'd had for nearly a day—a few bites of fish and bones last night. Or was that the night before?

I filled my pockets with a half dozen bunches of grapes, then returned to Hues. I lifted the netting and sat him up so I could feed him. I adjusted the netting around us and put two grapes in my mouth and chewed them to a juicy pulp. I then placed them in Hues's mouth and gently rubbed his throat.

As darkness settled in and the jungle resumed its nightly chorus, we ate most of the grapes, real or imagined. I kept one bunch of grapes in my pocket for breakfast. We weren't full, but our pressing thirst was sated a bit. We had a little food in our bellies. We were happy to be eating *something* again. And happy as hell we'd survived another day, one surrounded by visible enemies. We'd lived on the edge of death for one more day.

After Hues swallowed three mouthfuls of grape paste, he slowly shook his head when I tried to feed him a fourth mouthful. Was he saying he was too full? Or trying to tell me I needed the grapes more than he did? Or was he saying he was dying and didn't need any more?

"Just one more, Hues. Please. Eat it for me," I pleaded.

Hues shook his head again and refused. Just too tired and sore, I decided.

I settled him into a sleeping position on his right side, then laid on my side and backed up to Hues so he could tap my back if needed. I pulled the net over us. I expected Hues would close our day with a whispered psalm, but he remained silent. Maybe he was already lost in sleep. I gave in to my own exhaustion.

But as I fell asleep, I softly psalmed the words of one I'd heard several times before, MoCity Psalm #143.

Or maybe the quiet psalming voice I heard was Hues wrapping up our day.

Or a bird softly singing as it winged nearby.

Maybe I dreamed it all. It didn't really matter.

I simply took it as a sign Hues was still with me for another day.

> Lord, share your kindness in the morning.
> Tell us which way to walk at dawn.
> Save us from enemies and murder in their hearts.

Let your goodly spirit guide us through the jungle.
Shine your light upon our plight, our way home.
We have dwelled in darkness here far too long.
Grant us another day of life, Lord, to follow your light.

CHAPTER 20

—— MEMORY ROOM (5) ——

I only learned later in life my mother carried me safely to birth while she was locked in the painful chains of severe polio. It was little short of a miracle we both survived. In her picture, she's smiling and reaching out her hand to offer me a heel from a loaf of freshly baked bread.

Oh, those early Saturday mornings when I'd awake to the tantalizing aroma of baking bread and rush down the stairs, rubbing sleep out of my eyes. She'd greet me in the kitchen with a big smile, then slice off the heel (my favorite piece) of a fresh loaf, cover it lavishly with homemade strawberry jam, and offer it to me.

I'd take the bread, lick off some jam, take a huge bite, and watch her loving smile spread and fill the room like morning sunlight. That fresh bread, sweet red jam, and loving smile constituted key ingredients of joy and contentment then and throughout my life.

Her memory picture also brought to life the sound of her soft humming "Amazing Grace." She hummed it constantly as she cooked, cleaned rooms, washed dishes, or carefully applied makeup after a long, hot bath. I once asked her why she hummed so much.

"Because I'm happy," she said, smiling at me. "It's a way I express my happiness. And I'm always happy because I'm alive—I have the gift of life. And that includes *you*, my family, and many friends."

She leaned forward and kissed my cheek. "We all have problems in life, Brian, small and large. But just being alive, that's the greatest gift we have. I celebrate every precious minute of life when I hum."

"But Mom, why always the same song?" I asked.

"Because the words, the music are just right for about every moment and situation in life," she said. "They express the blessing of life even on dark days and nights. Grace kept me alive and you, too, Brian, at your birth. When I hum I celebrate the gift of life and you to love."

"Will you sing a few words just for me, Mom?" I asked.

"Of course," she said. She grasped and held my hand and softly sang for me. "Amazing grace, how sweet the sound that saved a wretch like me. I once was lost, but now am found, was blind, but now I see."

The beauty and power of that memory, along with the collective power of all the memory paintings hanging in the room, again provided a soothing antidote for my pain and fed my hopes. I celebrated the gift of life for Hues and me to live another day.

CHAPTER 21

— DAY 6: FIREBASE HOPE —

Sleep was reluctant to release me, and I wasn't eager to escape it, so I gradually awoke to a hot, muggy morning later than intended. I struggled through several layers of sleep and dreams to reach consciousness and inventory my world. Surprise: we were still in the jungle.

Hearing returned first: nothing unusual, just the normal jungle chatter and ever-present music of mosquitos. Vision was next. Through the bushes and branches of the banyan tree overhead the sky was a perfect blue with a few wispy white clouds floating by like steady puffs of smoke from an invisible giant's pipe in the heavens. The sun looked nearly full-blown in the east, maybe an hour after dawn. The early start I'd planned was long gone.

My body spoke next and protested loudly. Feet were cut and bruised, and my swollen left ankle was hot and throbbing. I hoped for another river today to wade and savor, if only briefly. Thighs and shoulders ached—a steady rhythm of pain beating and competing like war drums. My ribs hurt like I'd fallen hard on them, which I didn't recall doing. Hands and wrists were laced with cuts and insect bites, chafed and red. Face and neck itched constantly. Overall, I felt even more feverish today. Something hot and evil was growing inside me.

I was glad I couldn't see myself in a mirror. Not sure I'd recognize me. Would my family and friends? Sometimes I caught a brief glimpse of myself reflected in Hues's dark eyes, and I could look at Hues anytime and basically see myself: a clone of scarred and skinny desperation, looking more like a faint shadow of a man than a man, but one whose eyes still expressed some light of hope. Fortunately, our spirits remained a little stronger than our bodies.

Hues must have slept well too. I hadn't heard or felt him during the night, which was unusual. I scanned the immediate area again, listened closely for about fifteen seconds, then lifted the netting off myself and scratched my swollen left cheek. I drew blood on my index finger. I turned and lifted the netting off Hues. What little was left of him brought me near tears.

His black pajama shirt and leggings looked bigger than his body, which was little more than a dark shadow on the ground. He was a thin mass of knobby knees and elbows, a swollen and cracked left ankle, the thinnest arms and prominent wrist bones, sunken cheeks, a giant Adam's apple, beaky nose, and eyes closed. If life was a muscle, his muscle mass and strength were all but gone, and to top it off, he had no tongue.

But his spirit was so close it gave me a hug.

Then I noticed his sandals were missing. When had that happened? Why in hell was I just noticing this? I looked around but couldn't see them.

Get it together, man!

"We going, brother," I whispered, hugging him. "Gonna find a firebase today. Hang with me, man."

I cut and pulled three leeches off his right foot, then used my black shirt sleeve to wipe sweat and some dried blood from small cuts on his face. I sat behind him, pulled his head back against my shoulder, then put my left hand in front of his nose and mouth. I felt a small breath of air on my fingers. He was still breathing. Barely.

I pulled two grapes from the bunch in my pocket. Put them in my mouth, and chewed them, enjoying the tiny bit of moisture. I pulled the small pulpy mass out and placed it in front of Hues. "Take a bite, man. Still tastes great."

He didn't respond, just continued sleeping or unconscious. I checked for a pulse in his left wrist. I convinced myself it was there: faint and slow but steady. When the grapes were gone, I rose and scanned the area again. Still no sandals. Time to move.

We carefully descended the long slope of a low hill. The countryside was semiopen, a sea of waist-high grass dotted with clusters of pine trees, some bamboo stands, and brushwood scattered here and there. The sun's heat was already intense, the heavy air wrapping us tightly in a thick blanket of humidity.

I tried to remember if any time during our journey we *hadn't* been sweating or soaked in rain. Or both a lot of the time. Would constant moisture cause our skin to wrinkle and age faster? Had I read that somewhere?

Such silly, stupid thoughts!

At the bottom of the hill, we literally stumbled upon a dark pool of water. The ragged hole looked like an old bomb crater now partially filled with stagnant rainwater. Without thinking, I set Hues down, quickly stripped naked, and stepped into the cooler, dirty water. I reached into the air and grasped an imaginary bar of soap, then a thick sponge. Cleaning myself leisurely, I whispered to Hues the whole time.

"Feels just like the old city swimming pool," I said. "Or maybe that little lake back home, Silver Lake. I ever tell you about that? Lots of fish—gills and perch—and sometimes naked girls sunbathing! Bare boobs and butts! But it's a shit bit warmer in *this* water. Maybe twenty or thirty degrees! And there's a few hundred more bugs and skeeters hanging around this pool.

"And now, guess what, Hues? Feels like some little buddy bloodsuckers pulling on my feet. Wow! They going crazy on my toes. Other than those little bitty differences, hey: just like my pool back home! Maybe even a Holiday Inn pool! But where's the music? The girls?"

I climbed out, lifted Hues, and then set him by the pool so that I could put his feet and legs in the water and wash them off. As I did so, I watched his face for a reaction. There was none. "Hope you're living your dream, man," I said softly. I wiped his feet and legs with my black leggings, then put my clothes back on and brushed at tears in my eyes.

We set out to climb a steeper hill. A faint trail appeared through the brush and trees. I followed it for fifty feet or so where it turned left to ascend the hill, then stopped. Hues's single tap on my back confirmed my own sudden sense of possible danger in front of us.

I set Hues down, dropped to my knees, crawled forward, and carefully examined the path and grass directly around us. Then I saw it: a tripwire was stretched across the path about six feet ahead, nearly invisible in the long grass.

We worked our way cautiously around one end of the wire, then moved back into the edge of the jungle, thirty feet or so from the path. Despite my sore and weakened body, I was struck again by how light Hues felt in my arms. Like he was thinning away a little bit with each step. I was carrying the bones of my brother in his black pajamas. I looked at him often this morning to confirm he was still with me. Couldn't go on without him.

"Hang with me, man. We got this."

The vegetation grew denser as we ascended the hill, while I grew more desperate as the pace of our journey slowed dramatically again. Back to one tough step at a time. I leaned forward on the ball of my leading foot. Reached out with my left hand and grasped a small tree trunk, a bush, or tree, then pulled forward a foot or two. Prepared my other hand for the same maneuver. Loosened the hand holding Hues's legs, then reached out quickly with my right hand and grabbed a tree trunk or bushy limb to pull us ahead. One more step. I stood shaking.

Not many of those steps left in me.

"Hell of a park walk, ain't it Hues? Just out enjoying nature," I whispered, laughing softly. Imagined I heard Hues laughing too. It wasn't really funny but laughing together felt good. Damn good.

The Cobra gunship appeared out of nowhere, a moving dot against the sky, rapidly growing larger and louder. It dove out of view behind the hill we were climbing, opened fire on the enemy or something on the far side, and then soared back up, turned, and plunged back down over the area, rapidly firing its guns again.

Were the NVA or VC massing for an attack on a firebase? Was it simply a small patrol they'd spotted? Or were they sending a warning to the enemy we Americans were armed and ready for them? I felt more confident. We were closing in on a firebase. I could feel it.

We pressed on, still climbing the long hill I hoped would give us a better view of what lay ahead, maybe a glimpse of a firebase. I also was hoping for a new shot of strength.

At some point midday, with the sun overhead and sweat running steadily down my face while red ants left stinging bites on my left foot, I tipped over yet again. I found myself once more walking side by side and talking with Hues—another one of our religious discussions, which may have been triggered by the blasted Vietnamese village we saw yesterday.

We debated quietly as we climbed the hill, parting the sweet oil grass and skirting thick coffee bushes and dense clusters of ferns, while watching closely everything around us. We acted like it was the most normal thing in the world: two American POWs debating the Bible and walking side by side in the jungle where danger was pervasive, even though one POW was carrying the other, who couldn't walk or talk.

"Look, the Bible is words, man," I whispered to Hues. "Lots of words written by dozens or hundreds of men, right? You ever known a man without a political or religious point of view and a self-centered vision? You ever think maybe those words were written to control people and their beliefs—like a politically religious form of government control? Religious propaganda?"

"The Bible isn't political, man. Forget that," Hues said, shaking his head.

"Okay, but what about all those words that took more than a thousand years to write—more than fifty generations of people! Why did it take so damn long to write the damn Bible if the Lord can do anything and everything in a heartbeat? Why didn't he do it overnight?"

Hues shook his head again. "Those sixty-six books in the Bible weren't written by men."

"What? Wait a minute. Got their names on them. Who wrote them, then?"

"They are the *Lord's* words, Buck. He *breathed* them into those men's ears and minds, and they wrote down what he said. The words in the Bible are the words of the Lord, not men."

"*Breathed* them into their heads? Now *that's* a helluva stretch," I said. "Don't believe I ever heard *that* before."

"Trust me, Buck."

"Where's it written in the Bible?"

"Couple places. In the Psalms and Timothy 2, maybe. I met those words in the Psalms."

"Well, I guess if you believe the Lord *breathed* those words into the minds of men, who then wrote them down, you'd believe anything and everything in the Bible! Did the Lord also breathe the new words into the minds of the hundreds of editors in all the edited versions of the Bible over the centuries? All those words, all those versions of the Bible . . . You're blowing my crazy mind even crazier, Hues."

He nodded at me. "Just forget 'all the words' stuff, man. What really counts most are those eleven most important words in that big book. Just eleven little words say it all: 'Do unto others as you would have them do unto you.'"

"Now I know you're kidding, right?" I asked.

"Nope. That's the essence of the Bible, and it was captured in Jesus's life. He was the Lord in human form, and he showed us the way to live. He modeled it, man. Life's about living and doing, helping others by giving them love and hope. Anybody in any position in life can do that, right? You don't have to be rich, and you can do it even if you never attend church. You still can, man. *Living* the words is what counts—not reading them, praying them, twisting them to suit your fancy. That's what counts most, Buck. Is that so damn difficult to remember?"

"Nope. Easy to remember," I said, "but damn difficult to do for most of us, as our history has demonstrated again and again forever."

I smiled at Hues and winked. "Our actual history suggests eleven other little words that may actually better describe our great human race."

"And what are those?" he asked.

"Forget all the others—life is about me and the Devil."

"Not in the Bible," he said. "You made up those eleven words."

I nodded. "Yes, but they exist in more important places in our world—human minds."

Hues gave me four soft taps on my back: possible danger to our left. My mind returned to the present moment, and I dropped to my knees in the chest-high grass. Closed my eyes to listen better. A soft whisper of a breeze came from my left and lightly touched my cheek. At least we were downwind of anything to our left.

Then I heard it: soft rustling sounds in the grass, like people or animals slowly moving by. The sound slid closer to us, then stopped. Was someone or some creature aware of us and just watching, listening, and waiting for us to move again before they attacked?

I opened my eyes but saw nothing. I kept my head below the grass. The rustling sound slid further away.

Hues tapped me once in the back: danger now in front of us. I heard a faint grunting sound in front of us, an answering grunt even closer, and a third grunt farther off. I recognized the sounds.

"Wild boar," I whispered.

Thank goodness we were downwind. We'd not last long against wild boars. We'd seen several of them near the camp and the Banyan Tree Store. One charged Caveman one day when we were picking fruit south of the camp. It was a huge brown boar with a pointed head and snout and a thick neck, probably weighed three hundred pounds or more. It looked at least four feet tall and six feet long. Its tough skin was like layers of thick leather.

If Caveman hadn't been armed and shot the boar to death, it

would have knocked him to the ground, then proceeded to break his neck and tear off chunks of flesh, grunting happily. Boars eat virtually everything, from snakes and birds to animals and people. Their brains are tiny, but their strength and appetites are huge.

Hues and I never forgot that day because Caveman and Skinny sliced up the dead boar. We then carried big, bloody slabs of boar meat back to the camp, where it was seasoned and cooked. We could only imagine how tasty it must have been because we weren't given a single bite. Nothing. Nor were we allowed to get in the river and wash the blood off our pajamas.

The VC and NVA had feasted on the boar. We sat in our cage covered in blood and smelled the meat, a taunting scent that lingered through the night and into our dreams, where we were the guards who beat the VC prisoners daily and fed them nothing.

I no longer heard the boars nearby, but two louder grunts sounded further ahead. Eventually I raised my eyes above the grass. About thirty yards in front of us the top of a boar's head was sliding through the grass and moving away. One other boar rippled the grass beyond.

"Thanks, Hues," I whispered. "Saved us again."

We found some shade near the top of the ridge in a tangle of bushes and lay down to rest. My legs and arms were ringing with pain. I was fighting hard to hang on to my diminishing willpower. I fell asleep with Hues in my arms despite the intense heat.

A buzzing sound woke me later, and I shook my head. Brushed my ear to bat away what I thought was a bee or a big mosquito. The sound increased dramatically. My eyes popped open. A Loach helicopter soared over the brush and trees no more than one hundred fifty feet above us. With the trees and brush overhead, we were invisible to the pilot.

The helicopter and its sound disappeared but returned moments later some distance to the east. I sat up and watched it disappear behind the hill just east of us. Silence returned. I stared at the hill and wondered: Was a firebase just beyond it? Was the helicopter just taking a look around before something else was going down—a kind of prescreen flight before some bigger action? We needed to see what lay beyond that hill, at least a klick away and fairly steep. We needed to see. I'd climb a mountain if it was a firebase. Somehow.

I gathered Hues in my arms and rose, my balance shaky, my body slowly swaying as my mind tilted awkwardly. I ordered my damn muscles to listen, pay attention, and get their shit together for another walk: one more step toward the bottom of this hill, then up the hill we needed to ascend. Circle the bamboo, step over the creeping vines, duck under papaya tree limbs. No. Big. Deal. Just more steps.

Just do it!

The late afternoon heat grew intense. I was living and walking in a furnace. Every step now was a struggle. How many did I have left? I stopped and gasped for air, panting. My dry mouth made it even more difficult to suck air into my lungs. My lightheadedness competed with my lungs for attention. The solutions to my growing list of physical and mental problems were really quite simple: water, food, safety.

Water, food, safety.

Water, food, safety.

I timed my steps to this three-word counting rhythm and pushed on.

At the bottom of the hill, I was stunned to discover what looked like one of our solutions: water! A tiny creek or spillway glinted in the sunlight. As we approached it, I looked up the hill. It didn't look like a creek. It was running more on the top of the ground. I decided it was most likely a runoff of some of the heavy rain we'd experienced in the past few days.

I set Hues down then closely examined the water, which appeared quite clear. I traced it up the hill again; it looked increasingly like a runoff, a pretty clean and clear runoff. A safe source of water. Okay, not totally safe, but we were desperate for water.

I removed the black cup from my pocket and dipped it into the water, then swirled, smelled it, watched it closely: nothing but the faint scent of rainwater. Worth taking a chance? In the interest of life, yes.

"Here goes, Hues," I whispered.

I scooped some surface water from the runoff and sipped it slowly. Swirled it in my mouth to try to identify any danger, but it tasted wonderful! I gulped two cups quickly and moaned with pleasure. Maybe we'd die from the water or become violently ill, but the truth is, we'd die damn soon *without* water. We were close now, more than a long day waterless.

The risk disappeared in my mind.

The necessity of drinking took over.

I pulled Hues close to the runoff and sat behind him. I filled the cup again and whispered, "You gonna love it." I slowly poured the water into his mouth and stared into his closed eyes, which nevertheless shared that smile of satisfaction I remembered.

I opened my eyes again. "We needed this, man," I whispered.

We drank water until we felt bloated. I then poured cups of water over our faces and dirty hands. We could feel the water work inside our bodies to refresh us and slake our thirst. The water on our skin cooled and cleaned us just a bit, left us feeling fresh for a few minutes. Overall, it was our big ticket for another day of escaping and living. Water. So simple. So vital.

"Off to a good start," I whispered. "Who knows, maybe today is *the* day."

I resumed counting steps up another steep hill. Halfway up the hill I fought through another stretch of dense pines and teasing, dangling vines beneath the limbs of several giant Fokiena trees that darkened the jungle floor. I longed desperately for an axe or machete to cut a path in the tough underbrush, but I couldn't imagine I'd have enough strength left to carry Hues after swinging the machete a hundred or two hundred times to beat the brush.

My mind wandered off somewhere as I struggled.

I returned to the present moment once beyond the dense brush. I'd been fantasizing about food—not a rice ball but a big bowl filled with at least a pound of rice and big chunks of chicken and beef bathed in the foul-smelling but delicious-tasting *nuoc mam* sauce. We'd seen the old man and old woman at the mess hall making the stuff.

They cut up fish heads and put them in a cloth or some kind of a netting bag, which they left hanging for hours on a limb in the sun, fermenting. Juices from the bag dripped slowly into a jar or dish, to which they added other stuff like spices, maybe salt and pepper, some vegetables, and whatever. We imagined the awful smell carried all the way into Laos, but we still desperately wanted some to eat.

The urgency to keep moving increased in the late afternoon sun. We needed to see what was over the hill so we could make our plans for tonight and tomorrow. As we neared the crest of the hill and the vegetation thinned, we heard another helicopter coming from the south. The noise grew, and I knew it was a bigger helicopter, much bigger than a Loach. I dropped to my knees and laid a sleeping Hues in the grass nearby.

The helicopter thundered past us and turned toward the east. I smiled: it was a Chinook, one of the biggest American helicopters that ferried troops, weapons, and supplies to firebases and other locations. But my mouth fell open when I saw a cargo net below the chopper that was filled with what looked like bodies. Or was I seeing bags of water and boxes of supplies? I rubbed my eyes but couldn't tell for sure. The chopper descended out of view.

Got to be a firebase down there somewhere. I leaned and whispered to Hues, "Stay here, man. Gonna crawl up the ridge a bit, get a better look. Think we're close to a firebase."

A green finch with pink legs landed fifteen feet from me and then hopped and flitted ahead in the direction I was headed. I followed it as I low crawled up the hill to a kind of lookout point over the land below and more hills to the east. And there it was: a firebase below atop a smaller hill! My spirit soared. The firebase looked about half the size of FSB Bastogne. I had no idea what the formal name of this firebase was, but it didn't matter. It was an American firebase. It was our best hope for survival. It would always be Firebase Hope for me.

The hilltop below had been cleared by soldiers, bulldozers, or other equipment, as well as roughly two hundred yards of vegetation in a big circle around the base. This allowed soldiers to see anyone or anything moving toward the camp. From a distance I saw some bunkers, artillery positions, a helicopter landing zone, and a couple of larger tents. Some soldiers looked no bigger than ants. While I couldn't clearly see the details of the firebase, I knew the top of the hill would be surrounded by rows of trip wires, concertina wire, and tanglefoot—barbed wire staked close to the ground to prevent the enemy from crawling and sneaking into camp at night.

The Chinook had probably dropped off some soldiers and supplies, then picked up soldiers at the firebase who were likely headed to Camp Eagle or Camp Evans in the rear or to another area of operation. Studying the firebase and surrounding jungle, I decided the best approach would be from the southwest quadrant around the base. It also looked like potential cover for us for the night. Early morning sunlight would illuminate the quadrant nicely. I wanted to present myself to the firebase in bright light so my beard and hairy body could be clearly seen.

Satisfied with what I saw, and excited about the morning and our opportunity to finally reach safety, I thought about the night ahead as dusk was coming on. We'd need to find a hiding place to wait until first light, one not near a listening post or too much in the open that might lead to us being seen by the soldiers.

I low crawled back to Hues, who once more appeared to be sleeping. I lay by his head and whispered, "It's a firebase. We got a real chance to make it home. We'll find a safe spot near the firebase for tonight."

With the sun beginning to drop west over the ridge, I carried Hues as quietly and quickly as I could down the slope toward the southwest corner of the firebase. Coming down the hill wasn't so bad because we hadn't had rain for a day or more, so fewer muddy stretches slowed us down. The coming darkness was our biggest threat. We needed to be in position before our world was black. The closer we drew to the firebase, the more concerned I became about being seen and shot in the dusky light.

The ferns thinned a bit, but my view was still limited. I began counting steps again and following my instincts closely once more. We were so near the firebase I didn't want to make a foolish mistake. Birds, frogs, and an orchestra of other insects chattered at us as we slipped awkwardly through the jungle. Our personal cloud of mosquitos hovered nearby.

We settled into a good hiding and viewing spot about thirty yards into the jungle at the edge of the long bare slope leading up to the firebase. It was a low spot between two thick bushes surrounded by some thigh-high grass and long-armed ferns behind us. I saw no tracks on the ground in the immediate area in the fading light. I could lift my head and see a small portion of the cleared area near the southwest corner of the slope. I doubted we'd be seen or found unless the Americans, or enemy soldiers in the area, literally stepped on us.

We finished the day with no food, apart from several grapes, but we'd enjoyed fantastic water. As we settled in beneath the bushes and the bugs descended, I realized I'd lost or forgotten the mosquito netting somewhere. I sighed audibly and tried to remember how that might have happened or where. Had I left it or dropped it close by? Had I actually left it behind this morning after my bath in the dirty water? Or had I tossed it aside when I was tipped over today and talking the Bible with Hues?

Get it together!

"Sorry," I whispered to Hues. "Lost the netting. Just you, me, and bugs tonight. Get some sleep, man. Tomorrow's our big day. Gonna find out early if we live or die. Either way we go together, brother."

I lay next to Hues and held him in my arms. I so wanted him alive and laughing, flashing his lightning grin, telling great lies and stories, rolling with laughter, rejoicing in life. Psalming forever.

At that moment when thinking about Hues and the netting, I remembered a story he'd told me about the Reverend, telling him to "Forget what you lost and don't have, Hues. Focus on what you still got and can give others."

I still had life and my brother. A new wife and new baby. My family and friends. So many great memories. And hope.

I could be the netting tonight.

I spread my hands, arms, and legs to cover as much of his bare head, face, neck, and legs as possible to protect him from numerous bugs and mosquitos. The last thing I saw before closing my eyes was a cluster of tiny faint stars light-years away in the heavens, yet teasingly close, blinking on and off as the jungle night chorus expressed MoCity Psalm #37.

> Trust in the Lord, live and do good.
> He rewards you with life and light,
> shining like dawn, brightest noonday sun.
> Commit to the Lord and walk firmly.
> You may trip and stumble, but not fall.
> He's with us, stumbling, coming, and going
> sunrise to sunset to sunrise, forever.

CHAPTER 22

—— MEMORY ROOM (6) ——

I visited several pictures of Hues and me together. Shaking hands outside the redneck bar in Kentucky when we first met. Arms around each other's shoulder after completing the escape and evasion course at Ft. Polk. Holding and tipping beers the night I shared news about Jeanie and the baby. Being carried by Hues after the chopper crash.

The most recent picture, a close-up of his face, was my focus tonight. His face reflected light in the darkness of that moment: a soft smile and pinpoints of light shining in his eyes, though his face and body were bruised and swollen just hours after being brutally battered in the Beatdown Ring. The picture perfectly captured his spirit and the Lord's light, though just a breath from death. Hope and love were locked in his eyes as he grinned at me.

I'd kept that light blocked in my own mind behind a thick, rough door of anger and doubt. I knew it was simplistic, but if the Lord was the light, why didn't he eliminate or soften the darkness in the lives of so many who suffered due to the words and actions of others in life?

Hues cracked open the door for me. He was light. His spirit was ever-present, no matter the density of darkness in the moment. I loved and believed in Hues, but I carried nagging doubts and was unwilling to embrace the Lord and his light until our torturous escape and especially our experience the day before as we lay and watched the NVA crossing the river. We lay silent, just feet from them. Death was a cough, sniff, or sneeze away. We lived in hell. We watched death pass by daily. Yet, we were still alive, as was hope that night with Hues. I felt the Lord with me in Hues and his spirit.

At the far end of my memory room, I saw a small, faint glow about the size of a candle. I crawled toward it and stopped near it, stared into the soft, hypnotic flame, folded my battered hands together, and prayed my first real prayer in years:

Father in heaven, please hear my prayer. Forgive me my many sins. I have denied your light and truth for too many years. My own doubts shut out your light until my sweet brother Hues arrived. He had little or nothing, save you, Lord, and your love and light, which he lived daily in his life, focused on helping others. I love him like a brother, Lord. He's saved my life. He's given me love and hope in our jungle prison when I needed them most. He's breathed life into my shrunken soul. My prayer tonight is for my dying brother, Lord. Please give me the strength to carry him home.

At the end of the prayer, I found myself back on the jungle floor, a light rain falling in the humid night. Hues was in my arms. The last thing I remembered before sleep was the small light on the floor at the end of the memory room. That was our pathway home tomorrow.

CHAPTER 23

— DAY 7: LAST STEPS —

Sleep was punctuated by abrupt awakenings, triggered not by bugs, bullets, or bombs, but rather an accelerating kaleidoscope of competing memories, experiences, and images ranging from horrible to heavenly in my mind:

A piece of Hues's bloody tongue floating on muddy ground.
Mom's soft humming and the salivating perfume of baking bread.
Cruel beatings and cruder burials in the brutal Beatdown Ring.
Dad soaring like an eagle, toppling self-doubts in my mind.
Endless hours staked to the ground, a mindless X in the searing sun.
Jeanie wrapped warmly in my arms, nursing our blue-eyed baby.

A brief shower woke me just before dawn—one of those classic rain-on, rain-off experiences. A torrential deluge lasted maybe a minute then braked as suddenly, shifting into a slow drizzle for another minute before fading into light sprinkles, which vanished quietly at first light. A quick cleaning to begin the new day.

The rain cooled my mosquito-bitten face. I turned my head during the downpour, opened my mouth, and savored some raindrops. The value of a few droplets of rain in your mouth when you've been without enough water for too long . . . The little things in life are huge when absent.

I listened to soft dripping sounds from the shrubs and trees until they became lost in the growing chorus of jungle voices. I'd lived with these voices more than a year and grown familiar with many of them. I heard nothing unusual, save some banging or hammering sounds just now that probably echoed from the firebase up the hill. Sounded like construction or destruction to begin another war day.

The mosquitos returned, but I lay still, Hues in my arms. Daylight crept in swiftly as the sun erased several clouds and painted the sky a glossy blue—a perfect background for my performance "on stage" this morning.

Two bright green magpies trimmed in black, yellow, and red landed on a rose myrtle bush nearby, the limbs swaying under their weight. They nodded at us and chattered good morning, then flew off, their voices and bright colors lingering. The day was off to a good start.

I eased away from Hues, sat up, and cut and pinched several fat leeches off my feet and left hip. I removed three leeches from Hues's right foot. It would be wonderful to never see or feel another leech in life.

For a moment I sat and enjoyed the gift of another day. I hoped Hues was enjoying it too, wherever he was in his mind. His body was silent and unmoving, but he looked peaceful, comfortable, relaxed wherever he was. Like he knew this was our big day.

The growing sunlight flooded the open ground of the firebase just beyond our hiding place. The stage was fully lit. It was time for the biggest steps of our journey.

I leaned and hugged Hues. "This is it," I whispered. "I'm headed to the firebase. If you hear shots . . . well . . . forget that. Won't be any shots this morning. So, get ready, man. We're headed home. Going fishing next spring. Count on it. Love you, brother."

His eyes blinked open for an instant, just long enough for me to glimpse a tiny pinpoint of light in each pupil—two bright stars in the galaxy of his mind—just like the stars I'd seen last night in my memory room. His eyes closed again, but the twinkling stars in his eyes would remain forever whenever I looked toward the heavens at night. Maybe all the stars in the distant universe are the eyes of our deceased loved ones. I'd never felt closer to Hues, our spirits once more tightly embracing.

I slid beneath the brush and low crawled slowly and soundlessly on the muddy jungle floor to the edge of the cleared slope of land running up to the firebase. I saw nothing or no one, but I was certain some eyes were watching the wood lines around the base. It wouldn't take long for someone to spot me.

The big moment was here. Given everything I'd experienced in the past fourteen months, I wasn't frightened. But I was light-headed when I stood, swayed a bit but kept my balance. My whole body ached with every breath. No more fighting the jungle was left in me.

I pulled off my black pajama shirt and dropped it at the edge of the wood line, a marker for Hues's location. My bony, scarred body looked pitiful. But maybe all the scars would catch their attention and help them realize I wasn't an enemy. Just a skinny, scarred brother.

I raised my arms straight in the air, stepped out of the jungle onto the open slope, and faced the firebase at the top of the hill. I waved my arms slowly up and down along my sides, took another hesitant step, and then several more. I imagined someone had seen me by now and was studying me closely with binoculars or a sight on a rifle, alerting others to my presence. Probably lots of rifles focused on me.

One, two, three, four more steps, hands still in the air. I realized I probably looked like a long-haired skinny Hippie. Hippies didn't like soldiers. And vice versa.

Two more uneasy steps . . .

"Stop! Stand still!" a voice commanded me through a megaphone. "Don't move!"

I kept my arms in the air and remained perfectly still. The sun was in my eyes so I could see little up the hill. I posed like that for what seemed like hours but was likely little more than a minute.

"If you understand my words, take your left arm and lower it slowly to your left side!" the voice commanded.

I did as ordered and remained still.

"Now, take your right arm and lower it slowly to shoulder height!"

I did so. More quiet time passed.

"Raise both arms over your head again, and stay where you are, hands in the air!"

I raised my arms into position and saw several soldiers start down the slope. As they gradually drew closer, I counted six of them: two on each side spread about ten yards from each other and the two in the middle. One of the two men in the middle was carrying a megaphone, while the other was carrying a radio and appeared to be speaking into it.

I felt the increasing heat of the sun and began sweating. A few mosquitos remained with me. Many things raced through my mind as the soldiers cautiously descended the hill. The images from my dreams last night flashed again. Other moments of life also passed quickly in my mind. I'd nearly died in my mind dozens of times in Nam but was still alive.

They halted about thirty feet away and formed a loose half circle around me, their rifles at the ready. The man with the megaphone, an older man with what looked like sergeant stripes on his jungle fatigues, said in a normal tone of voice, "Identify yourself."

"I'm Brian Charles Kinder, that's K-I-N-D-E-R. I'm a PFC who was serving with the Casualty Branch of the 101st Airborne Division at Phu Bai in 1969. I can't remember my service number, but my hometown is Farewell, Michigan.

"My injured buddy lying nearby in the woods is Jameis Jones, that's J-A-M-E-I-S Jones, PFC, who was serving with the Graves Registration Unit, 101st Airborne Division, Phu Bai. I don't know his service number, but his hometown is River Rouge, Michigan."

As I talked, the soldier with the radio was also talking, probably relaying the information I shared to someone on the firebase, or at Phu Bai, or maybe the records office in the admin center. When he finished talking, we stared at each other for several minutes. A voice on the radio finally broke the silence. The radioman nodded at the sergeant.

"You can lower your hands, soldier. What's your situation?" the sergeant asked.

"Sergeant, in early September 1969, I don't remember the exact date, Jones and I were in a medevac chopper that went to firebase Bastogne to pick up some dead and injured men in the 101st. The fighting was heavy. After we loaded the bodies and took off, maybe a klick or so later, heavy machine gun or rifle fire ripped through the chopper. The pilot was killed, and the copilot injured. Then the chopper went spinning down and crashed into some trees. Only three of us aboard were alive after the crash, and we all had injuries. One of the men had serious injuries and couldn't walk.

"The VC came out of the dark and surrounded the chopper. They killed the injured man. My buddy carried me until I regained consciousness and could walk on my own. They marched us west for two days to a POW camp not far from the Laotian border, we figured. We spent fourteen months in a cage there and finally escaped at night during heavy rain a week ago.

"My brother has a smashed ankle, and they cut off his tongue, so I carried him. This is our seventh day. He's dying, close to death. I want to carry him up the hill, get him medevacked to a hospital. That's our situation, sergeant. It's pretty damn urgent. Please help us."

The sergeant moved closer and looked my body over carefully, then studied my eyes. "You sure look like you been to hell, son. But you survived and found your way here. And carried your brother. I'm proud of you and what you done, so welcome back. Now, let's have a look at your buddy."

"He's over this way, just inside the jungle," I said and stepped off. The sergeant moved beside me while the other soldiers cautiously approached the wood line.

The radio broke the silence with some static and a voice I couldn't understand.

"Both check out," the radio man said to the sergeant. "Listed as MIAs for about a year. Changed to KIAs a couple months ago."

"So, our parents and family think—" I started to say.

The sergeant nodded and interrupted. "But they'll be notified in hours, and you can talk with them soon."

"Great!"

As we neared the place where Hues lay, the sergeant said, "My two men will carry your buddy up the hill. I'm sure you're worn out. And we'll get a medevac as soon as possible. Get you both to the rear and some help."

"Thanks, Sergeant," I said. "I'm wiped out, but I want to carry my brother up the hill. He's been with me every step of the way. Truth is, he's the reason I'm still alive."

When we reached Hues, I pointed at him. "As you can see he's hurt bad. Not much of him left. I hope they can still save him because he's a great man. He's the finest man I've ever known. He's the reason we made it."

The soldiers looked down at Hues, then at me, then at each other. One soldier said, "I don't—"

The sergeant held up his hand, and the soldier stopped talking. The sergeant took a step closer to me and nodded his head. He put his hand on my shoulder and gave me a sad smile. "Son, carry your brother. We'll call in a medevac. We got water, coffee, food up there for . . . both of you. You can be damn proud of what you've done for your brother."

I bent and gathered Hues in my arms and followed the sergeant up the slope, whispering as we climbed as I had for the past week. "Almost there, brother, just a few more steps . . . we gonna make it and get some water, food . . . get you to a hospital . . . just a few more steps . . . almost there . . . one step at a time . . . and we did it, didn't we, man? We're headed home . . . you and me are going home . . . love you, man and here we are . . . our last damn step! We did it, Hues . . . damn well did it together . . . couldn't have done it . . . without you!"

I dropped to my knees, then sat cross-legged, holding Hues in my arms. I looked up to the pure blue heaven and the majestic sun. I closed my eyes for a moment of peace, the first real peace in my mind in a long, long time. "Thank you, Lord, for lighting our way home," I prayed aloud. "And thank you for my brother being with me every step of the way."

I looked down at my lap where Hues's black pajamas lay. I took a deep breath, picked them up slowly, and hugged them fiercely to my chest. My brother, Hues.

And I cried, my tears a blend of immense joy and deepest sadness.

CHAPTER 24

—— THREE MONTHS LATER ——

I spent five "medical" days in Vietnam and a hospital in Japan before flying home. Underwent a variety of tests. Blood samples were drawn. Urine and stool samples were examined. Injections and medications were administered. I tipped the scales at 112 pounds versus the 170 pounds I'd registered when I arrived in Vietnam. In my first glance in a mirror in more than a year, a haunting thousand-yard stare looked back at me from a face I barely recognized.

My left ankle was diagnosed as severely sprained. Two ribs were badly bruised, and the little finger on my left hand was broken. I didn't remember injuring my ankle, ribs, or finger, but their associated pains were quite familiar. They lightly taped my ribs and splinted and taped my little finger. My ankle was wrapped in a thick boot brace. I hobbled on it and got around fine. Hobbling was much easier than fighting the densely jungled up-and-down hills. Dozens of scars tracked my body. Some were still painful. Many would remain forever, they said.

They cut my hair, which reached my shoulders, and trimmed my beard short, as I requested. It would cover some of the scars on my neck and face. Showers and soap felt wonderful. Bliss was an hour in a cool bathtub one morning while familiar rock music played loudly somewhere in the background: "Don't Be Cruel" by Elvis, "Roll Over Beethoven" by Chuck Berry, "The Twist" by Chubby Checker, and "Eleanor Rigby" by the Beatles. I fell asleep in the water, remembering and dreaming about life before Nam, which was mostly simple, fun, and sweet, though I hadn't realized it then.

I spoke briefly twice with my family and Jeanie via telephone before flying home. Jeanie's first words to me were, "Yes, I accept your proposal!" We agreed to marry shortly after I returned home. I was thrilled to learn of our new daughter whom they had named Brianna, after me. They all called her "Bree." While my family was eager to talk, I found it difficult to say much beyond "I love you;" "I miss you;" "I can't wait to see you;" "Tell me about the baby;" "What are you up to?" "I hope you're well;" and "I'm okay."

An Army psychiatrist, a friendly but serious man who'd served in combat in the Korean War, met with me each day We talked directly and indirectly about Hues and other stuff in my mind. Like the Beatdown Ring. My memory room. My fears and anger. The long pilgrimage with my brother's spirit in the jungle. I wanted to talk more, but finding the right words was impossible at times even with an expert listener. Our sessions were often quiet.

Numerous scars marked my mind too. The psychiatrist explained most of them would remain; I would never totally escape Vietnam. But I could learn to live with it, he said. That was the key. Meet it, acknowledge it every day, then push on in my mind. "Don't get trapped in that big Vietnam cage inside your head," he counseled. "Step outside your mind." Just one more step, right? I could be stronger than the gruesome memories. Most of the time.

The day before I flew home, I studied Army maps of the countryside where the prison camp was located, more or less, and the firebase I'd arrived at the seventh day. I tried to remember and reconstruct my route to the firebase. It was impossible.

In the end, our escape appeared to be a meandering semicircle marked by several turnaround loops and too many stretches of blindness—unknowing and sometimes unseeing where I was in those long days, nights, and heavy rains in the dark jungle. But overall, we'd moved slowly north and east, as planned and hoped. Little short of a miracle.

Jeanie and I were married in a small private wedding four weeks after I returned. She was even more beautiful and loving than I remembered. One of the first things she told me was, "I never stopped believing you were alive, Brian. And on dark nights when I couldn't stop worrying and crying, I felt your arms hugging me. You were here with me. Always."

"You and Bree saved my life too," I said. "You were the hearts of my hopes. Every day."

Bree was the blond-haired, blue-eyed baby Hues and I had envisioned. Her eyes sparkled with joy, just like her mother's. She and I grew to spend much of each day together—walking, feeding birds, reading books, playing with toys, or just talking quietly in the swing on our back porch with Jeanie each night.

She was like that sweet, curious little puppy that follows you everywhere, nosily checks everything, begs to sit on your lap to be loved and hugged, falls asleep in your arms, and awakes suddenly and sweetly to do it all over again. She made the world an even bigger and brighter place where good things not only seemed possible but likely.

On this morning we were gathered in Reverend Martin's meeting room in the small Methodist Church in Farewell. It was a cold but sunny and bright Sunday morning in early February 1971, the kind of winter day that hints at warmer spring and summer days ahead for Michiganders. Jeanie, Bree, and I sat nearest to Reverend Martin. My mother, father, brother, sister, and her husband also were present, as were Jeanie's parents and brother.

My family was uneasy. I was probably the most relaxed of them all. I still wore a short, trimmed beard and remained thin, though I'd regained twenty pounds of the nearly sixty pounds I lost in Vietnam. My body was slowly healing, and so was my mind. One day at a time.

Sometimes I'd break down crying or wake up screaming in the night—trapped once more in the cage, the dense jungle, the Beatdown Ring. Thank God for Jeanie. She'd hold me close and whisper her love and support until I stopped. Then she'd bring Bree into our bed to spend the rest of the night with us. I'd hold Jeanie in my left arm and Bree in my right. Sleep would come.

I was more nervous in larger groups, which is why in our churchgoing we'd arrive late, sit in the back of the sanctuary, and depart first at the end of the service, speaking briefly with just a few other families. Given this experience, my family was uneasy because I'd asked the minister the previous weekend if I could tell my story to parishioners today—some big lessons I learned in Vietnam. And I wanted them to meet Hues.

They were surprised when I made the request. To date I'd said little about my life in Vietnam, apart from sharing some painful stories with Jeanie and explaining how important Hues was to my survival. The family knew only through Jeanie about my occasional emotional breakdowns. Now, I suddenly wanted to tell my story. What was that all about? They were a little concerned about what I might say but more worried about my state of mind and the delicate emotional balance I struggled to maintain. Could I share my story without breaking down and taking a step back in my recovery? I thought so. My family wasn't so sure.

On the other hand, Dr. Warner, my psychiatrist at the clinic in the VA Medical Center in the county, supported me. Jeanie told me he'd cautioned my family never to pressure me to talk about Vietnam. But if I wanted to do so, he said, then listen carefully and be empathetic. Talking about the war could be a sign of some healing going on. And maybe there was something important I wanted or needed to discuss. He was intrigued by what I might share on Sunday and how I would do it, so he made plans to attend the church service. And if I ran into trouble and needed some help, well, he'd be there.

At the moment the minister was describing some coming changes to the church—several new additions for the structure; a bigger parking lot; a small, park-like area with flowers, trees, and a fountain; and an enclosed playground for children. Our small village was growing a bit, and so was membership in the church.

I listened with one ear as he talked, while I watched through a window as cars and trucks gradually filled the parking lot. I saw many familiar faces and people I knew walk into the church. Many saw me sitting near the window and waved or smiled. I took a quick trip to my memory room as the minister talked on.

I'd added several new pictures of family. The largest one captured those first few minutes arriving home when I landed at a small regional airport in southern Michigan. I was dressed in formal Army greens, while my left ankle was dressed in a black brace.

I stood atop the steps leading down from the airplane in the early afternoon sunlight in November 1970. The air was cold and fresh. No mosquitos. Just family. They were gathered outside in a tight circle near the terminal entrance. They waved and called out my name. I gimped down the steps and walked slowly toward them. Seeing them, being with them again, was both wonderful and awkward. So much had happened in my life away from them. And so much in their lives too.

They hurried toward me. My mother, father, brother, sister, and her new husband were there, as were Jeanie's mother, father, and brother. Four cousins were standing and waving behind them, along with several longtime friends from high school and college. Jeanie, in the center of the group, appeared even more lovely than I remembered. She waved with one hand, while in her other arm was Bree, a curly-haired blond baby with a big smile on her face too.

As I drew closer, Jeanie's eyes filled with tears as she smiled, as did many eyes in the group. We crowded together in a tight circle, hugging and kissing; touching shoulders, arms, and backs; and murmuring words of love, welcome home, and how much we'd missed each other. Then the magical moment unfolded.

Standing in front of me, with Bree in her left arm, Jeanie pointed her finger at me and said to Bree: "Dada, that's your Dada, Bree. Remember? We talked about Dada coming home? And now he's here! You want to hug Dada? You want to go to your Dada?"

I held out my arms. Bree stared at me, seeing a stranger wearing an odd hat, a funny suit, and a big black boot, then looked at her Mom again, who nodded and grinned. Bree looked shyly back at me. A smile lit her face, and she suddenly thrust out her little arms toward me. I lifted her and kissed her tiny forehead. Hugged her to my chest. "Oh, Bree, I love you," I whispered. "I dreamed of you all the way home!" Then I cried for a moment, as did the others. Our crying turned into smiles and laughter as we entered the terminal and headed home.

In the background of that picture—my family gathered at the airport when I returned home—I saw the faint outline of another smiling face. Hues celebrated with us.

Jeanie and I were married four weeks later in a small ceremony at the church in Farewell. Twenty-four family members attended and celebrated at a private dinner party. Afterward, Jeanie, Bree, and I spent a weekend in a rustic cabin on Lake Michigan. Though it was winter, the weather was mild and the cold, clean, bugless air felt wonderful. We took long walks on the mostly empty beach north of South Haven, Michigan. I carried Bree in my arms or in a rucksack on my back. At night we built a fire in the fireplace, roasted hot dogs and marshmallows, and read stories to Bree.

My body and mind still suffered as they healed. At times I woke back in the cage and broke into tears. But we became a family of three, inseparable those first months home. I went for counseling once a week at the VA Medical Center. Jeanie and Bree always went with me. They walked the grounds or read books while I spent an hour with my psychiatrist. We talked briefly about the sessions after I returned to the car. When we drove away, we discussed where we might live when our rental lease expired. I wanted to get back to teaching in the fall. If I could get my head squared away and land a job at an area school . . .

I returned abruptly to the present moment when I realized they were staring at me.

"Sorry, daydreaming," I said. "Did you ask me something?"

The minister smiled. "No problem, Brian," he said. "I just asked whether you're sure about today, telling your story? We all want to hear it, but I want you to be absolutely certain you're ready to share it. And it's certainly okay if you aren't."

I nodded, looked around at my family, and saw the questions in their eyes. "Yes, I'm sure. I want to share my story. I'm ready."

Reverend Martin had spread the word I was going to talk about Vietnam this morning. He imagined the church would be full because so many knew me and my family, and other veterans who lived in the community too. In fact, the church was overflowing. All pews were filled. The walls were lined with people standing, and a group of fifteen or so were gathered near the entrance to the sanctuary.

Reverend Martin paused at the entrance. "Ladies and gentlemen," he said, "please stand and join me in welcoming home our church member, Brian Kinder, and his family. Let's all thank him for his incredible service in Vietnam on behalf of our nation."

The minister led our procession down the aisle. I followed him, holding Bree in my left arm, my right arm around Jeanie's shoulder. Our family members followed. Everyone stood and applauded as we walked the aisle. I recognized many faces, and some nodded, smiled, or called out my name as I walked past. These people were part of my larger extended family.

Reverend Martin welcomed all, shared a brief prayer of thanksgiving for being together, then introduced me.

"As you know, Brian served in Vietnam. He went there in May 1969. In September, he and a buddy were in a helicopter crash. They survived but were captured by enemy soldiers and marched to a prison in the jungle. They literally disappeared and were declared missing in action.

"His family, friends, and neighbors here in Farewell, we were deeply saddened and worried. One year later, just a few months ago, the Army changed Brian's status from missing in action to killed in action. We were devastated. But his mother and his now wife, Jeanie, refused to accept his death. They believed Brian was still alive. And they were right!

"After fourteen months, Brian and his buddy escaped the prison. They spent seven long days finding their way to safety, and they made it! Many of us know Brian well. We prayed for him and I'm delighted this morning to have him in our church. He's going to share some important lessons he learned in Vietnam. Ladies and gentlemen, please welcome Brian home."

MY STORY

I walked to the front of the sanctuary and looked out on so many familiar faces, nodded to all, and began. "On this beautiful Sunday morning in February 1971, I'm standing in the church where I was baptized as an infant. I feel embraced by your warm smiles and memories. After everything that's happened in my life, at this moment I cannot fully express how utterly wonderful it is to be . . . *alive*.

"To be alive and to be . . . *home*.

"To be alive, home, and with . . . *my family*.

"To be alive, home, with my family, and with . . . so many *friends and neighbors* today.

"My mother once told me the gift of life is the greatest gift we receive, and she was right. And how we live that gift is then what matters most. The best gift we can give with *our gift* of life is to pass it on—share hope and love with others. As my Vietnam brother Hues put it, 'Sharing love and hope costs us nothing but feeds and grows *our* hearts and souls.'

"In Vietnam, I learned several powerful lessons, but the most important one is this: They can take away your freedom . . . your family and friends . . . your home, possessions, clothes . . . food and water . . . even your sleep.

"But two things they *cannot* take from you, even in the most horrible conditions: the power of good memories, and the strength of your spiritual beliefs. They cannot take away your good memories or spiritual beliefs—unless you let them.

"This morning I want to share my story about the long and powerful reach of good memories and the incredible power of the human spirit. Both of these were demonstrated and lived by my Army brother, Hues. My good memories and Hues's spirit saved my life in Vietnam, and some of those memories were created by people in this church today.

"The power of good memories: What do I mean? How can they help us? Well, we know people are complex—physically, psychologically, emotionally, and so forth. But we often judge others, and they judge us, based on a pretty simple formula: what we say and how we say it, and what we do and how we do it. Our words and behaviors are the basis for creating good memories. Or nightmares. Or total indifference.

"Most important, every time you are with someone, you have the opportunity to create a good memory. And good memories, as I discovered in Vietnam, help us live because they give us the great gift of hope. Hope! And hope is like water: you can't live without it.

"As I look around this morning, I see people who created good memories for me. My mother and her constant humming of 'Amazing Grace.' My father and his never-quit attitude. My sister, brother, new wife and baby—all created wonderful memories that kept me alive in Vietnam. And there are others in this room too.

"I see a former neighbor here, Miss Cora. As a boy every morning when I saw this elderly neighbor outside her house—fetching the newspaper or tending flowers in her garden—she always, *always* gave me a warm smile and said in her sweet voice, 'Good morning, Brian! May you be blessed today!' Those eight words? Every day. That warm smile? Every day. The memory? Forever.

"And there's a young lady here too, Alicia, I once tutored in math. And one night each week, when her mother attended a meeting, I stayed on to babysit and fix dinner. And every time I asked her what she wanted for supper, she said 'hamburgers!'"

"So, we had a deal: I cooked the burgers, she picked the toppings. She asked if the toppings could be anything? I said as long as it's food. Well, that opened the door.

"You ever put Cheerios on your burger? How about jelly? Peanut butter? Celery? Carrots? Ever give cottage cheese or maple syrup a try? She'd always ask me to take the first bite. I would, and then I'd make a sick face and pretend I was choking. And Alicia would laugh and laugh and laugh—*real* laughter that filled her eyes with joy and delight.

And I could still see and relive that joyful laughter in Vietnam, where I sure as hell needed it!

"Now, in the prison camp, there was a circle of mud in the grass we called the Beatdown Ring. Each prisoner was forced into the ring about every five or six weeks. Here's a picture of what happened there: I'm standing in the ring, my hands tied behind my back. Two or three NVA soldiers armed with thick bamboo clubs enter the ring. Then they attack me with their clubs and beat me and other prisoners as close to death as possible. I saw two Americans beaten to death in the ring. And my first beating took me to the edge of death, where I lay for two days filled with aching pain and struggling to hang onto life.

"I know what I tell you next will sound crazy, but the truth is I *was* sometimes crazy—what Hues and I called 'tipped over.' In those desperate hours after my first beating, I retreated to a small corner in my mind where I created a special little memory room. I hung pictures on the walls of that room—my good memory pictures, faces or images of people who had given me the gift of good memories.

"So, when I received another beatdown, or when I was badly sick or ill with some disease, or being punished in some other way, I'd race to that little memory room in my head. Close the door behind me. Walk or crawl the room. Stare at those pictures. Relive those good memories and . . . *hang on to life*.

"Those memories saved my life! They saved my life by giving me the most crucial gift we can receive when we find ourselves in a hell on earth: the gift of hope! Hope *is* the bridge to tomorrow, and hanging on to hope kept me alive. And some of those memory pictures were of people here in church this morning. I can't thank you enough for your good memories . . . for giving me life.

"Those memories, along with the human spirit and light of the Lord, guided me for seven days in the jungle with my dying brother in my arms. In religion we hear the words *Lord* and *light* and *spirit* a lot. I have since I was a kid. I believed them most of the time, looked up to them, wanted my life to be filled with the light and spirit of the Lord.

"But like others, my belief in the Lord was sometimes darkened with doubt. With so many evils in our world—poverty, hatred, murders, race riots, unending wars, and destruction—we can't help but wonder: where is the Lord's so-called light? Where in *hell* is the light in our so often bitter, angry, divided, and warring world? Where?

"In Vietnam, I discovered the light and spirit of the Lord were present in my Army brother Hues, which he spelled H-u-e-s. He called himself that because his bloodline was a rainbow of colors: he was Black, White, Brown, and Yellow. He was every shade and color; he believed he was everyman. But at the same time, he possessed nothing in life!

He lost his family growing up. His mother and sister died in a car crash when he was ten. At age fourteen, his father was shot and killed before his eyes in a robbery attempt in Detroit. He had no family, no home, no possessions, no money, no bright future.

"He then lived for a time with a Baptist minister and his family, who took him into their home. They helped him see again the many possibilities in life and to help others whose lives were as tough or even tougher than his own. With the minister's help, Hues's motto became: *Forget what you lost or don't have in life—focus on what you still got and can give.*

"So, Hues took stock of what he still had. He was a good listener. Had a great singer's mellow voice. He loved poetry. His smile and laugh were contagious. He was good at sharing and great at connecting. And he possessed a huge heart. So, what did he do?

"At age fifteen, that's right, *fifteen*, Hues began walking the rough streets of River Rouge here in Michigan—a poor, Black community near Detroit. Some of you know it: a city seething with racial tensions and marked by homelessness and poverty. No matter, Hues walked those grim streets greeting all and psalming—his way of singing his poetry prayers to them.

"He memorized dozens of psalms. He could change the lyrics to fit any situation. He became a friend to so many who had so little: the homeless—old, alone, broke beggars living on the streets. Through his smile, psalming, laughter, and caring, Hues made good differences in *their* lives.

"How? He gave them *hope*! The streets of River Rouge became *his* church. The poor and lonely walking them were *his* congregation. And they were delighted and looked forward to seeing his smile and hearing his soft, sweet psalming. At age fifteen!

"I know some of you may be thinking that Hues sounds crazy! And he was—absolutely crazy in the most wonderful way. He lived and expressed the light and spirit of the Lord every day. He was everyman. He focused on others. He saved my life in Vietnam after the helicopter crash when he carried me in his arms to keep the enemy from killing me because I couldn't walk.

"He was my brother, my spiritual guide! He lived and was the daily light, the spirit of the Lord. I wouldn't be here today without him.

"When we finally escaped the prison camp, Hues was so hurt and suffering he couldn't walk on his shattered ankle, so I carried him. And two nights before our escape they cut off part of his tongue to stop his psalming. He could barely eat—swallow but not chew. I fed him food I had chewed for him. His personal radar warned us about dangers. And he closed each day by softly psalming a prayer in his faint, gurgling, guttural voice. Hues gave me love. He gave me hope. He gave me life even though he couldn't walk or talk!

"On the seventh day, when we reached the firebase, we were so happy. Somehow we'd survived together—the war, the prison cage, the Beatdown Ring, the seven days in the jungle, and so much more. When we got to the top of the hill on the firebase, I sat down with Hues in my arms, crying and hugging him. Then I looked into the blue heaven and thanked the Lord for lighting our way home and keeping my brother alive and with me every step. But when I looked back down at my lap, Hues was *not* in my arms—just his *black pajamas* lay in my lap. No Hues . . . just his black pajamas . . . in my lap.

"Only at that moment could I finally accept what had *actually happened* to Hues that night after they cut off his tongue. They shot him, killed him . . . four feet in front of me. Then they made me carry him to the Beatdown Ring, where I was forced to dig a hole in the mud and bury my brother. Bury my dead brother in the rain and mud.

"But in my desperate mind, see, he wasn't dead. No way! He was still bigger than life. I refused to accept his horrible death because I needed him with me. How could I survive alone in the jungle? I couldn't. I needed my brother . . . and his incredible life spirit . . .

"And so, as I sat on the firebase and stared at his black pajamas and cried, I finally fully realized I had *not* carried his body for seven days. On the contrary, Hues's *spirit*, his wonderful human spirit, had guided and carried *me* to safety *every step* in the jungle. *He* carried *me*.

"Now, I'm not saying Hues was Jesus, the son of the Lord. But in my heart he was *a* son . . . *a* son of the Lord. Why? Because *he lived it*! He didn't just talk it, or preach it, or pray for it. He *lived* it every day! He gave himself to old, poor, and lonely people walking the streets of River Rouge. He gave it all for me in the prison cage and dark jungle in Vietnam.

"So, in my long journey home, I've come to believe other sons and daughters of the Lord exist too. They aren't names or stories in the Bible; they live *with us*. Some are in our church this morning, and, like Hues, they give love and hope. *Their* spirits enrich *our* lives.

"Most importantly, this is not *my* story, even though it's about me. No, it's *our story* . . . *our story* of what *might be* in our world. We have but to open our minds and hearts to understand and accept that light, then live it. That's what counts most. *Saying* you're a Christian means nothing. *Praying* like a Christian is better. But *living* a true Christian life is what counts most. Deeds not words. We must live it!

"Memories can make positive differences in our lives. And embracing the light and sharing our spirit gives us the opportunity and capability to create warm memories for others.

"We can fight anger, despair, and fear with hope and love.

"And the best news is, ladies and gentlemen, young and old, the enrollment window for sons and daughters of the Lord is always . . . *open*!

"There's no age barrier, gender barrier, or racial barrier. No religious or nationality barrier. The only barrier is in *your* mind. I urge you, pull it out. Examine it. Then set it aside . . . and move on. Live . . . live and share your spirit. You can do it no matter your situation in life."

I paused and slowly scanned the room. So many memories of others in the church this morning intermingled with Hues's warm spirit. The mellow, peaceful possibilities of life . . .

"Let me close this morning by reading a psalm I wrote about Hues. The poem expresses what he believed. How he acted. How he lived it. Every day. My psalm for Hues goes like this:

> Ankle shattered, butchered tongue,
> my brother cannot walk nor talk,
> but his spirit glows ever bigger, brighter,
> a bursting sunrise lighting our world,
> enlightening meaningful life for all.
>
> How we live and share our life
> is the true measure of who we are.
> The light of the Lord can lead us,
> christen us as light bearers too.
> We can spread this embracing light,
> brighten others' lives anywhere, every day.
>
> Eleven little words in the Bible
> characterize Hues and meaningful life:
> *Do unto others as you would have them do unto you.*
> The simple notion of sharing light,
> spreading love and gifting hope,
> to ease the heavy life burdens
> so many hungry, lonely, hopeless bear.

What finer thing can we do
in our life in this often-angry world
than birth good differences
in the lives and minds of others?
Costs us nothing but a breath of time
that nurses our heart, grows our soul.

EPILOGUE

At least once each month for several years, I shared my story in churches in Michigan and nearby states. Occasionally I spoke with veterans' groups too. Jeanie and Bree always traveled with me. Over time we built a network of new friends, some of whom referred to themselves as part of the "Hues family."

In late spring of 1971, I received a phone call from Reverend Brown in River Rouge. I was delighted he called because I'd lost his contact information. Before I could say much more than hello and briefly introduce myself, the Reverend asked three rapid-fire questions: First, was the story I shared in church the story of "his" Hues? Second, was I the close "brother" Hues had written about in letters home? And third, how soon could I visit River Rouge and share my story in his Baptist Church?

Two weeks later Jeanie, Bree, and I drove to River Rouge. We met Reverend Brown and his family and talked for hours about Hues. The Reverend was so moved by my story in church the next morning he broke into tears and subsequently held a lengthy conversation with Hues in the form of a prayer that eventually closed the service.

That afternoon he gave us a tour of some streets Hues had used to walk and psalm. He carried a picture of Hues, and when we encountered older people who saw the picture and remembered Hues, the Reverend introduced me as his brother, Buck. We talked with smiling, happy people much of the afternoon while Hues's spirit lingered nearby.

We also met Sena Park. The Reverend had invited her to church to hear my story. Sena then invited us for dinner that Sunday evening. We shared stories and toasted Hues. She remained sad at his passing because she loved him but never got to tell him so. I assured her that Hues did know, whether she'd told him or not. And he loved her deeply too, talked about her often, and wanted to marry her. Sena became our close friend over time.

Hues still walks with me.

He still carries me.

Every day.

ACKNOWLEDGMENTS

I want to thank my wife, Joan, and sons Byron and Eric, for their rich love and lives over the years. They helped me finally "come home," and I cannot imagine life without them.

I also want to acknowledge several relatives and close friends who served in Vietnam: my brothers-in-law, Mark Kastner and Mike Luck; close friends Gerry Bentley, Phil Bohm, Ray Harter, and Richard Meade; and the men who served with me in the Casualty Branch in 1970.

Thanks as well to my great longtime friends Don and Betty Tyler and Nick and Maggie Miles for their thoughtful and helpful reviews of the book.

Finally, I want to acknowledge publisher John Koehler, editor Becky Hilliker, and designers Lauren Sheldon and Danielle Koehler for their excellent work on the book.

www.ingramcontent.com/pod-product-compliance
Lightning Source LLC
LaVergne TN
LVHW041910070526
838199LV00051BA/2568